Praise for
Sugarplum Surprises

"This book is a diamond of the first water and a perfect example of the best the Regency genre has to offer its devoted fans. Ms. Fairchild's *Sugarplum Surprises* shines a joyous light on the Regency era and transports readers into the heart of the *bon ton*."
—*Romantic Times*

"This rich, frothy, and funny book is just the thing to read before trimming trees and sipping eggnog. Wonderful!"   —*Affaire de Coeur*

"Not a book to be raced through—neither the subtle growth of the romance nor the fresh glimpses of Bath's local color. For a gentle (for the most part) holiday tale told with humor and poignancy, you can't go wrong with *Sugarplum Surprises*."
—Romance Reviews Today

Praise for the Novels
of Elisabeth Fairchild

"A treat for Regency lovers."   —Mary Jo Putney

"Mesmerizing fiction at its best. . . . Add Elisabeth Fairchild to my list of must-read authors."
—Mary Balogh

"Gracefully written, tenderly nuanced."
—Diana Gabaldon

Sugarplum Surprises

Elisabeth Fairchild

A SIGNET BOOK

SIGNET
Published by New American Library, a division of
Penguin Group (USA) Inc., 375 Hudson Street,
New York, New York 10014, USA
Penguin Group (Canada), 90 Eglinton Avenue East, Suite 700, Toronto,
Ontario M4P 2Y3, Canada (a division of Pearson Penguin Canada Inc.)
Penguin Books Ltd., 80 Strand, London WC2R 0RL, England
Penguin Ireland, 25 St. Stephen's Green, Dublin 2,
Ireland (a division of Penguin Books Ltd.)
Penguin Group (Australia), 250 Camberwell Road, Camberwell, Victoria 3124,
Australia (a division of Pearson Australia Group Pty. Ltd.)
Penguin Books India Pvt. Ltd., 11 Community Centre, Panchsheel Park,
New Delhi - 110 017, India
Penguin Group (NZ), 67 Apollo Drive, Rosedale, North Shore 0632,
New Zealand (a division of Pearson New Zealand Ltd.)
Penguin Books (South Africa) (Pty.) Ltd., 24 Sturdee Avenue,
Rosebank, Johannesburg 2196, South Africa

Penguin Books Ltd., Registered Offices:
80 Strand, London WC2R 0RL, England

First published by Signet, an imprint of New American Library,
a division of Penguin Group (USA) Inc.

First Printing, November 2001
First Printing ($6.99 Edition), October 2008
10 9 8 7 6 5 4 3 2 1

PUBLISHER'S NOTE
This is a work of fiction. Names, characters, places, and incidents either are
the product of the author's imagination or are used fictitiously, and any resemblance to actual persons, living or dead, business establishments, events, or
locales is entirely coincidental.

The publisher does not have any control over and does not assume any
responsibility for author or third-party Web sites or their content.

Dedicated to
Deb, Pat, Melissa, and Julie,
who in the face of adversity
never fail to see the silver surprises

Chapter One

Bath, 1819

Fanny Fowler, an accredited beauty, one of Bath's *bon ton,* slated to be the most feted bride of the Christmas Season, was not in her best looks when she burst through the door of Madame Nicolette's millinery shop, on a very wet December afternoon right before closing. The violent jingle of the bell drew the attention of everyone present. And yet, so red and puffy were Fanny's eyes, so mottled her fair complexion, so rain-soaked her golden tresses, she was almost unrecognizable.

"Madame Nicolette!" she gasped, noble chin wobbling, sylvan voice uneven. Bloodshot blue eyes streamed tears that sparkled upon swollen cheeks almost as much as the raindrops that trickled from her guinea gold hair. "It is all over. Finished."

Madame Nicolette's elaborate lace-edged mobcap tipped at an angle, along with Madame's head. The heavily rouged spots on her heavily powdered cheeks added unusual emphasis to the puzzled purse of her mouth. She spoke in hasty French to her assistant, Marie, shooing her, and the only customer in the shop, into the dressing room.

Then, clasping the trembling hand of this, her best customer, she led her to a quiet corner, near the plate glass window that overlooked the busy, weather-drenched corner of Milsom and Green Streets.

"Fini, chéri?" she asked gently, taking in the loom-

ing impression of the Fowler coach waiting without, the horses sleek with rain, their harness decked with jingling bells to celebrate the season. Gay Christmas ribbon tied to the coach lamps danced in the wind.

"The wedding is canceled!" Fanny wailed, no attempt made to lower her voice. "He has jilted me. Says that nothing could induce him to marry me now. Ever."

The distraught young woman fell upon the matronly shoulder, weeping copiously. Madame Nicolette, green eyes widening in alarm, patted the girl's back. "*Vraiment!* The cad. *Abominable* behavior. Why should he do this?"

"Because I told the truth when I could have lied." Fanny gazed past Madame with a sudden look of fury. "I should have lied. Might so easily have lied. Any other female would have lied."

She burst into tears again, and wept without interruption, face buried in the handkerchief in her hands, shoulders heaving.

Madame offered up her own handkerchief, for Fanny's was completely sodden. "What of the *trousseau*?" Madame asked, for of course this was the matter that concerned her most.

Fanny wept the harder, which brought a look of concern to Madame's eyes, far greater than that generated by all previous tears.

"Papa . . ." Fanny choked out. "Papa is in an awful temper. He refuses to p-p-pay." This last bit came out in a most dreadful wail, and while Madame continued to croon comfortingly and pat the young woman's back, her lips thinned, and her brows settled in a grim line.

"And your *fiancé*? Surely he will *defray* expenses."

"Perhaps." Fanny made every effort to collect herself. "I do not know," she said with a sniff. "All I know is that he intends to leave Bath tomorrow morning. Now, I must go. Papa waits."

"Allow me to escort you to the coach." Madame solicitously followed her to the door.

"But it is raining." Fanny wielded both sodden handkerchiefs in limp protest. "And Papa is in such a mood."

Madame insisted, and so the two women ran together to the coach, under cover of Madame's large black umbrella, and Madame greeted Lord Fowler, his wife, and younger daughter standing beneath her dripping shield just outside the fulsome gutter. "An infamous turn of events," she called to them.

"Blasted nuisance," my lord shouted from the coach. "Frippery female has gone and lost herself a duke, do you hear!"

"Fourth Duke of Chandrose, and Fourth Marquess of Carnevon." Lady Fowler's voice could barely be heard above the pelter of the rain that soaked Madame's hem, but as the door was swung wider to allow Fanny entrance, her voice came clearer. "A fortune slips through her fingers."

"Silly chit," her father shouted as Fanny climbed in, cringing. "I credited you with far too much sense."

Fanny's sister kept her head bowed, her eyes darting in a frightened manner from parent to parent.

Fanny resorted to her handkerchief as she plopped down into her seat.

"Do you know what she has done to alienate him?" Lord Fowler demanded of Madame Nicolette as if she should know, as if he were the only one in Bath who was not privy to his daughter's thinking.

Madame shook her head, and gave a very French shrug as she leaned into the doorway of the coach. "My dear *monsieur, madame,* I sympathize most completely in this trying *moment,* and while I understand you have no wish to pay for the *trousseau* that has taken six months work to assemble, the *trousseau* Miss Fanny will not be wearing, I wonder, will you be so good—"

Lord Fowler sat forward abruptly, chest thrust forth, shaking his walking stick at her with ferocity, the sway of his jowls echoing the movement. "Not a penny will I spend on this stupid girl. Not one penny, do you hear? More than a hundred thousand pounds a year she might have had with His Grace. Not a farthing's worth shall she have now." Like a Christmas turkey he looked, his face gone very red, his eyes bulging, his extra set of chins wobbling.

"I comprehend your ire, my lord," Madame persisted calmly. "But surely you intend to offer some compensation for my efforts, my material?"

His lordship's face took on a plum pudding hue. "Not a single grote. Do you understand? Not one. Make the duke pay." He thumped the silver head of his cane against the ceiling, the whole coach shaking. "Jilting my daughter." Thump. "Disgracing the family name." Thump. "Two weeks before the wedding, mind you." Thump-thump. "Bloody cheek."

With that, he thumped his cane so briskly it broke clean through the leather top so that rain leaked in upon his head, and in a strangled voice, the veins at his temples bulging, he ordered his coachman, "Drive on, damn you. Drive on. Can you not hear me thumping down here?"

The horses leapt into motion with an inappropriately cheerful jingle, and Madame Nicolette Fieullet leapt back from the wheels.

"Fiddlesticks," she muttered in very English annoyance as the coach churned up dirty water from the gutter in a hem-drenching wave. She took shelter in the shop's doorway to shake the rain from her umbrella.

The wreath on the door seemed suddenly too merry, the jingle of the door's bell a mockery. *Christmas. Dear Lord.* Christmas meant balls and assemblies, and dresses ordered at the last minute, and she must have fabric and lace and trim at the ready. But how was she to pay for Christmas supplies now that so much of her capital was tied up in Fanny's *trousseau*?

"*Madame!* You are soaked," her assistant, Marie, cried out as she entered.

"*Oui. Je suis tout trempé.*" Madame kept her skirt high, that she might not drip, her voice low, that their customer might not hear. "You will give Mrs. Bower my excuses while I change?"

Marie followed her, a worried look in her deep brown eyes. "Is it true, Madame? He refuses to pay?"

"*Oui.*"

"*Mon dieu!* The material arrives tomorrow. However will we pay?"

"I shall think of something. Do not torment yourself." Madame sounded confident. She looked completely self-assured, until she locked herself in the back room, pressed her back to the door, and sinking to the floor, wept piteously at the sight of Fanny's finished dresses.

More than a dozen beautiful garments had been made up to Miss Fowler's specific measurements, in peacock colors to flatter Fanny's sky blue eyes and guinea gold hair. Thousands of careful stitches, hundreds of careful cuts, and darts. How many times had she pricked her fingers in the making of them? How many times had she ripped seams that they might fit Fanny's form more perfectly? It was heartbreaking just to look at them. Tears burned in Madame's eyes. Her breath caught in her throat.

The masterpieces were, of course, the wedding dress, and two ball gowns, one in the colors of Christmas, an evergreen satin bodice, vandyke trimmed in gold satin cord, Spanish slashed sleeves that had taken several days to sew, a deeply gored skirt of deeper green velvet, with a magnificent border of gold quilling, and twisted rolls of satin cord that had taken weeks' worth of stitching.

"Fanny must have something entirely unique," her mother had insisted, "something worthy of a duchess."

The results were exquisite. Madame's best work yet. They were the sort of dresses every young woman dreamed of. Head-turning dresses, and yet in the best of taste, the perfect foil for youth and beauty. They were the sort of dresses she had once worn herself in her younger days. Gowns to catch a man's eye without raising a mother's eyebrows. Gowns to lift a young woman's spirits and self-esteem as she donned them. She had hoped these dresses would be the making of her name, of her reputation.

Now they were worthless, completely worthless. Indeed, a terrible drain upon her purse.

Defeat weighed heavy upon Madame's shoulders. Tears burned in her eyes. Sobs pressed hard against her chest, her gut, the back of her throat. What to do? Panic rose, intensifying her feelings of anger and regret.

She had believed the future secure, the holiday fruitful, her worries behind her at last.

But no! Life surprised her most mean-spiritedly, at Christmastime, always at Christmastime.

The tears would not remain confined to her eyes. It had been long since she had allowed them to fall. They broke forth now in an unstoppable deluge.

She clutched her hand over her mouth, stifling her sobs, choking on them. But they would not be stopped. Disappointment surged from the innermost depths of her in a knee-weakening wave. She was a child again, unable to contain her emotions. She thought of her mother, lying pale and wan in her bed, the familiar swell of her stomach deflated, the strength of her voice almost gone.

"My dear Jane," Mother had whispered, cupping the crown of Jane's head, stroking the silk of her hair. She could still feel the weight of that hand, the heat. "I had thought to bring you a baby brother for Chr-Christmas." Her mother's voice had caught, trembled. She had given Jane's hand a weak squeeze, her hand hot, so very hot. "But, life never unfolds as one expects, pet."

Jane had been frightened by her mother's tone, by the strangled noises of distress her father made from the doorway. She had not understood it was the last time she would have to speak to Mama. She had patted the feverish hand, then held it to her cheek and said, "Do not cry, Mother. If you have lost my little brother, Papa will buy you another for Christmas. Won't you, Papa?"

Her father had made choking noises and stumbled from the room.

"Jane!" Miss Godwin, her governess, had sounded cross as she snatched her up from the side of the bed.

But Jane had clung to her mother's fingers, the strength of her grasp lifting her mother's arm from the bed. Something was wrong, terribly wrong.

Her mother's clasp was as desperate as hers. "Cherish what is, my pet, not what you imagined," she said, the words urgent, the look in her eyes unforgettable. And as Miss Godwin had gently pried their hands apart, she had said with an even greater urgency, "Promise me, Jane, my love. Promise me you will not allow regret to swallow you whole."

Jane had nodded, not knowing what she promised, looking back over Miss Godwin's shoulder with a five-year-old's conviction, no comprehension of the words. Promising was easy. Honoring that promise was not.

"Look for the silver surprises, my love, in the plum pudding at Christmas, and know that I put them there for you." Her mother's words were almost drowned out by the muffled desperation of her father's cries. He sat, bent over in the dressing room, a balled handkerchief stuffed in his mouth. His shoulders had shaken in a manner she had never before witnessed.

"Is Papa all right?" she had asked Miss Godwin, all concern.

Miss Godwin had made comforting noises and carried little Jane off to bed, her own cheeks wet with silent tears, her shoulders shaking like Papa's, as hard as Jane Nichol's shook now as she rocked back and forth, her fist pressed to her mouth.

The wet hem of her skirt had soaked her petticoats. Her legs were cold.

"Oh, Mother," she whispered as she stood to wring out the wet. "What silver surprise am I missing? 'Tis all soggy pudding, this."

The rack of clothes mocked her silently. They were dry, and perfect, a reminder of her past in so many ways, and yet she must remember they promised to throw her carefully constructed present into chaos.

Jane turned to the old mirror that had been tucked into the corner behind the door. Clouded at the edges, it had been removed from the dressing room, replaced by a newer, less timeworn cheval. The buxom, brightly dressed woman that stared back was still a stranger to her, not the picture of herself she carried in her head. Her frizzled brown wig was even more frizzled from exposure to the rain. Her oval spectacles were speckled with raindrops. The careful veneer of face powder and rouge was much besmeared by her tears.

Jane had to laugh, a tragic, pitiful gust of a laugh, as she took off the horn-rimmed spectacles that so completely dominated her face, and wiped at the streaked powder with the damp sleeve of her gown, exposing smooth, youthful flesh, complexion quite at odds with the sad horsehair wig and matronly mobcap.

A sight—a proper sight she was. She could not face customers looking like this. She needed a fresh powdering—dry clothes.

The wedding dress caught her eye, the ball gowns and walking dresses, morning and evening gowns, the capes, and pelisses, and negligees. Dry clothes. Beautiful dry clothes, so beautiful any young lady would be tempted to wear them.

The silver surprise of it made her smile as laughter filled her chest and shook the weight from her shoulders.

She rose to examine her choices with a devil-may-care tilt to her head, a daring idea taking hold—a silver surprise of an idea. She laughed again, and fingered the fall of satin flowers at the sleeve of the second ball gown.

A light rap came at the door, and Marie called out, "Madame, Mrs. Bower has gone. Shall I lock up?"

"*S'il vous plaît.* Do not wait for me, Marie. I have a bit of work to do." Jane fell into the French accent she affected without blinking, without thinking. It came so naturally now, the pretense.

Time to stop pretending, if only for an evening. What a relief it would be. What a joy.

She needed joy. It was a Season of joy, was it not?

She peeled off the dreadful wig and undid the ties on her dress. The false bosom fell away, the padded hips. She felt lighter, smaller—herself again. A different silhouette looked back at her from the mirror—a tear-streaked face, and swollen eyes. She ruffled her fingers through flattened flaxen tresses, exhaled heavily, and straightened her back with a rising sense of resolution.

Lord Fowler had left her with good advice if nothing else. His words still rang in her ears.

"The duke must pay!"

And so he must. It was a necessary solution. She needed the money desperately, and she would not allow His Grace to leave Bath before he had given it to her.

Chapter Two

His Grace, Edward Brydges, fourth Duke of Chandrose, fourth Marquess of Carnevon, heir to the Brydges, Chandrose, Carnevon, and Kinro fortunes, formerly referred to as Lord Kinro, wished himself anywhere but at the Assembly room ball that night. One does not wish to be required to make conversation, much less to dance when one has just cast off one's fiancée, canceled a wedding only two weeks hence, and attempted to explain the whole to one's irate mother and three astounded siblings, all the while knowing that one's explanation would be judged wanting.

At His Grace's suggestion that he had no desire left in him to escort them to an Assembly ball that evening, those same astounded siblings raised such a hue and cry as to come close to deafening him.

He was in no mood for it. But his mood mattered not to them.

His furious parent had insisted harshly, "You are not to be allowed to disappoint every female in your life now that you have disappointed the female closest to your heart, Edward."

Edward might have thought she meant Fanny, had not his mother already said twice that day, "Surely a son is closer to his mother than to a woman he only thought he wanted to marry."

Heaven protect all women for the manipulative creatures that they were! Heaven protect him for giving in to them!

As he had already dashed their spirits in his intention to whisk them away from the entertainments of Bath, ruined the wedding, his mother's hopes for a grandchild, and their forthcoming holiday, Edward felt he had little choice in the matter. Duty called, and he had been schooled since birth on the importance of his duties.

"If you've nothing to be ashamed of in jilting Fanny," his mother had said, "you must be seen in public, head held high. Do not allow anyone to think she has broken your heart. Meet your peers cheerfully, and they will believe a perfectly good reason must have prompted such an astonishing action in a sober man of good reputation."

He had not turned from the window, where he stood looking out at the rain-swept street, thinking it appropriate that the sky should weep today. God knew he could not.

His mother did not sound so sure of herself in asking, "A perfectly good reason did prompt such drastic action, did it not, Edward?"

"Of course," he said shortly. What do you take me for? he had wanted to snap, and yet he restrained himself. He prided himself in his restraint.

Of course he had a perfectly good reason. And, of course, his mother would most certainly not agree. Thus, it was wisest not to reveal too much in the way of detail.

"Was she unfaithful, Edward?"

He could not be angry with her, such a depth of concern and ready rage possessed her voice.

He merely clasped his arms a little more firmly in the small of his back and said, his voice remarkably even, admirably unemotional, "The reason we are not to be married is our business, Mother. Mine and Fanny's."

"And the solicitors," his sister Celia had piped up from her seat by the fire—heartless scamp.

"Poor Edward." Beth was more sympathetic. "What has Fanny done to you?"

Anne had looked worried when he turned at last from the window. "Lord Fowler is sure to demand some sort of settlement for breach of promise."

"Let him," Edward said smoothly, as if it did not matter, when of course it did. One did not like to be sued, did one? "I promised to marry Fanny, but find I cannot."

"Why?" Anne persisted.

Rather than skirt the question again, he simply ignored it in saying, "Had you not best be getting dressed if we are to make an appearance at the Upper Rooms?"

Beth and Celia had brightened and run to do his bidding. Anne had stood there a moment longer, staring at him.

"Go on," he prompted. "You know how I hate to be kept waiting."

"You will tell me eventually, Edward. Won't you?"

"Perhaps," he said, "but for now you try my patience."

"I like Fanny," she said.

He sighed, and turned his attention to the window again. "So did I."

His mother had watched this exchange, and shoved Anne out of the door, before opening her mouth on more questions. He stopped her far more brusquely than was his habit, with an abrupt wave of his hand.

"Not now, Mother. I've no patience, and no intention of revealing anything more than you already know."

"I was only going to suggest you ought not wear black tonight, my boy. Too gloomy by far."

And so, he stood at the end of the ballroom farthest from the music and dancing, away from the scowling matrons, equally distant from the long wall of would-be dancers. He wore deep blue, not black, chalk white breeches, and white stockings, the only black his shoes, nothing gloomy but his mood. He could not bring himself to smile, to pretend nothing had happened. He could not glibly fall into conversation, or act as though he was not in any way affected, or pretend that he did not hear the whisper of his name, of Fanny's, as he stalked across the room. Of all things, he hated most making himself conspicuous while gossip was rife.

And so he stood half hidden by a potted palm, staring stonily at the glitter of chandeliers and the silvered sheen of oval mirrors that dotted the upper walls beneath faux columns, watching the dancers obliquely, the whirl of skirts and coattails like the wink of sunlight on water.

He shot an occasional puzzled glance directly at the dance floor, trying to imagine what these whirling couples had to smile about. What brought them such joy while he had none?

Had they discovered love when he was only fooled by it? He, who prided himself on never playing the fool?

He dared not look his mother's way. She would beckon, and insist he dance with his sisters or some worthy matron who had a yen to kick up her heels, or, heaven forbid, with one of the hopeful-looking wallflowers who stood about in colorful clusters between the doors that led to the tearoom, trying not to look partnerless, trying not to look as though they noticed him, trying not to be too obvious in their whispered discussions behind fluttering fans.

His mother had arranged his first dance with Fanny almost a year ago. He remembered the moment, her beauty, his instant infatuation. Silly gudgeon!

He must not allow his mother to play matchmaker again. If he wished to speak to a woman, he would speak to her. If not, well, he would not be drawn in again. He would not play the idiot twice. He deserved better—a truthful woman, no dissembling or devices. He would not settle for anything less.

Word was out. The wedding was off. The Duke of Chandrose was always observed with interest—tonight more so than usual.

"You are, in an instant," Anne reminded him between dances, "an eligible bachelor again."

"A trifle tainted perhaps," Beth said later. "For no one is quite clear on why your union with Fanny ended." Her brows rose in hopeful anticipation.

But he had no intention of clarifying the matter. Beth would not understand—she might even agree with Fanny.

His mother had been unable to drag the truth from him. None of his sisters' gently wheedling queries had met with an unburdening. It was too humiliating, really. He did not care if anyone ever knew. Let them speculate. He was done with it. Done with her. What a fool he had been, a perfectly naive fool.

"Go and dance, Beth," he suggested gently. "Tomorrow we return to Candon Manor."

"No, Edward!" she whispered, stricken. "Not home again. So soon."

"Christmas will be lovely in the country," he assured her. Far preferable to a Christmas in Bath, he thought, where every sight and sound must remind him of Fanny, of his own stupidity.

"Piffle!" she said under her breath. "Christmas will be a dead bore at the Manor, and you know it. We know everyone, and there is nothing to do."

He waved her away with a flick of his hand. He had only to survive the night, the stares, the whispers, the insufferable attempts to learn specific details straight from the source, his sisters' questions, his mother's . . .

A young woman skirted the dance floor, turning heads, turning his head, a rather attractive young woman dressed in the height of fashion. Not beautiful as Fanny had been beautiful. Her nose was too ordinary, her hair fair, but not of the golden variety. It possessed no hint of Fanny's much envied curl. Smooth as silk, it was pulled back in a simple French-style chignon, with none of the popular kissing curls and fringes. Her figure was good, perhaps a trifle too slender. Yes. She had not Fanny's curvaceous form, but she did turn heads as she crossed the ballroom. Her dress was quite fetching.

"Who is that?" An old woman to his left peered into her quizzing glass as she wondered aloud.

"I've no idea." Her companion carried a hearing horn. He announced his responses a trifle louder than was necessary. "Pretty frock."

Indeed, it was a pretty frock. Edward had never seen anything quite like it. He decided at once that he liked the young woman, for one reason, and one reason only. She diverted tongue waggers. He no longer served as the center of attention.

"Breeding," he overheard one of the dancer's speculate as they whirled past. "Observe her proud carriage."

"Wealthy," someone else murmured. "Only look at that gown."

In a room full of fine ball gowns this one shone like a star. The bodice was gold satin, the body white lutestring with a silvered sheen, the waist high, the neck round and very low with a line of silver and gold bullion. The sleeves were fashionably short, silver net over gold Spanish slashed satin, the points attached to reverse points from the shoulder in deeper gold. But what set the dress apart were the festoons of delicate white and silver silk flowers that dripped from shoulder to elbow.

Matching silver rosetted satin slippers peeped from beneath the deep border of gold bias gauze that spilled even more dainty, festooned flowers into the vandyked and scalloped hem. She was a confection, a marzipan-wrapped, sugar-dusted bride's cake. Just a glance at her and Edward must think of his wedding, of how Fanny might have looked in the wedding dress she had mentioned with anticipatory glee.

Whose heart, he wondered, did this dazzling young woman mean to break?

She paused on the dance floor to speak to, of all people, his mother. And then they were both turning, the slender grace of her neck arched, that she might look in his direction.

Oh, for a trapdoor through which he might sink!

His stomach turned, as did the gossip. His mother led the well-dressed dazzler toward him.

No chance of ducking out unseen, no possibility of tucking tail and running. Such behavior did not suit a duke—it certainly did not suit him. Ordinarily such an idea would never have so much as crossed his mind, but Fanny had made a cynic of him—an irritable, impatient pessimist.

Could it be the dowager duchess was matchmaking already?

Edward had his mind set against the ever-so-eye-catching young woman before ever they were introduced. In mind and mouth a word formed, a single, brutally rude word. He would wield it at once if his mother dared suggest he should dance with anyone other than his sisters.

No. He did not care to dance.

No. He did not care to be introduced.

No. No. No.

"Edward, do you know Miss Jane Nichol?" his mother asked.

"No," he blurted harshly.

The young woman flinched, but did not retreat. Like a willow in a gale she leaned away from him.

Feeling rather foolish, he tempered the word, adding a stiffly polite, "I have not had the pleasure."

Miss Nichol held forth her slender, gloved hand rather tentatively for salute, and bobbed an elegantly languid curtsy as his mother made formal introductions. He looked into the pleasant symmetry of her features, into the cedar green depths of her eyes and thought, *You time this meeting most ill, Miss Nichol, for I've no interest at all in women today, most especially not young or pretty women who think to capture my eye now that Fanny offends me.*

"Your Grace," she said, her voice as reed-thin as her figure.

With a tight little smile, his mother excused herself.

"I come with a message." Miss Nichol did not wait for him to initiate conversation. Wise of her, as he might have stood there silent, gazing at the dancers for some time without encouraging her to speak.

His brows rose. She was not smiling, as he had expected. Indeed, the green depths of her eyes held a hint of severity.

"A message from whom?"

"Not from, but on behalf of a woman to whom you have done a great disservice today."

His back stiffened. Did this stranger dare to address him directly with regard to his jilting of Fanny?

"You have placed her very future at risk . . ."

By God, she did!

". . . and as she is a dear friend . . ."

His eyes narrowed.

". . . and as I know you intend to leave on the morrow, I come to you tonight on her behalf . . ."

The cheek! The unmannerly gall!

". . . to beg your sympathy . . ."

Fat chance!

". . . for her plight."

He made no effort to disguise the chill in his voice. "You waste your breath if you would beg sympathy on Fanny's behalf."

"Not Miss Fowler," she said, surprising him.

He felt knocked from the high horse of his own self-centered pride when she said, her tone severe, and oh-so-politely formal, "I refer, Your Grace, to Madame Nicolette Fieullet, the dressmaker who has not been paid for a very beautiful, if completely useless *trousseau*, and wedding gown."

Dressmaker? What had he to do with dressmakers?

"You come to the wrong man, Miss Nichol." He turned dismissively, ready to be rid of this bothersome gadfly.

He caught her off guard. She was a moment in responding, in stepping swiftly to a position that forced him to face her once again. The wind of the dancers who whirled past them blew whiffs of mingled perfume his way, sweet and heady, jasmine and roses—her perfume.

"I think not, Your Grace."

Edward sighed. As a gentleman of means and title he was well accustomed to quashing impertinence, and this elegant but intrusive young woman must be put firmly in her place. "Surely this arrangement was made with Lord Fowler?" he drawled slowly, as though speaking to the thick-headed.

The flaxen sheen of her hair caught the light as she nodded. "Yes, but—"

"Apply to His Lordship for sympathy." He shooed her away with an irritable gesture. "I have no use for dresses."

She frowned, and had the temerity to step in front of him a second time as he attempted to walk away. So gracefully was this intrusion made he felt for a moment as if they danced, and again the floral odor wafted near, light and sweet.

Nothing light or sweet about what she would say, however. "Lord Fowler refuses to pay."

"A pity."

A pity, too, he felt none of the emotion he professed.

Green eyes sparked with contempt. "Is this your habit then, Your Grace?"

"What? Refusing to pay other men's bills?" he asked dryly.

"No." She lifted her chin. When she spoke, she enunciated every word with crisp clarity. "I mean, do you make a habit of cruelty to women? The dress-maker will be ruined, just as your fiancée's reputation has been. Six months' work, sir. Not a penny to show for it. Do you think it fair?"

She was quite attractive in her righteousness. It steeled her posture and brought fire to her eyes.

"Life is not fair," he said, his voice imbued with uncustomary ice.

A sudden flash of pain crossed her fragile features, like a bird on the wing. "No. It is not fair."

And with that she stepped aside, head bowed, to allow him free passage, her hair palely silken in the

candlelight, her sudden acquiescence after such a show
of righteousness, surprising.

He was tempted to walk away at once, but the
wounded anger in him would not allow it. Deep within
he had to acknowledge a sense of guilt, of a cal-
lousness completely at odds with his normal behavior.
He felt as if he stood outside of himself, observing the
overbearing rudeness of a stranger.

"This dressmaker?" he snapped.

Her head rose, expression guarded, gaze cool, flaxen
hair so smooth he longed for a moment to cup the
crown of her head.

"She made the frock you are wearing?"

She nodded.

His gaze strayed the slender length of her, and again
he thought of Fanny, of Fanny's deception. His anger
flared anew.

"A pretty thing," he said lazily.

Her cheeks flushed under the intensity of his examination. Green eyes flashed.

"It must have cost a pretty penny."

Her voice crackled with anger. "Your point?"

He was unused to women snapping at him. The second time today. It did not bring out the best in him.
He kept his voice cool, but the white-hot intensity of
suppressed rage surfaced momentarily in an uncharacteristically snide retort. "You fight most ardently for
this dressmaker, Miss Nichol. Is it the contents of your
own closet you fear suffering the loss of?"

She gazed at him a moment with something akin to
loathing, and when she spoke it was very slowly, her
voice low, that none but he might hear. "You are a
cold and heartless man, Your Grace. How ever did
you convince Fanny to love you?" she asked. Without
waiting for an answer, she turned on her heel, silver
and gold roses glinting, trembling from both shoulders,
like a garden in a gale as she stalked away.

He watched her go, his expression grim. "That's the
problem," he muttered. "I didn't."

Chapter Three

Jane thought she would never see him again—never see that proud, troubling mouth—never hear the brittle chill of his voice—nor look again into the icy blue of his eyes. She dared not approach the duke again, after such an unpromising, indeed, unkind reception, and as a result this day might be her last in the trade.

But she dressed as carefully as ever in her French-woman's disguise. As Madame Nicolette she powdered and rouged her face, propping the unnecessary pair of horn spectacles upon her nose, pulling the dark, riotously curling wig over her smoothed-back hair, topping the wig with a lace lappet and deeply brimmed bonnet. Carefully, she arranged the fur-trimmed red woolen cloak about her shoulders. It was a cheerful color, but today it would take the color of money to cheer Jane Nichol.

The morning was frosted and foggy, the paving stones, the brick and glass of every storefront glittering, silvered with it, her breath a thin white cloud against a sky that lay like a blanket upon the ground. The air smelled of winter, of coal fires, of damp wool and ice. She shivered.

The cold had new meaning this morning. It nipped at her nose, at her fingers and toes. Such weather posed serious threat to those without a roof over their heads, without the means to feed or clothe themselves adequately. Would she soon number among the wraiths who haunted the back alleyways and rubbish heaps, looking for crusts of bread?

She shivered again. She would never survive Christmas without payment for Fanny's clothes. Her stepmother would prove correct. She was not as clever as she liked to think. A young girl setting out to make something of herself, convinced she could leave her mark in the world. Her dreams were nothing more than that—dreams.

Doubts and inadequacy added lead to Madame's square-heeled shoes. The cold crept under her cloak. Jane was a few minutes later than usual turning into Milsom Street, keys jingling in her hand, the Christmas tune of her mother's voice running through her head—"Cherish what is, my pet, not what you imagined."

She must not lose hope—her mother's last gift—her most cherished gift.

She realized with surprise that a graceful black carriage stood cloaked in the silvered layers of drifting fog that veiled the shop, a carriage with a crest on the side panel picked out in silver, the wheel spokes in silver as well. Even the horses were silver, or as close as one could get, four perfectly matched grays, all white stockinged, with white stars on their foreheads, blowing silvered plumes of heated breath into the silver morning.

Her mother's voice rose from the back of her mind, "Look for the silver surprises, my love, and know that I put them there for you."

A lump formed in the back of Jane's throat. Tears burned at the back of her eyes.

Dear Lord, she thought. Who can that be at this hour of the morning?

As if in answer, the Duke of Chandrose stepped from the carriage, sweeping his gleaming black hat from gleaming dark hair, an azure blue wool cape with sable collar swinging heavily just above his heels.

The keys slipped from her hand, and he, gaze following them, thrust forward his hat with swift agility. He caught them before they hit the ground! It seemed an impossibility, that he was here, that he had caught the keys. The air crackled with the magic of it.

"Madame," he said, presenting the hat, and thus her keys. The blue of his eyes was not at all cold. The tone of his voice proved not so distant as she had expected. She took the keys from the hat still warmed by the heat of his head.

His mouth tilted, as it had the night before, at a wry upward slant—not a smile—but a look that spoke of his superiority without a word said. That mouth lent him the look of a man who knew things—all manner of things—some of them secrets he had no intention of sharing. "Madame Nicolette?"

"Oui," she said breathlessly, dipping into her most obsequious curtsy, and yet she stole a glance at that captivating mouth.

"Bonjour," he said politely, nothing snide in his tone, though it was a mouth capable of great snideness, she was sure. She had experienced it.

She forced her most professional smile, heart lifting. Had she shamed him into coming after all! "A beautiful morning, *non*?" she said in her heaviest accent.

"Is it?" he asked, brusque as ever, looking about him as if for the first time.

His cheeks had creases that ran vertically, lines that spoke of smiles, of laughter, and yet she had not seen him smile, nor heard hint of laughter.

He looked tired, she thought, giving him a most searching look, far more searching than the night before, when all of her concentration had been on what she must say to him, and how forbidding he looked, and how puzzling the captivation of his mouth was, even in its censure of her.

Something changed in his eyes as he looked about him—perhaps it was only a change in the brilliance of light reflected in them, and yet he said, "I suppose it is a fine, brisk morning."

The keys played a familiar music through her hands

as she searched for the right one, as she stole glimpses of him in the shop window.

He was tall, slender-built, perfectly postured—blessed with an appropriately noble profile. His dark brown hair was pomaded smoothly back from high temples and an intelligent brow. All had been haughty and cold at the ball. The set of his lips, the flatness of his gaze, the dismissive tilt of dark brows. His features had hidden all feeling other than disinterest, contempt, and boredom. She might have judged him an unfeeling, cold-blooded fish, but for the contradiction of his mouth.

This morning he seemed changed. As if, out of the public eye, out of the crowded ballroom full of his peers, the defenses came down. He definitely looked tired—defeated, the proud line of his mouth strained at the corners, as though it took great effort to refrain from frowning.

She wondered what Fanny had done or said to earn his displeasure. What truth had she revealed? Did it pain him enough to lose sleep? Shadows smudged the skin beneath bloodshot blue eyes.

He looked almost pitiable in the morning light. She felt a sharp stab of guilt. She had kicked this gentleman while he was down.

"*Que voulez-vous?* Please come in," she coaxed, holding wide the door.

He strode into the shop with the lean, elegance of a thoroughbred racer, cape swaying, stirring the fog.

The premises she took such pride in seemed suddenly small in his presence, as if the shop crouched in too deep a bow, unworthy of a duke.

Chandrose's bearing had lost none of its starch, despite his dispirited air.

"I have come to pay for the bride's clothes," he announced to the ceiling.

"But, of course," she said, removing her bonnet and gloves.

"Your friend . . ." His jaw tightened. The well-shaped mouth pursed. "Was most persuasive."

"Mon ami?" she asked, patting the lace lappet, checking the wig's placement, pretending again. Always pretending. How weary she was of it.

He cocked his head and looked out the window. She was free to stare at his mouth again.

"Miss Jane Nichol."

Her name sounded strange. Too brisk, and hard, as if he did not care for Miss Jane Nichol.

She blushed and looked away as she asked, "Do you wish to see the *trousseau*?"

"No."

It needled a bit that he would not so much as look at her work.

He drew from his pocket a bank draft. "Have you a pen?"

"Where shall I have the things delivered?" She rattled about in her desk for a sharp quill and a bottle of ink. Her fingers seemed clumsier than usual.

He moved, blocking the window's light.

She turned to find him almost on top of her.

He said, with a bit of heat, "I do not care if I ever see the clothes. You may do with them as you will."

She stepped aside, gesturing to the chair, busying herself in lighting lamps. "You have sisters, *non*? Alterations could be made."

He ignored the chair, leaned over the desk instead, taking off his gloves to write, taking up the pen impatiently, stabbing it into the ink. "No," he said briskly, and then, "Blast! I have bent the thing."

"No matter. I have a knife. We will sharpen a fresh one."

Such an elegant, slender hand for a man, a handsome hand. Fanny had walked away from these hands. *Stupid Fanny!* Jane's fingers accidentally brushed the duke's when she handed him the knife.

At her touch, at the electric crackle that sprang between them, he looked up abruptly, startled, spattering ink. The ponce box rolled to the floor.

"I do beg pardon," he said.

What was that? she thought. That tingling jolt of

feeling! She must look at his mouth. The shapely lips were for the first time apologetic, and something else, something she could not quite place. She held her breath, as surprised as he, waiting. Something was coming—must happen—had happened—like the flash of lightning—like the distant rumble of thunder.

"Clumsy of me," he said, looking past her with a sudden stillness, as if he drew all of his emotion within, as if he carefully shut it away.

"No matter." She stepped in beside him to fetch a fresh quill, head bent, eyes averted, pondering the change in him, that sudden guardedness—the air still heavy with potential—the stillness before a storm.

Madame Nicolette's lace lappets flapped at her cheeks like a spaniel's ears. She shook her head, wondering if she would ever grow accustomed to them, and from the corner of her eye found he watched her most intently, his gaze disturbing in its fixedness. She turned, and looked directly into the blue heaven of his eyes. Until that moment he had not looked directly into Madame Nicolette's eyes, simply looked past and around her, as did most of her customers.

He blinked, tilting his head as if what he found in her was most curious, his lashes sable against his cheeks. "That perfume you are wearing. Is it French?"

Perfume? He noticed her perfume? Her father had been the last gentleman to notice her perfume.

The duke opened his eyes again, his gaze far too delving, far too inquisitive. Questions hovered in the azure eyes, and a hint of doubt. She thought in that moment he saw to the very heart of her, that he knew in an instant her subterfuge—not completely perhaps—but his curiosity had certainly been stirred.

She shrugged and shook her head, the wig's curls bouncing. He could not unmask her. She would not allow it. "*Anglaise*. Jasmine and roses. Do you like?"

Nostrils flaring ever so slightly, as if he tested the air, he said with unexpected certainty, "Your young friend wears something similar."

Oh, dear.

Jane forced herself to remain calm, to think quickly. Her very hesitation might be enough to deepen his suspicion. "Her *favori*," she said with a bored shrug, a little gesture. "She gave me a gift of it."

"Ah," he said, and held out his hand for the quill. "I see."

She gave it to him, avoiding his gaze. She could feel the intensity of his regard, like a weight upon her shoulders. She did not want such an examination. She did not want him to recognize what no one else had— that a young woman hid in this older woman's clothes.

Their gazes met, a fleeting glance. He had felt it, too. The pinprick of suspended lightning.

She looked away quickly, bent to find the ponce box, rose to find the little sharpening knife fallen into the ledger that stood open upon the desk, her debts revealed, indeed punctuated in red.

He was bleeding. She grabbed up a muslin sample from the desk and pressed it to the cut, struck again by the jolt of contact between them.

"Knife slipped." Tone apologetic, curt as always, he pulled hastily away.

"We will bind it," she said. "I have tincture of iodine."

"It is nothing." He was dismissive. An amount was carefully inscribed on the bank draft with his good hand, while he thrust the injured one into his pocket. As he deftly shook the ponce box and blotted dry the ink one-handed, he looked up to say, "As for your offer of refitting the dresses. You will understand it would only pain me if my sisters wore them?"

"*Oui*," she breathed, rather reluctant to so much as glance at the bank draft. So much money. And he took away nothing, nothing but a cut hand and the memory of the dreadful things she had said to him.

"*Vraiment!* Your coat."

A spot of blood seeped through the coat pocket, staining the pale blue, threatening the lining of the cape. "You must allow me to bind your finger," she insisted. "The bleeding has not stopped."

He glanced down, pulled his bloodied hand from the ruined pocket, nodded thoughtfully, and murmured, "If you would be so kind."

"I shall fetch the iodine." She swept through the curtain to the back room, never expecting him to follow, shocked when the curtain rattled behind her and he stood, like a peacock in a hen yard, looking about him in the cluttered space, half-finished dresses draped on straw-stuffed dummies, patterns scattered on the tables where she cut and pressed fabric, the row of flatirons by the fire. Fabric crimpers and pleaters and rollers hung from the wall like ancient torture devices. His gaze found at last the rack of finished dresses. The wedding gown. The ball gown she had worn the night before.

"I was certain to drip on the rug," he said calmly, as if her furnishings were more important than his injury. From the cutting table he took up a fresh scrap of fabric and pressed it to his finger.

The wedding dress!

She was sure he stood staring at the wedding dress, felt sure that he meant to say something about it, about Fanny, but what he said with the mouth that so distracted her, was, "Miss Nichol was not happy with her ball gown?"

Oh, Lord! How to explain away the dress being here rather than in Miss Nichol's possession?

"No, no," she said at once, waving the shears with which she cut a clean strip of muslin. "She loves the gown. It suits her quite well. *Oui?*"

"But why do you have it?"

"A small tear in the hem." Another shrug. Madame was wont to shrug just so. She finished her snipping. "I repair it."

"Ah." He tipped his head to better study the fall of flowers at the sleeve. "However did she manage to get it to you so quickly?"

A polite question, politely voiced, and yet it stymied her temporarily.

She rolled the muslin into a neat ball, fingers shak-

ing, mind racing. "On her way home from the ball. I
was working late."

He cocked his head, one brow arched when he
turned to look in her direction, lips pursed, as if to
hold back a smile. Such a knowing look, such a knowing twist to his incomparable lips. "And she went
home without the dress?"

She would not allow those piercing blue eyes to
rattle her. *"Tout nu,"* she said evenly.

Dark brows rose, bird's wings taking flight. His elegant mouth fell slightly ajar. "Nude?"

She wanted to laugh, but thought better of it.

He clapped shut his captivating mouth, lips thin.
"You are a liar, Madame."

She flushed, embarrassed by her own audacity, glad
of the powder and paint on her cheeks. He could not
see how deeply she blushed. Her father would have
laughed. But whatever had possessed her to say such
a thing to this tight-lipped stranger?

"But of course!" she agreed. "I am a liar *extraordi-
naire*. Miss Nichol went home in a garment already
accompli." She waved a negligent hand at Fanny's unwanted dresses.

"I see," he said, lips easing a bit, his gaze searching
hers again, most intently. "Impertinent of me to suggest otherwise."

"Oui," she said. "And most impertinent of me to
respond as I did. You will forgive me by sitting here
that I may bind your finger?"

He obliged her in sitting by the window where she
and Marie usually took advantage of the light to do
fine work, and held out his hand.

She thought she would be prepared this time, for
the frisson of electricity that ran the length of her
spine when she cupped his bare palm to hers. She was
not prepared at all.

She took a deep breath—how loud it sounded—like
the beating of her heart.

This hand, as no other hand before, stirred a

trembling awareness in every cell of her being, awareness radiating outward like the light of a star, from
the heated universe that sprang alive in the meeting
of their two hands. She did not look at him, at his lips
when they parted. She merely tried to repress the
wave of heat rising from chest to throat, and stifled
all inclination to sigh.

Odd. He flinched at her touch, but did not so much
as quiver when she dabbed his finger with iodine.

She took up the muslin and pressed it firmly against
the cut to stop the bleeding the iodine had begun
again. The slender grace of his hands struck her once
more. So elegantly powerful they looked next to hers.
So tanned by the sun. No calluses, like the one she
had on her pointer finger from years with the needle.
His were not a laborer's hands, but there was strength
to the muscles and tendons, the thickness of the wrist.
She wondered what it would feel like to clasp this
hand, fingers twined.

She thought of Fanny again, of what she had said
when she came in from the rain. She had "told him
the truth, when she might have lied. Should have lied.
When any other woman would have lied."

What truth? What truth had ended the relationship
with this man? What truth so horrible he had canceled
the wedding and jilted the bride?

She snipped the last of the bandage and knotted the
end. *"Voilà!"*

"A neat little package you make of me," he said,
rising, so tall he overshadowed her, blocking the light
from the window. "Is your stitch work as tidily done?"

She need not lie to answer this question. Her chest
swelled with pride. She jumped up to lift the scalloped
flounce hem of the dress on her straw mannequin and
flipped the fabric over that he might see. "Beautiful
work, *non*?"

He studied the green-sprigged day dress rather intently where blond lace insertions had been set in
deep green satin cording, her favorite part of the

dress. For a moment she thought he studied even more intently the turn of her wrist, the ball of her thumb.

She twisted the fabric in a new direction the better to display her work, the better to hide her work-worn fingers.

His own manicured nails trailed along the edge of the lace, a provocative gesture, though his voice held no hint of seduction. "My sisters love this sort of thing." Affection softened his voice, softened the line of his lips. She wondered for a moment what it would have been like to have such a brother.

"You must bring them to me for new *toilette,*" she said.

"Perhaps I will. I thank you for the invitation." With that he was up and on his way briskly through the shop, and she was certain as the bell over the door jingled that in this instance it was he who lied. She would never see the duke, or his sisters, again.

Chapter Four

Edward Brydges smiled for the first time since he had ended things with Fanny, not so much because he was happy, but because he felt he had stumbled upon an interesting mystery that required investigation. Something to take his mind off of Fanny, and the devastating reality of what she had said, and the nightmare that was to come in the courts should her father sue for breach of promise.

As he settled himself in the coach, he eyed the front of Madame Nicolette's shop with its cheerful, red-ribboned wreath and shining brass fixtures and considered what he ought to do.

The woman was a fraud, a liar. He was convinced that Madame Nicolette and Miss Jane Nichol were one and the same.

Perhaps her ruse was harmless; indeed he found himself so drawn to her in an indefinable way that he wanted very much to believe her harmless, but then again, perhaps she was not. He could not understand why an attractive young Englishwoman should pretend to be an older, bespectacled Frenchwoman if she were not in some way practicing guile, perhaps a scam that involved defrauding the local citizenry.

As an MP it was his duty to dig deeper, and he meant to do just that. It would take his mind off of another liar—Fanny.

Returning to the house his family had taken in Great Pulteney Street, Edward surprised his mother and sisters in the midst of directing footmen to carry their trunks and bandboxes downstairs to the second of his carriages—a carriage brought into town specifically for the transport of all of the clothing and servants originally required for the staging of a wedding.

"I intend to remain in Bath a while longer." His voice echoed in the stairwell.

His mother leaned over the railing with an expression of disbelief. "Are you quite serious, Edward?"

"I do apologize for troubling you to pack." He tipped back his head to look up at her.

"Splendid!" Beth called down, while Anne and Celia laughed and waved the footmen back to their rooms, caroling, "We are staying. We are staying!"

"Whatever possessed you to change your mind?" his mother asked as he met her on the stairs.

He shrugged and whispered in her ear. "Unpack, Mother, and I will buy you a new dress."

"Hmph." She looked at him most suspiciously. "I've no real need of a new dress, Edward, but your sisters . . ."

"I will buy each of you a new dress," he said airily, which earned him a trio of whoops as he continued up the elegantly sweeping stairs.

"And have you plans for some entertainment this evening?" she called after him. "There is an Italian singer at the Assembly rooms."

"By all means. An aria it is, though I would much prefer someone French to sing me another tragedy," he said lightly.

Beneath him he could hear his mother mutter. "French tragedy? Whatever do you mean?"

The Italian singer was well received that evening by all who attended the event, almost as much so as the Duke of Chandrose and the duke's party, for though the glances in his direction were more discreet, and generally did not involve the use of opera glasses, they were almost as frequent as those cast toward the singer.

Here was an eligible *parti,* a handsome young man of means and title. There was only the small matter of his recent refusal to marry his fiancée to get past. The night was rife with speculation as to why the duke had done such a thing, as well as how much he would be made to pay for it, but no one had definitive answers on either account, and none could be pried from his mother or his sisters. Enviably discreet, the lot of them. An admirable trait, really, if a trifle irritating.

His Grace seemed preoccupied it was noted during the intermission, both by those who knew him not at all, and by those who knew him most intimately. He settled himself in a position to watch the main entrance. Most unlike him, it was whispered. The duke generally preferred a quiet corner.

When his mother questioned him about it, he whispered an answer only she was privy to. "You suggested I be seen in public, Mother, and that I must not appear to be suffering a broken heart."

"A dutiful son," she was overheard telling his sisters. "Most admirable in a brother."

His lovely sisters were circumspect in their responses, voices kept quiet enough that what they said to one another could not be repeated.

"He looks as if he waits for someone," Anne said to Celia. "Only see how he examines everyone who steps past the door."

"It is odd," Beth agreed from behind her fan.

"A clever ruse," his mother murmured. "Your brother deals with his disappointment exceptionally well."

The duke said nothing, though he felt a pang of sadness, of regret, in realizing it had been several hours since he had really contemplated Fanny, or his loss of her.

Could one really lose what one had never had?

He resolved to consider the matter later, when his emotions were less likely to be affected by the wrenching sentiment of an Italian love song. He must not allow himself to be distracted from his current purpose, said purpose being to discover more of the mysterious Miss Jane Nichol, Bath's biggest liar.

And so he rose at the intermission, and additionally startled his family, in making a point of furthering his acquaintance with the Mayor of Bath, a gentleman he might have otherwise considered beneath his notice. But who, of all the people in the room, might tell him more about a shopkeeper, and a young woman residing in the town?

"Madame Nicolette?" The mayor's face lit up when he said the name, and on either side of him there were those who wondered, who is Madame Nicolette? And why should the duke show an interest in her?

"But of course, I know her." The mayor nodded benevolently. "My wife has recently had a dress made up by her own hand, and quite pleased with it she was. 'The height of fashion' she called it. Demned expensive, I say." He chortled at his own wit. "But I know that will not stand in your way. As you do not want for money, Your Grace, I would highly recommend you take your sisters to her, for while Fieullet is dear by Bath standards, I am sure the quality of her work is equal to any I have ever seen in London. Perhaps better, for you know how highly French couture is regarded."

"I am pleased to hear you approve. And her friend, Miss Nichol? Can you give me her direction? I must thank her for recommending the dressmaker."

The mayor tapped at his chin, thinking. "One of Lady Nichol's daughters? Arrived yesterday?"

"I would not know when she arrived, only that I spoke with her at the Assembly ball last night."

"Yes. Yes. The Nichols arrived yesterday afternoon. I ordered the bells rung for their arrival myself, and they were good enough to sign in at the guest register and have paid subscriptions for the Assembly rooms, the library, and the private walks. If you saw them at the ball, I daresay they may very well be here tonight."

The duke looked about dubiously. "I do not see her."

"Yes. Yes. There they are. Come. I will be more than happy to introduce you."

And then the fat little man was barreling across the room, toward three women the duke had never seen before, and before he could stop the mayor, he was bowing and scraping, and announcing his presence, saying, "His Grace, the Duke of Chandrose begs an introduction."

The ladies, all three of them, lit up like candles at the mention of his title.

Edward could not very well correct the mayor in saying he did not beg for anything. His manner guarded, he bowed to each of them: Lady Nichol, Miss Rose Nichol, and Lily Nichol. No Jane Nichol.

There was no resemblance between these women and Miss Jane Nichol. These Nichols were full of figure, like their mama, and rather florid of complexion. All three of them had brown hair and brown eyes. Stout chestnuts, not a willow. He did not think they could be related to Miss Jane Nichol.

"And which of Lady Nichol's lovely daughters have you met?" the mayor asked.

His words brought a pinched look to Lady Nichol's mouth. She glanced sharply at her daughters as if she would ask them the same question in a far more strident tone.

The two young women shrank under their mother's gaze, before turning to glare at each other suspiciously.

Edward knew at once he was going to regret this introduction. He watched them without speaking, and at last they realized he watched them, and all three strove to hide their unhappy expressions.

"I have not had the pleasure," he said.

"But you said . . ."

The mayor was not the brightest of men.

Edward responded politely, perhaps a trifle imperiously—he was on occasion quite dreadfully imperious his sisters were fond of claiming. "It is a Miss Jane Nichol I have had the pleasure of speaking with."

He might just as soon have said he had met a ghost for the reaction his utterance received.

All three of the women froze, eyes wide, mouths gaping, and then the youngest blurted out, "Jane? You have seen Ja—?"

Anything more she might have said was cut short by the grasp Lady Nichol took upon her daughter's shapely arm, a rather forceful grasp. Lily Nichol's face drained of color.

"You have met my stepdaughter, Jane, Your Grace?" Lady Nichol asked, voice silken. She released her daughter. How pleasant she sounded, and yet her lips thinned in saying Jane's name, and Lily Nichol's wrist bore a red mark.

"Have you another daughter, my lady?" the mayor asked with a fatuous smile, oblivious to the growing tension. "Is she as pretty as her sisters?"

"She is not my sister," Lily Nichol declared indignantly. "She looks nothing like either of us, and she has completely disgraced herself in running away with the d—"

Lady Nichol interrupted, correcting her offspring in the gentlest, the most cloyingly sweet voice—a voice that won instant silence from both her daughters. "She is your stepsister, my dear. A trying young woman," she confided inappropriately to His Grace, "quite fractious since the death of her father, my dear, late husband, Lord Nichol, may his beloved soul rest in peace. As much as I hate to admit it"—and yet she did—"it is true, she has run away from us. We are worried sick about the poor, foolish girl. Any clue you might give us as to her whereabouts would be greatly appreciated, for that she should be returned to the loving bosom of her family is my dearest wish."

Edward watched them without speaking—watched the two young women exchange looks of surprise at their mother's admission. He observed with blank-faced interest the mother carefully choose her every word.

Are all women liars? he wondered.

"I regret to say I cannot reveal her whereabouts," he quietly added to the lies, for while it was true he did not know the young lady's whereabouts, he felt no regret in disappointing this two-faced woman.

The mayor, endlessly jovial, ceaselessly helpful, and completely without discrimination, said with an incessant smile, "Perhaps the dressmaker will know."

"Dressmaker?" Lady Nichol's eyes lit up. She leaned forward and took the mayor's arm.

"Of course," Rose Nichol said with hushed urgency to her sister, as if such a connection made great sense.

"Which dressmaker would that be?" her ladyship was ever so polite in inquiring.

His Grace, the Duke of Chandrose, caught the mayor's eye as he opened his mouth to blurt out the answer, pinning him with a quelling stare, giving his head a quick, subtle shake.

The mayor choked back his reply in surprise as the duke said smoothly, "Where was it she said she hailed from? Bristol?"

The mayor's eyes nearly popped from his head. His mouth sagged open in surprise.

"Bristol?" Lady Nichol asked. "Is Bristol very far from Bath?"

Chapter Five

Jane sat by the back room window, the silver wink of her needle clicking against silver-cased thumb, carefully basting a sleeve into a Christmas gown for the mayor's wife, thinking of the Duke of Chandrose in this very room—of his unexpected kindness—of the way his hand had felt in hers. It did not hurt to remember, to dream a bit, to imagine the duke meant to leave her in peace as Madame Nicolette—that he did not begrudge her making a living—indeed she allowed her mind to wander even further.

She imagined herself in Fanny's shoes, pondered deeply what truth Fanny might have revealed to so alienate the duke. She imagined her stepmother insisting she marry this man rather than the old baron. She imagined her father's reaction to him, her mother's. She dreamed her life as a different story, a story death had not put its grim mark upon. Change the circumstances, and the characters that played in them, and life would be different, so very different.

But she could not change what had already happened. It was foolish of her to imagine too much of what might never be. A waste of time, and thought, and dreaming.

As it was, she was now a dressmaker, not a baron's daughter, and a dressmaker had too much time for imaginings and daydreams, as she set neat stitch upon neat stitch. None of them were likely to come true, of course. Not where a duke was involved at any rate.

When the bell jingled, announcing a customer at the front of the shop, Marie jumped up from the box of ruffles she was examining, bits of sewing they had jobbed out to three elderly ladies who regularly did fine work for them. Jane was in no hurry to rise, to let go completely the fast-dwindling memory of the duke. She was glad Marie took the initiative to sweep through the curtain, saying brightly, "Good afternoon. How may I help you?"

"My sisters require dresses."

That voice! Could it be? Her dreams came to life! Jane could not believe her ears.

"Christmas ball gowns."

That silver surprise of a haughty voice! No mistaking it. It ran the length of Jane's spine like the pricking of a needle.

"Does Madame Nicolette have time to add them to her schedule?"

The duke! Jane's pulse raced.

Setting aside her work, she ran to the curtain. A quick peep. Three exceptionally well-dressed young ladies crowded her shop. *His sisters!* Lord, she thought, he really had brought his sisters to her for dresses! Would wonders never cease? She stifled a breathless laugh.

Heart racing, she swung the door to the back room hastily shut that she might eye the tilt of her cap. Straightening her fichu, smoothing stray locks of the dark, curling wig, and dabbing fresh powder on her nose, she suffered a moment's pang. That he should see her thus—as an older, heavier woman, a woman in trade—completely beneath his touch—ran contrary to the silvery anticipation that surged through her.

But what did it matter? He was there for dresses— dresses for his sisters. Dresses for Christmas! She must cherish this moment for what it was, not what she had dreamed of. It was, indeed, the most she could expect of him.

She took a deep breath, straightened her backbone,

and reminded herself she had chosen this life, this identity, this place. It was all that she wanted and more, was it not?

"*Bonne chance!* Your Grace!" She stepped through the curtain with a businesslike smile, at her most effusively helpful. *Bless the man. Dresses for three!* After overpaying her for a score of dresses he would never see, he came to commission more. She began to like this stiff-rumped, unsmiling duke in every way imaginable.

His eyes met hers at once, a piercing blue gaze that looked down the length of his proud nose into the very heart of her, so keenly, indeed with such a level of unexpected cool suspicion, that she paused in her enthusiastic approach. At once the look disappeared.

Had she imagined it? A trick of the light? She could not be certain, could not stop darting glances at him, studying the tilt of his lips, the tone of his voice.

In his actions he was all that was polite and proper. He introduced the young women as Anne, Beth, and Celia. She greeted them warmly each in their turn. She did not understand the distant manner in which he looked at her, unless . . . unless he knew!

But he could not know. No one knew. Not even Marie suspected.

"*Que voulez-vous?* How may I help you this afternoon?" she asked, and dared to look at him again only to be disconcerted further by his piercing gaze.

"My sisters will tell you what they want," he said.

"We differ decidedly in our tastes," his sister Anne spoke with such confidence, with such a warm smile for Beth and Celia, that Jane liked her at once, and could not help wishing herself so fortunate in sisters.

With that, the duke sat himself in a chair, drew a small book from his pocket, and only now and again lifted his eyes from its pages to watch with a bored air as his siblings bent over fashion plates and fingered fabric swatches, and eyed the racks of laces and trim samples. He was correct. They were quite ready to tell her what they wanted.

So still did the duke sit, barring the occasional turning of a page, and so caught up was Jane in the process of choosing the most flattering cut and colors for each of the young women, she almost forgot he observed her. Not his presence—she could not forget his presence. He was too vibrant an energy, even sitting motionless. The shapely musculature of his legs drew her attention on more than one occasion, as did his mouth, that uptilted, secretive mouth! But now and then she looked up to find his hooded gaze, not bored at all, not reading the book either, but watchful and keen, observing her. And each time she caught him at it, her heart raced.

He veiled that keenness with a bored look, or a yawn, and returned to his pages, but she knew better than to believe him completely absorbed in Plato's works. She found his presence disconcerting, his furtive curiosity vaguely alarming, his mouth absolutely distracting.

She managed, for the most part, to keep her mind on the work, on what was best suited to his sister's forms, figures, and coloring. Anne wanted lace, and lots of it, but Jane managed to dissuade her from a lavish draping at the bodice. A full bosom ought not be overaccentuated.

Beth liked lively color. Jane thought it suited her quite well, but steered her away from a popular rosin-colored satin that jaundiced her complexion. Deep green enhanced the color of her eyes. A much better choice.

Celia was easy. She chose white upon white, which brightened her complexion nicely, and was still very much the fashion. She had only to be convinced that a sheer long sleeve might keep her more comfortable in winter than the off-the-shoulder puffing she chose, and as it could be removed when the weather warmed, the dress might prove useful all the year round.

Decisions made, the young women were eager to set off for the shops for the purchase of shoes, gloves, and shawls to match their recent choices. Their brother rose accordingly, and held the door for them as they departed, a watchful look in his eyes, a knowing curve to his lips.

Jane stood ready to breathe a sigh of complete relief in the wake of such an invasion, but His Grace paused in the doorway, sleek sable hair and sable collar ruffling in the breeze, eyes the color of the sky turning her way one last time, as he said, "Oh, by the by, Madame, will you be so good as to inform Miss Jane Nichol I have had the pleasure of meeting her stepmother and sisters?"

Jane inhaled abruptly, shocked into momentary speechlessness. "Here?" she said at last, forgetting the French accent, forgetting all but this sudden paralyzing fear that she would be found, and made to go back.

His penetrating gaze missed none of it. That look of amused superiority played about his lips. "They attended last night's concert."

The room seemed to close in on her. Her heart thundered, her blood ran cold, her breath came fast. Black spots flickered before her eyes. Fear sat heavy upon her shoulders—it froze her mouth and stilled her brain. What could she say? What should she say?

His eyes narrowed, and he turned more fully, genuine concern in his tone, to ask, "Are you ill, Madame? You look as if you are ready to faint."

Jane took a deep breath to keep from doing just that, and shook her head with undue vehemence, dark curls bouncing against her shoulders, lace lappets fluttering against her cheek. "No. No. *Tout cela est bel et bon*. I am fine. And happy to pass along the *message*. Miss Nichol will be most pleased to have been warned."

His eyes widened, regarding her with even more interest than before. "Warned? Of her own family?"

"Yes. She will wish to avoid them."

"Why should a young woman avoid the care and concern of her family? I am told she is a runaway. That they would welcome the return of their prodigal daughter."

Jane laughed bitterly, gesturing broadly, as Madame had a habit of doing. "In that you are misinformed, Your Grace."

"Am I?" he asked, dark eyes narrowing as he straightened a windblown ribbon on the Christmas wreath that bumped his shoulder. "How so?"

She looked out at the carriage, where his sisters peeped from the windows.

"It is a long *histoire*, *monsieur*. Best heard from Miss Nichol herself."

"It is a story I insist upon hearing," he said crisply, his back very straight, his tone just as stiff. "It went very much against the grain not to reveal at once her whereabouts."

She met this revelation with hope and astonishment. "You did not tell them she is here?"

"I came very close to it."

So righteous his expression, so proper, even haughty, and yet he had not given her away. She wondered why.

"I will allow nothing that endangers a young woman's safety to continue," he said firmly. "Do you know if Miss Nichol means to attend the private Christmas concert this evening at the Assembly rooms? If so, I might ask her about this story firsthand."

Jane pressed her lips together, brow knitted. She did not make a habit of attending the concerts, generally because she had too much work to do. Christmas concerts were not the pastime of a dressmaker. She could not tell him he was almost the only reason Miss Nichol made public her person—that she had no intention of an encore appearance. She most certainly could not risk exposure as Miss Jane Nichol if her stepmother was in Bath with Rose and Lily.

But then an idea occurred to her. There was one place she frequented daily, in which her stepmother would never set foot. She brightened and asked, "Are you an early riser, Your Grace?"

"How early do you deem early?" His lips twitched. She thought he might actually smile.

"At *exactement* six o'clock, when the baths open for business, Miss Nichol visits the King's Bath without fail. If you care to indulge in the *curatif* waters, you are bound to see her."

His Grace's lip curled upward, the knowing look more pronounced than ever. He gave her one last raking glance before he tipped his hat and said, "I am an early riser, Madame."

Chapter Six

Edward descended from his carriage in the predawn mist that shrouded the steps leading to the King and Queen's Bathhouse, in a most suspicious mood. The air smelled of the morning damp and wet stone. It reeked, he thought, of a trap.

Why would Miss Nichol insist they meet here? At this hour? And why, in Heaven's name, had he agreed to it? He knew Miss Nichol to be a liar, who foisted herself off on the public as something she most certainly was not. It seemed likely to him that she wished to place him in a compromising situation, in a most compromising setting.

He scanned the area for witnesses. To place him in a situation worthy of blackmail would require the presence of witnesses.

As if on cue, a Merlin chair emerged from the fog-shrouded line of columns at his right, an aged gentleman pushed by his nurse. The bald head bobbed as the wheels of the little vehicle rattled briskly across the paving stones. The old man peered at him with the baleful glare of a carrion crow. The nurse glanced at him, disinterested.

Surely, he thought, these two were natural elements in the scenery of Bath—surely they had not been corrupted to any scheme that Miss Nichol might have formed. But could he be sure of anything, or anyone, since Fanny?

He watched the pair trundle off down the street, the mist swallowing them. How would he fare as age crept upon him? Would he depart as quickly as his father had, hale and hearty one moment and gone the next? Or was it his fate to be wheeled about in a chair, glaring at fools in the mist?

Edward took a deep breath. He had once thought it did not matter. Come what may he would be a happy man with Fanny at his side. Now his future was uncertain, his happiness suspect. Fanny had done that, Fanny and his own gullibility, made him suspicious of everyone and everything. Certainly he was suspicious of a young woman like Miss Nichol.

With a sigh he stepped into the gloom of the bath-house, gave his overcoat and the change of clothes he had brought into the hands of an attendant in the changing room, and insisted he did not care to remove his frock coat or waistcoat. The attendant had bathing coats for rental, and wooden pattens that his leather shoes might not get wet, but he waved them aside. He had worn this black coat, his least favorite, with the expectation of its being soaked, and he did not care for wooden shoes that other feet had trod.

Accepting the length of linen he was offered, and the japanned tray he was instructed to tie to his wrist, he proceeded down the steps into deeper gloom, emerging from an archway into the silvered square of morning fog where the King's Bath itself bubbled greenly, steam rising thick as smoke. The columns and galleried rooftop that boxed in the bath rose gracefully in the mist, houses towering grayly just beyond, lamp-light in the windows, the smell of bread baking, of sausage grilling, rich upon the air.

His stomach growled. He had skipped breakfast, intent on being prompt. Now he wondered why.

The water appeared empty, the mysterious Miss Nichol nowhere to be seen. Had she gulled him into coming with no intention of arriving herself? Had she boarded a post coach for parts elsewhere? Frightened away? What had she to fear? Why would a young woman flee the bosom of her family? Lady Nichol and her daughters were a trifle unpleasant, but worthy of flight? He hardly thought so.

He leaned against the aged base of a Roman column to slip his shoes from his feet and to pull off his stockings. His calves looked very white in the predawn gloom, vulnerable in their nakedness. His feet felt like blocks of ice.

He imagined one of his sisters running away, throwing herself upon the mercy of the world in the middle of winter—as a dressmaker. The vision was as incomprehensible as an Englishman in wooden shoes. He could not conceive of it—imagined all the ills that might befall her, and shivered. The damp paving stones beneath his feet were unbearably cold.

Dear God, he wondered, where was the foolish, deceitful young woman? How foolhardy for any young woman of means to abandon her home, a position in society, all for pursuit of a trade? It seemed such a lonely endeavor—and risky in the extreme.

The sounds of the water intruded on his thoughts—flowing, dripping, slapping the sides of the pool. The sound of movement, of change—like his life.

No sense in standing here shivering, he concluded. He dipped a toe into the steaming water, surprised by the lure of its heat. Despite the flatiron stink, the green depths looked enticing, and the rest of him felt suddenly cold. He yearned for warmth, for the buoying comfort of water all around, and so in he stepped, the bath even more soothing than he had expected as he doused himself slowly, hot water wrapping his bare calves, soaking his breeches, clutching at his thighs, teasing his private parts.

When his coattails floated like a blackbird's wings on the murky green surface of the bath, when his abdomen tensed against the water's encroaching embrace, he felt a fresh surge of anger. She had tricked him into coming. He soaked himself and a perfectly good set of clothes in this stinking green water for no good reason.

His chest trembled in the chill of the waterline, despite his waistcoat, despite the drenched weight of the black coat that seemed determined to pull him deeper, pockets bubbling as they submerged. In or out, he must decide. He closed his eyes, and sank down into water's warm arms, until the wet lead stink of it cupped his chin.

He made waves with such sudden movement, waves that rippled over his shoulders, waves that slapped the heel of his chin.

The air smelled suddenly of roses—jasmine and roses.

He started, eyes flying open, warmth spraying his mouth as he whirled, an unpleasant taste, much like the underlying mineral smell of this place. Not jasmine. Not roses.

Miss Nichol. She stood less than four feet behind him, half-submerged in the water, looking even more slender than before, too slender—as if she did not eat enough—almost wraithlike in the long, black bathing dress that ballooned about her hips, still partially dry, pockets of air lifting it away from the suggestion of pale legs in the murky water. She batted at the fabric, noisy bubbles rising, the skirt not at all anxious to drown. She looked embarrassed as she did so, face flushing, her hands anxious.

The flaxen silk of her hair had been gathered in a graceful knot at the crown of her head. The rising cloud of humid air beaded it with diamonds of light. Damp wisps plastered brow and temples. He thought of long-necked swans, of dew-drenched lilies, of fallen angels.

The dress succumbed at last to her coaxing, trailing about her like a cloud of wet seaweed.

His heart thundered. He had not really expected her to come—had convinced himself she was in all ways the liar, the costumed deceiver.

But she wore no disguise here, no pretense of powder, no rouge to color her heat-pinked cheekbones. So young she looked. A perfect, youthful complexion

was bejeweled with water pearled by the misted light.
Her green eyes had gone pewter-colored, golden
lashes starred with moisture.

She seemed to him to be staring at his mouth. But
surely not, surely he imagined any fixedness in her
gaze.

"Wonderful, isn't it?" She waved her arms through
the water, dark sleeves trailing.

Could this creature really be the same powdered
and rouged, matronly-shaped woman he had stared at
for hours the day before as she measured his sisters
for Christmas gowns? It did not seem possible she
could so completely transform herself. It certainly did
not seem right. Just as it was not right that he should
feel drawn to her.

"Do you come here often?" he asked, his shoulders
as cold as his voice, his soaked shirt, waistcoat, and
coat heavily clammy against his skin. He sank down
to warm himself, teeth chattering, heart thumping, his
body roused to her despite his mind's complete understanding that the bewitching Miss Nichol was dangerous.

"I try to," she said, and turned, a dancer in the
water, graceful and lithe. The tray of comfits that trailed
from her wrist teetered and bobbled in her wake. She
ended up looking at him over her shoulder—the little
coquette. He must not be charmed by her, must not
give in to the impulses of the flesh. She was a liar—
and of all things he detested liars most at this point
in his life.

He looked about, sure she would need witnesses for
anything nefarious. But for the present they had the
baths to themselves. He wondered if that, too, was
planned. Lure him to a lonely, provocative place, clad
in wet, provocative clothing, and see to compromising
him when others arrived. It was a public place. Other
bathers would arrive eventually.

"I do love a hot bath." She sank down, as he had,
so that the water embraced her shoulders, and kissed
her chin.

Temptress. Angel. He resolved not to be taken in, not to be deceived by feminine wiles. They were so blatant when one stood back and observed them coolly.

"I used to frequent only the Queen's Bath." She rose in a sudden wash of water to point, the dark fabric of her bathing costume clinging most provocatively, steam rising from heated cloth, from heated neck and hands.

He looked away, rather heated himself.

"The water flows out of the King, and into the Queen."

She said it without so much as a blush.

"Thus it is cooler, but I am not happy anymore unless I have stewed in the King's heat." She tilted her head and brushed a strand of light-silvered hair from her cheek with a wet hand.

Did she know, he wondered, how much heat her words might stir in a man?

"One grows accustomed, I suppose," she said.

He wondered if men ever grew accustomed, even resistant, to woman's wiles.

"How long have you been in Bath?" he asked. Safe ground, he thought. Safe question, for he must question her. That was why he came, was it not?

"Six months," she said.

He thought back to the ledger on Madame Nicolette's desk. The first entry had been almost exactly six months ago. He might assume, therefore, she did not begin with a lie.

"Why did you run away?" he asked coolly.

"What?" She backed away, eyes wide, water sluicing.

"Do not pretend." He pushed after her, the water resistant. "I know who you are. I know they pursue you. What I do not know is why you chose to leave them in the first place."

She slowed her backward flight, hands rising to the water's silvered surface, balancing her stance, chin rising as well, obstinance in her gaze, in the tone of her voice. "Why should I tell you?"

"Because otherwise I will tell them a young, unprotected female is trying to pass herself off as a matronly French seamstress in Milsom Street."

She sighed, head bowed, water trickling from her hair to her cheeks like a rush of tears. Her breath came fast, as though they ran a race. "I see. I might just as well ask, why did you leave Fanny?"

An unexpected turn in the conversation, to be so questioned when his questions went unanswered. The water pushed him toward her. He swayed when he would not be swayed, and yet his feet would not be still. They led him closer to her. It made him angry with his body, with his lack of control.

She did not back away, simply looked at him unblinking, her lashes pale gold, the light touching the green of her eyes as he said, voice low, "That is none of your business."

"Why?" she snapped. "Because I have no threat to hold over you with which to make you tell?"

So defiant she looked. And in her defiance, eyes sparkling, back ramrod straight, chest thrust forward, she was beautiful. He tried to imagine Fanny in this young woman's position, and wanted to laugh. Fanny had no intention of supporting herself by any means other than a rich husband's purse. Odd, that her choice should be deemed entirely acceptable by society, while this young woman would be condemned, even scorned, for hers.

He responded quietly, the sibilant hush of his voice whispering back at them from the stone walls. "*I* am not a woman alone who may be imperiled by her own foolishness."

Imperious. He realized he sounded imperious. A bad habit of his, and he knew he had done it again the moment she inhaled abruptly, as if he had struck her. Gaze falling away, she wiped the droplets from her forehead with the flat of her hand, a look of sad desperation in eyes gone deep green with the growing light. "You think me a fool?"

Water starred the pale fringe of her lashes. It beaded upon full lips, kissable lips. Edward could not tell her he thought her beautiful, and vulnerable, and while that ought to rouse the most protective and brotherly part of him, it roused something else entirely. He could not stop watching the emotional rise and fall of her chest, standing as she did, so straight and indomitable.

There was far too much intimacy in such a meeting. He could not help thinking that the same water that soaked his shirt to clinging transparency washed up against the soaked folds that clung to her bosom. That, in this way, they touched.

"I do not know you," he said, carefully modulating his tone. "I know not what to think of you other than that you sew as well as you spin tales."

She studied him a moment, eyes wide, breath misting the air. As the light grew, her hair looked more golden than silver. She must be cold, standing as she did, half in and half out of the water. Was it passion or the cold made her breasts rise and fall with such vehemence?

He could not look away, and that made him rather impatient with himself, for he prided himself in avoiding crass temptation. He had never been drawn to many of the passionate pastimes his peers relished. He had never visited women of ill repute, indeed, had never so much as attempted to fondle Fanny. And yet this slender wraith managed to stir him to an unfamiliar yearning.

She thrust her chin forward mulishly, her own passions focused elsewhere.

"I see no reason to confide in you if you will not confide in me." Her voice was deep in its intensity. She did not speak loudly, but with force. "Why should I trust a stranger to have my best interests at heart, any more than my family was supposed to?"

So her family had not her best interests at heart?

This was the first indication she had given as to why she might have run away.

She turned, wet hair slapping her shoulder, and pushed away from him through the misted water.

He did not want it to end this way, when so much promise hung upon the damp air, when need and curiosity still spurred him to know more of her motivations, her designs.

"You leave me no choice," he said, voice low.

The words had the desired effect.

As if pinned by the slanted bar of morning light, she stopped, head turned slightly, the side of her face gilded by the light, the profile of her upper body steaming, haloed golden by the mist.

He could not allow this mysterious water sylph to slip away.

"Tell me why they had not your best interests at heart," he said quietly, the earnest tone of his voice echoing back at him from the side of the pool.

She turned more completely, face damp, lips damp, and with a surge of deep need he realized he wanted her. Against his better inclination, against reason, he wanted this woman. He wanted to erase the pain of Fanny's rejection, to feel whole, and wanted, and desirable again.

"Have *you* my best interests at heart?" she asked quietly, her manner intense, as if the question were important to her. He could read the tension in the line of her neck, in the focus of her gaze. The steam from the water seemed risen from her.

He licked lips gone suddenly dry. Did he have her best interests at heart? In what way did he want her? Were his intentions honorable? She was a dressmaker, he a duke. It had been his intention to expose her for the scheming liar she was. What exactly were his intentions now?

He looked away, watching the awkward upward flutter of a dove, heavy against the light. Its wings beat the air, the clatter of feathers loud, a single, downy bit of silvery gray fluff floating free as it gained height.

She stood wordless a moment, unmoving, her expression unchanged. "Do what you will," she said at last. "I have heard you are a man of honor, righteous and fair, of spotless reputation until . . . until Fanny." She shook her head and sighed. "Of all people, I thought you would understand."

"Understand what?" he demanded, patience worn thin. "You have given me no reason to understand."

"My circumstances echo your own."

He dared to suggest wryly, "You canceled a wedding?"

She shook her head, the light gleaming in her hair, winking on the droplets on her cheek. "It never got that far."

He waited for more.

She slid a guilty look his way, head down. "I ran away."

He remembered what her stepsister had blurted at the Assembly rooms. That Jane Nichol had completely disgraced herself running away with the . . . With whom? Whom had she run away with, he wondered cynically, and where was he now that she was disgraced?

"Go on," he prodded.

Voices and footsteps stilled her. The echo of wooden shoes on wet stone. A gaggle of old women in bathing costume passed the King's pool, pattens clacking, their tongues clacking almost as loudly. He thought of Miss Nichol's mother and sisters—fond of gossip—all too ready to tell him their version of the truth. With Jane he must extract every word like a pearl from its shell.

"You were saying?" He turned back to resume their conversation, only to find her halfway across the pool, water rippling in her wake. One thing was certain. She had not come here with the intention of compromising him. Could it be she was what she said, and nothing more?

Rather than give chase, he headed for the nearest set of steps, his hope to move faster outside the resistance of the water. If he hurried, he might be able to make it around the pool by way of the pavement, ready to offer his hand as she made her watery exit.

And so he would have, had his progress not been impeded by the mayor, who beamed at him jovially from the door to the men's changing room, and waving his toweling as he approached, said, "Your Grace! You are the early riser, and just the man I have been wanting to see!"

With regret Edward watched Miss Nichol make good her escape from water's clutch before he turned to face the mayor with a polite "Good morning."

Had the man any other facial expression than an ear-to-ear grin, Edward wondered. Had he any other manner than that of closest friend and confidant?

The mayor leaned close, breathing peppermint and hot chocolate on him to say in a whisper that echoed, "I must say I was surprised you told Lady Nichol that our fine French dressmaker is to be found in Bristol."

She passed them as he said it. Drenched and shivering, her length of linen toweling draped about her shoulders like a limp cape. Her wooden pattens tapped loudly on the stone flooring. He wondered if she heard, if she understood. She did not look in their direction.

"I've good reason," he said.

"No doubt!" The mayor laughed, and leaning closer, in the most comradely way imaginable, a twinkle in his eye, he clapped Edward on the back to ask, "Is she pretty? Good reasons often are," before he plunged into the hot bath with a splashy groan of sheer delight.

Chapter Seven

The duke waited for her in the colonnade outside the bathhouse, in the drizzling rain, an umbrella hoisted along with his coat collar. He looked cold, she thought, his hair standing out in wet spikes. She had never seen him look anything but calm, collected, well-groomed. He seemed more human with his hair gone all hedgehogish. She wondered how long he had stood there, and why he had not bothered to dry his hair.

Her own hair was damp, but bundled up in a mob-cap, topped by a bonnet, to keep out the chill. The rest of her felt very warm this morning, heated by the bath, by the presence of the irritating gentleman who fell into step beside her, umbrella large enough to shelter both of them if she did not mind walking rather close.

The duke seemed to expect it of her.

She chose not to object. Perhaps there was still hope she might convince him to keep her secret.

"I still have questions," he said.

"I suspected as much."

"And yet you walked away."

"The place echoes dreadfully. You did not wish our conversation overheard, did you?"

"No. Best not."

She nodded, then set both pace and direction away from the shadow of the cathedral, into the High Street, north. The wind off the river sweetened the air as they crossed Bridge Street into Northgate past pubs and shops still shuttered and dark.

She had to confirm what she thought the mayor had said. "You told them I was in Bristol?"

He examined his feet rather than look her way. "Who?"

She made an impatient noise, warmth rising from the very core of her being. A surprising comfort, his kind action coupled with his reluctance to brag about it. "You know exactly who I am talking about."

He slid a faintly amused glance her way, dark brows arching. "People do have a tendency to misinterpret. I might have mentioned a dressmaker in Bristol. I never told anyone it was you."

A silver surprise, this man. He seemed impatient with her most of the time, even angry, and yet he had done such a thing. She wondered why. She longed for the briefest instant to throw her arms about his neck in gratitude—but he quashed the inclination at once in saying, "I must warn you. It is not at all my habit to lie, indeed, even to prevaricate. I do not care for secrets. Far better to have the truth behind one."

But of course it was, she thought. What did he take her for? An idiot? An incorrigible liar?

Perhaps he did! Dreadful thought.

She did not dwell on the idea, preferring to imagine instead, her stepmother, who hated to travel, on her way to Bristol.

"Are the roads to Bristol well paved?" she could not resist asking.

"They are."

Canny, the way in which he looked at her, as if he read her mind.

"A pity," she said, and stopped in front of a baker's window, arrested by the smell of fresh-baked bread, by the sight of golden loaves piled high. She closed her eyes, inhaling the wonderful smell. Sugar and yeast and cinnamon. She must remember to buy a plum pudding for Christmas—in remembrance of her mother. She opened her eyes to find him staring rather hungrily—though not at the baker's goods.

Oh, Lord! Why had she not realized at once? Did he hope to obligate her? Heat rose to her cheeks. "And do you think I owe you something for this wild-goose chase of a favor?"

One moment he was looking at her as if he would never look away, the next he tilted his head, frowning, and seemed quite preoccupied with the placement of the umbrella as the breeze buffeted its spokes. "You owe me an explanation," he said quietly.

He twirled the umbrella, flinging water, flinging an offended look her way as well.

An explanation? She supposed she did owe him that much.

"You must join me for a concert breakfast at the Assembly rooms," he said as if the matter were already decided. "To tell me the rest of your story, that I may not regret having sent three ladies on a long, arduous, and completely pointless journey."

Three ladies who would most certainly hear gossip of any young woman who breakfasted with the duke at the Assembly rooms. Jane pursed her lips, watching the milkman's dray as it trundled up the street. Not a sensible or polite offer this peremptory, even pompous demand. No. The duke ordered her about like a lackey, his lackey. Had he no comprehension of the demands on a working woman's time and energy? Of the risk she would be taking in being seen in public with him?

He turned to look at her, brows arched, his look imperious—every inch of him the gentleman. But was he really? Did he wear the disguise of gentility as she wore the disguise of Madame Nicolette? She could not be certain.

She shook her head. "I think not. It would be risky. You are too much the center of everyone's attention, especially now. And I must open the shop. Christmas ball dresses to sew." She arched an eyebrow to echo his. "Marie will not recognize me without my wig, so I've . . . changes to see to."

His mouth curled in disdain. "Of course."

She felt a twinge of guilt. She did not mean to deny him an explanation any more than she enjoyed living a lie. She did not care for the heavy warmth of the wig every day, the awkward addition of padding about hips and waist. What woman would? And yet, she saw no other solution, no other way.

"The woman who works with you does not know?"

She glanced at him by way of his reflection in the lamp-lit window, willing him to unbend a little. Stiff his back, stiff the manner in which he asked. "She knows I wear a wig. She tells me often I wear too much powder, but no, I have not told her. Only one person in Bath knows other than . . ." She gave a wry nod in his direction.

"I see," he said briskly.

Did he see? she wondered. Did he have an inkling of how important his silence was to her continued success? Her future? So calm the line of his jaw, so resolute, as if he had no doubts how he must deal with her.

She stared vacantly at the baker's loaves, rows of Bath buns blurring. What could she tell a gentleman to convince him the path she had chosen was not only best but necessary?

It would seem she was not to be given a chance.

"Will you wait here a moment?" he asked, handing her the umbrella, which hardly seemed necessary as the rain no more than misted. The heavy silver handle was warm from his grasp, as warm as the breath of air that swept from the door as he stepped into the bakery. She closed her eyes a moment, savoring that warmth, the umbrella's shielding weight, the comforting smell. When she opened her eyes, he was looking at her through the window, as he stood at the baker's counter, a speculative look, a pucker in his brow, as if he did not know what to make of her.

She wondered, as she gazed back at him, clutching

the engraved handle of his umbrella, why this man, a very personable and wealthy gentleman of title, took interest in her, of all the women in Bath. Why had he not revealed her whereabouts to her stepmother at once? What had she to offer him other than Christmas dresses?

What other than the basest of human exchanges? The sort of activity she had vowed never to sink to when she left her father's house, when she struck out on her own. Not that. Never that. She considered for the briefest of moments walking away, but the wind caught at the umbrella, baffling the waterproofed fabric, showering raindrops in a glitter of silvered light.

She tilted the umbrella at a fresh angle and took firmer hold on the silver handle, the engraving catching her eye, an acorn and an oak leaf. She turned the umbrella the better to see it.

The movement caught his eye. He glanced her way again, no smile upon his lips, no come-hither gleam in his eyes.

Indeed, her mind ran away with her. He had no seductive airs, seemed not at all interested in her physically. The bath had surely tested his intent.

A man who did her favors.

Was she so jaded to the efforts of a Good Samaritan that she expected signs of lascivious intent?

Barring a certain intensity of gaze, followed by an avoidance of looking at her, and the occasional quirking of his mouth, she had observed nothing to worry her as much as his touch had. She could not forget his touch—the quick flare of heat in his glance.

He was out again before she had time to speculate further, bringing with him warmth and good smells and a warm paper cone. He handed it over in exchange for the umbrella.

"What's this?"

"You looked hungry."

She blinked, surprised he should care. The cone was stuffed with Bath buns, glistening with butter, sugar, and raisins.

"Thank you. I am."

"As am I."

Again he surprised her, in admitting he felt anything. He seemed so careful all the time to hide emotion, feelings, or desires.

She shifted the paper cone, paper crackling, that he might take one.

He rummaged among the soft, rounded nest of buns, their gloved hands on either side of the paper, his pushing downward, hers pushing up. Physical tension hovered between them like the glinting raindrops that clung to the edge of the umbrella, growing fat and bulbous before falling. He refused to look at her, and yet seemed always on the edge of glancing her way. She, to the contrary, could not look away from his mouth, lips locked in their perpetual expression of lofty amusement.

He plucked a sugared raisin from the top of the bun and popped it into that mouth, breaking the spell. She blinked and looked away.

"You mentioned a connection between your circumstances and mine," he said.

The bun in her hand was warm, the bite of yeasty dough a good excuse not to answer immediately. She supposed she would have to tell him.

"Mm." She turned her head.

He paused in his chewing, his gaze settling on her mouth of all things. So often had she looked at his, she found the mirrored attention quite unsettling until he tapped the corner of his lip.

"Have I crumbs?" she asked, heat rising to her throat, flaming in her cheeks.

He nodded.

She brushed at her mouth.

He raised his hand, as if to touch her. It faltered in midair. "Other corner," he said, and looked away.

The tip of her tongue found the sweetness. Sugar, not crumbs.

"That's got it," he said, his gaze politely averted. "I am sorry to have interrupted. You were telling me why you ran away."

She rolled down the top of the coronet, paper crack-ling, anything to delay addressing this subject, of all subjects. How did one discuss such a thing with a com-plete stranger? A stranger one wished to impress, who already had a less than favorable opinion of one?

With a sigh, she stopped fussing and said, "Lady Nichol was keen on the match."

"You were to be married?"

He was admirably direct. She decided to answer him in kind. "My father would have objected to the gentle-man in question."

He did not respond immediately, and when he did it was to ask the unexpected. "How long ago did you lose him?"

She inhaled deeply, the pain still fresh enough to leave a dull ache. The mouthful of bun seemed to lodge itself deep in her throat. "Almost two years now."

"And your mother?"

She stared at the rain that misted in tarnished sil-vered sheets across the street ahead of them, blurring the edges of the buildings. "I was a child."

"A pity, to lose one's mother so young."

She leaned her nose into the comforting smell waft-ing from the paper cone. "A pity to lose one's mother at any age."

She turned the corner into Bond Street and paused to peer in a stationer's window. Her reflection looked sadly back. She shrugged, forced a smile, and noisily unrolling the paper again, turned to offer him an-other bun.

He peered into her eyes rather than into the prof-fered cone. "Life never unfolds as one expects."

She almost dropped the buns. Indeed, she clutched the paper cone to her chest rather than spill its contents. *Her mother's words exactly!* She could not believe he had uttered her mother's words exactly.

Oblivious to his impact on her, he leaned close and plucked out another bun, careful not to stir the paper too much, careful not to press his hand to hers, or to venture too close.

Startled, she looked up, thrusting the crushed paper cone away from her person, knocking his hand in the process. He paused, his regard intent beneath the radiating spokes of the umbrella, his eyes the inky blue of the rain-darkened sky.

"One must cherish what is, rather than the dream of what might have been," she blurted.

He blinked, looked faintly puzzled, faintly pained, and then his gaze sharpened. The bun no longer interested him.

"What dream? What might have been?"

So intense his voice, his manner, as though she spoke directly to him of his life, his dreams.

Fanny. Of course. He thought she meant to remind him of Fanny. Not her intention at all.

"Had my mother not died," she said quietly.

He blinked before meeting her gaze once again, sympathy weighing his gaze, pulling at his mouth.

"Had my father not . . . remarried."

He closed his eyes, as if to better absorb what she told him, and then, lashes fluttering, he pinned her with the deep blue depths, and said, "We would not be standing here now, enjoying Bath buns." He bit into the bun, his jaw strong as he chewed. His gaze flickered in her direction as he swallowed. "Why would your father have objected to the gentleman?"

She could not take her eyes from the strength of his mouth, from the youthful fullness of his lips, from the healthy sheen of his hair. Had he any idea what he possessed in his youth? In good health?

"The baron is a contemporary of Father's. A man whose habits and history we both knew well."

He cocked his head, "Ah! A vast difference in age, then?"

She peered down at the buttery buns, the clusters of sugared raisins. Hard to imagine the dried fruit had been plump and firm in its youth.

She turned away, no longer hungry. "Twenty-two years."

"A man of means?"

She sighed, then tucked the bundle of buns under her arm. "Wealthy, yes. But forty pieces of silver made a traitor out of the best of men."

"Do you not sacrifice your youth, your beauty, your status, Miss Jane Nichol, in order to earn the very silver you scorn?"

She stared at the rooftops, dark gray, disappearing into the pale gray of the sky. Like life, she thought, and truth, gray upon gray. "The difference being, I choose how the sacrifice is made."

He blinked in surprise.

She spoke quickly, impassioned for her subject. "Does not marriage bring a woman a living by way of a husband? And does a woman not sacrifice youth, beauty, status, even security, certainly her independence in becoming a wife, and mother, in the very legalities of marriage, which transform all of her worldly goods into her husband's possessions? Those possessions to be taken away from her if he should die without issue."

With a look of consternation he tossed what remained of his bun into the gutter, and dusted crumbs from gloved hands, from the facing of his lapel, umbrella swaying. Then he glanced sideways at her, and said with a wry twist of his lips, "You've a bleak way of regarding the institution of marriage."

She shrugged. "I have seen poor example of it."

His brows shot upward. "But surely you will agree most women do not take upon themselves a disguise, as you have, when they marry?"

She was not at all prepared to agree. "You would ask a dressmaker if women disguise themselves?" She laughed.

Did a smile hover briefly about his lips? Hard to tell, he was so abruptly brisk and proper, and inquisitive.

"Who helped you with your disguise?"

She wished she might better disguise her impatience. "My old governess and my stepmother, if you must know."

"Lady Nichol? Really? Does she know the part she played?"

"Oblivious."

He was amused. The slight twitch of his lip could be identified in no other way. She began to think she misjudged him. He was, as his expression suggested, perpetually amused. Catlike the tilt of his lips. One almost expected him to purr.

She had not thought to amuse him. It buoyed her spirits—offered fresh hope—unless of course he found her no more than a temporary amusement, and meant to play with her until she ceased squeaking.

"She used to speak often of the dressmakers in Paris," she said, still fascinated by the play of emotion in his oh-so-subtle lips, "of their superiority to English seamstresses. I really must credit her for inspiring the notion of Madame Nicolette."

They turned into Milsom Street. Not far now to the shop.

"And does Madame keep you safe?"

His was a logical mind.

Jane pulled her keys from her reticule, taking comfort in the weight of them, in their familiar silvery jingle. "Yes. Madame encounters fewer obstacles in business than Miss Nichol would have. She is more mature, a woman of the world, less likely to be seduced or bamboozled."

He waited while she put key to lock, the lock clicking open. She swung the door ajar with a jangle of the overhead bell. She stopped there, blocking the doorway, not intending to ask him in.

"The price seems high." He said it gently, as gentle as the rain, as resonant as the echo of the bell.

She sighed. His words, meant to comfort, served only to render her weak and wistful. She stood up straight as she pocketed the key to her door—her millinery shop—her dream come true.

"I could see no alternative," she said briskly. The perfume of the fabrics, of fresh dyes, met her nose in an eye-watering wave. She blinked back unbidden tears and said, "Bath promises opportunity enough for success if I can but avoid being found out. You must tell me, Your Grace, do you mean to expose me?"

He tilted the umbrella behind his head, no need to cover her anymore. She stood sheltered in the doorway.

"There is no one else in the family to whom you might appeal? An uncle? A cousin?"

She shook her head, wondering if the whole day meant to be gloomy.

"No one," she murmured. The lack of good light would be hard on her eyes, hard on the evenness of the stitches. "Your answer, Your Grace?" she pressed, not backing down, not asking him in. She had too much to do. The buns beneath her arm had gone cold.

"How soon will my sisters' ball gowns be ready for a fitting, Madame Nicolette?" he asked.

He caught her off guard with the question.

She eyed him a moment, considering what it meant. "A week, maybe less," she said, warily, hope rising. Did he mean to give her hope?

"I will give you my answer then," he said, and tipping his hat, he walked away, coattails swaying, footsteps echoing.

She stood for a moment, watching him go, watching the rain fall, the taste of Bath bun gone flat in her mouth.

Chapter Eight

"My dear Jane! I began to think you would not come today," Miss Godwin sat by the window in her Merlin chair, her favorite spot, for from this vantage point on the first floor of St. Joseph's Hospital, she could look out over the street, and in the distance got a glimpse of the river.

"My dear Miss Godwin." Jane took her hand and warmed it between her own. "I do apologize for coming later than usual. I could not get away sooner, but I would never forget Madame Nicolette's favorite customer—her very first customer."

Miss Godwin leaned forward with a wink.

"Your dress is finished, as promised." Jane drew the garment from the valise she had carried in with her, and held the high-necked, blue woolen dress in front of her old governess. "It is lovely, do you not agree?"

Miss Godwin nodded. Her rheumy blue eyes gleamed as she held the fabric close in order to study the pretty row of pin tucks across the bodice. "Just as you said, Jane. And I am very glad you talked me into the heavier cloth. This damp does seep into these old bones of mine. It will be lovely to have a warmer frock."

"Do you wish to try it on?" Jane rose. "It would be a pleasure to help you into it."

"Not right now, my dear. I will too soon be in bed to fully enjoy the effort of changing. Tomorrow I will start the new day with a new dress." Her eyes sparkled with anticipation.

"You will be wanting your shawl?" Jane wrapped her shoulders in the crocheted wool.

"How very kind you are, my dear." Miss Godwin patted her hand. "You are busy then? Christmas custom? I hear the Duke of Chandrose brings his sisters to your shop. That his patronage has finally awakened all of Bath to the beauty of your work."

Jane's mouth dropped open. "You hear of this already?"

Miss Godwin laughed the same heartfelt chuckle that had captivated Jane so many years before. "I may be confined to my room, my dear, but I have my sources for finding out what goes on in the world."

Jane beamed at her. "Indeed, you must. The bell over the door has not stopped ringing all day. And all the duke's doing."

"Really? His patronage means so much?" Miss Godwin sounded disbelieving.

Jane nodded. She could not tell her old governess how completely the duke's life and her own were now linked. She could not speak of how she had arranged to meet him in the quiet heat of the bathhouse, how they had walked together in the silvered mist of morning. Miss Godwin would not understand. She certainly would not approve. It would only worry her more. It had been men Miss Godwin had worried about most when Jane had come to Bath, determined to set up shop as a seamstress.

"He knows," she said. "Madame's secret."

"Oh, dear," Miss Godwin said. "However did he find out?"

"He is clever, and I was careless. But, that's not the worst of it. Lady Nichol and my sisters are in Bath for the Season."

"Oh, dearo dearo." The worry lines in Miss Godwin's brow deepened. "Have they come looking for you?"

"It would seem that way. Do not be surprised if they come to you with questions of me."

Miss Godwin rubbed at her forehead in the same way she had in the schoolroom when Jane had not completed her lessons. She had been such a young woman then. It was only now, as an adult, that Jane could see it clearly. Miss Godwin had given Jane her own youth, her strength, her wisdom.

"Do you mean to leave?" The frail chair-bound woman asked querulously. "Please do not tell me you mean to leave."

Jane frowned. She did not want to go, to leave Miss Godwin alone, as she had found her in Bath. She sighed and said, "That very much depends upon the duke."

The duke heard himself mentioned more than once as he strolled languidly through the hallways of the hospital his grandfather had been instrumental in building, a hospital that numbered among many he contributed to charitably. The staff knew he was there. Word had gotten out that the roof, long in need of repairs, was to be mended at the duke's expense. The water closets, which had been a problem since inception, were also to receive attention. Three workmen had given him their suggestions. He studied three different scrawled accountings as he walked, flipping from one page to another, viewing the problems firsthand.

Thus he did not think much of it when, in leaning against a wall rather near one of the patient's door frames, he heard himself mentioned. Nothing unusual in it. His status preceded him. His grandfather's name and money had been instrumental in shaping more than one area of the town.

What surprised him was the voice. A voice he recognized immediately from that very morning—the voice that had impressed itself on him only a few days before by insulting him—a voice he had begged to divulge its secrets. He had not expected to hear Miss Nichol within these walls. What had she to do with the aged and ill?

"The duke is entirely responsible," she said.

Her voice was low. One might hear it clearly only in standing very close to the open doorway, closer than he now stood. Dribs and drabs he could make out, but not the whole cloth of what was being said.

"Twice as much purchased . . ." he thought she said. Then, "Must not let opportunity be wasted."

He hesitated to move closer. First because it involved eavesdropping on private conversation, a practice he abhorred, and second, because if he was not very careful, either one of the women might look up and see him.

And yet, he could not resist, if only for a moment. What if his attractive little liar meant to dupe a defenseless old woman? He sidled closer to the door, pretending to be engrossed by his paperwork.

"Four extra dummies," she said.

Dummies! Whom did she consider dummies? he wondered.

"Wise, my dear, with so much new business," the old lady said.

"Is it?" Miss Nichol did not sound convinced. She paced the room as she said, "Only imagine if this sudden flush of good fortune were to be snatched away by the very hand that granted it in the first place!"

"A reverse Midas touch," the old woman said with a laugh.

Whose touch? His? He frowned. It had not occurred to him that he might be snatching anything.

Jane Nichol sighed. "Marie spent half the afternoon scouring Bath for women who might be interested in making a bit of Christmas money doing piecework. Flounces to go here, ruffles there. Hems and seamwork in a dozen different hands."

The old woman chimed in. "She came to St. Joseph's. Mrs. Blessing and Mrs. Montfort have both agreed to do hems."

"Have they? Good of them."

"Good *for* them, to keep their hands and minds active, my dear, and to be able to bring in a few extra pennies at Christmastime. Sounds as if a great many nimble-fingered women in Bath stand to profit from Madame's sudden flush of prosperity."

"Yes. They also stand to suffer if Madame's secret is revealed." The chair creaked as Jane sat forward to speak in a conspiratorial whisper. "He holds my fate and future in the palm of his hand. Does a duke's passive largesse give him the right to rescind it? How can I in good conscience promise the women who come to me, 'Yes. Your dress—that ball gown—those pelisses will most assuredly be ready in time for Christmas?' I cannot be sure of anything until the duke decides how he means to deal with me."

Edward almost walked away at that point. He stood away from the wall, frowning, but the old woman kept him right where he was in asking, "Why does he care so much, do you think? Why should a duke choose to meddle?"

He had to hear her answer, and most disappointing when it came.

"I do not know."

"Rather avuncular of him."

His brows rose. *Was it?*

"He is not my uncle," she said impatiently. "Too young."

Quite right.

"Is he handsome?" the older woman asked.

He leaned closer to the wall, undeniably interested in her reply.

She made none.

"I have heard he is a fine figure of a man," the old woman said. "He does not make unseemly advances, does he?"

"No. Certainly not! The very idea makes me blush."

His own cheeks heated.

"The idea has probably crossed his mind."

How would she know that?

"Men think about such things far more often than you might imagine, my dear. Far more often than women do."

"That does not concern me," Jane Nichol said tartly. "I have no room for advances in my life other than that of my business."

"You may end up a lonely old woman, my dear, if business is all that concerns you. Trust me, I know."

The duke's guilt in eavesdropping overrode his curiosity. He walked away, chastened, his mind in a whirl. He had not realized how much effect he had on Miss Nichol's life. No real comprehension. He paused at the admissions desk on his way out, to ask about the woman in room 212.

"That's Miss Godwin," the attendant was happy to tell him. "Dear old thing. So well spoken. A governess she used to be, for a fine gentleman like yourself."

"And can you tell me who pays for her stay here?"

The attendant said fondly, "That would be Miss Nichol, Your Grace. Lovely girl. She comes to see the old woman most every day about this time, and employs a dozen of the old ladies doing stitchery. I should be happy to introduce you."

"No need," Edward said, and walked briskly out the door.

He was glad of the fresh air, of the white light of the moon, when he stepped into the night. He needed to think.

To the dowager duchess's dismay, her son, the Duke of Chandrose, had already left the house when she rose the following morning. "Two days in a row he is gone before we have risen!" she complained over breakfast to her daughters. "How unlike your brother. He never rises early unless it is to go riding. Where has he gone?"

"To the baths," Anne said.

"Tells me they are quite wonderful," Beth confided.

Celia suggested, "Perhaps we should give them a try."

"Bathe in a great pool of water where dozens of diseased people have been traipsing about? I should think not. It is not at all a proper place for a young lady to be seen, I am sure."

"Edward says the water is drained away every night, and fresh put in," Anne said.

"He also says there is hardly anybody about that early in the morning," Beth said.

"Other than the mayor." Celia was not to be outdone. "With whom he chatted briefly."

"Hmmm. One can only wonder who the 'hardly anybody' is to hold your brother's interest for two days running," the dowager duchess murmured.

She was not there when he arrived.

He soaked himself for a good half hour, and she did not come.

Skin gone pruney, he finally admitted to himself she was not coming.

Too much sewing to do, he thought as he rose from the water, warmed to the heart, and feeling much refreshed, mind alone dissatisfied. He had hoped above all things to see her again there, to speak to her once more.

In leaving the baths there was nothing for it but to retrace their steps from the previous morning. He must speak to her after what he had overheard.

He stopped at the bakery as before. Almost bought another bag of Bath buns as a peace offering, but a miniature plum pudding caught his eye. Rum-soaked and aromatic, it seemed the perfect gift of the Season—the four silver trinkets he chose seemed entirely appropriate for his purpose. The baker poked them in, one by one, before covering the holes with a sugar glaze.

Fruity bounty tucked inside his coat, he walked on to Milsom Street. A lamp glowed in the front window of the dressmaker's shop, making it a golden oasis in the morning's half-light. Deep within the premises he thought he saw movement. Jaw set, he tapped upon the glass.

To no effect. She did not come to the door. No further signs of life met his peering in the window.

Perhaps she did not hear him.

Undeterred, he made his way to the end of the block and down and around into the nose-wrinkling stink of the alleyway that ran behind the building. Discreet tradesmen's doors led to the backs of each of the premises, most of them unmarked. He was unsure which might lead to the dress shop, until he saw lamplight again, and framed in its glow Madame Nicolette, no sign of Miss Nichol. The head that bent over the cutting table was bewigged in dark curls, the cheeks powdered and rouged.

She had a pretty neck, Miss Nichol. She could not hide her neck, even in the Frenchwoman's disguise.

He tapped on the narrow window.

Madame turned with a smile, her expression changing when she saw who it was. The harsh spots on her cheeks looked even harsher than usual now that he knew the fresh complexion that hid beneath.

Expecting someone else? he wondered, as her smile faded. He could not be sure what emotion he read in Madame's eyes.

He held up his paper-wrapped offering. "Breakfast?" he called.

She opened the back door warily, her gaze darting along the alley, a woman concerned for her reputation, the careful brown curls of her wig blowing in the morning's breeze.

"Your Grace?"

He stood within arm's length of the door, just close enough to hand her the baker's offering. He had no expectation, indeed, no desire to interrupt her work.

"A fruitful Christmas Season, Madame Nicolette. Your secret . . ." how anxious the face she turned to him . . . "is safe with me." He said it quietly, earnestly, and then he walked away, heels clicking on the cobbled alleyway, his every desire to look back, for she stood framed in the doorway watching him. He knew it was so without looking. He could feel the power of her gaze, like a touch upon the back of his head.

Chapter Nine

Jane was stunned by the duke's visit, by the completely unexpected gift of his promise to keep her secret safe, Christmas come early.

She was even more surprised by the contents of the heavy, paper-wrapped bundle he had pressed into her hands. A plum pudding! A tiny, rum-soaked plum pudding.

She thought to share it that morning with Marie, who always set a pot of coffee to boiling the moment she walked in the door, but Marie had brought croissants with her, and so Jane set aside the treat and took it with her that evening to share with Miss Godwin.

"Plum pudding! He brought you plum pudding? Does he know then? What your mother said on her deathbed?"

She shook her head. "How could he? Eerie though, isn't it? That of all things he should choose to bring me it would be a plum cake?"

"I daresay he is sweet on you, my dear."

Jane frowned as she poured them each a steaming cup of tea. "I do not think so, Miss Godwin. He does not know me well enough to have any great affection for me, and what he does know . . . No, it cannot be."

"And you? How do you feel about the man? Do you hold no tender feelings for him?"

Jane carefully cut the pudding and carefully placed it on plates. Her cheeks were hot.

Miss Godwin nodded as she took her slice.

"Thought as much," she said. "You are smitten. I can see it in your eyes."

Jane ran a hand ruefully over her eyes to hide whatever had given her away. She could not help smiling as she did so, however, for it was true. She was smitten.

"I cannot stop thinking of him," she admitted. "Foolish of me, really, for all day I work on dresses for women far more likely to see him than I. He will be at the ball I create so many beautiful gowns for. It begins to annoy me to think I may be sewing just the dress that will catch his eye, turning his attention to some other, more worthy, young woman."

"More worthy? I will not hear such nonsense!"

"A dressmaker and a duke? You know that would never happen."

"Unless the dressmaker is also daughter to Baron Nichol, a much-respected gentleman of Dorset."

She sighed. "My sisters have better chance at him than I. They are going to the Christmas ball at the Assembly rooms, and to Christmas Day services at Bath Abbey, where my stepmother will most certainly thrust them under his very nose."

"And so she might, but neither the Rose, nor the Lily smell sweeter than you. Why don't you go to one of these Christmas balls?"

"Madame Nicolette has neither time nor invitation to any balls."

"Not Madame Nicolette. You."

Jane shook her head, feeling a trifle wistful as she poked her fork about in the slice of pudding, looking for the silver surprise. It would be fun to go to one of the balls she had heard so much about, fun to be Jane Nichol again in a room other than Miss Godwin's—as she had been on the night she met the duke. Her fork clinked on something hard. She broke open the cake to extract the little trinket.

"What is it, my dear?" Miss Godwin asked, holding up her own silver prize. "I have just bitten into good luck."

The horseshoe.

"I have a silver star," Jane said.

"Excellent, my dear. Wishes come true. There is nothing for it. You must go the ball now, for you were wishing to go. Do not tell me otherwise."

Jane polished the little star with her napkin. "Too risky," she said. "My stepmother would spoil any joy I might take in dancing. I am sure of it."

"Your stepmother is not invited to this ball." Miss Godwin held out an embossed invitation.

"What's this?" Jane wanted to know.

Miss Godwin clapped her hands in delight. "My good luck. I have been invited to Prior Park. I've no idea why, indeed my dancing days are long past." She patted the arm of her Merlin chair with a chuckle. "But I've no desire for the invitation to go to waste. I understand they are rather hard to come by."

"Indeed they are!" Jane studied the invitation in awe, her imagination taking over.

"It is settled, then? You will go? As my companion? I've no desire to go alone, knowing no one, conspicuous in my chair."

"All the way to Prior Park? I shall need transportation, a proper dress. I cannot afford the one, nor have I the time to produce the other."

"Do not allow silly little details to stop you. Simply decide you've every intention of going, and make it happen. It is exactly what you did when you decided to leave your stepmother's care," Miss Godwin scolded. "Do not tell me it took any less courage."

"I should like to dance again. I should love to have something to look forward to for Christmas, other than the next stitch."

"And our Christmas morning together," Miss Godwin reminded her pointedly.

"Oh, Miss Godwin! Do not think me ungrateful. I love our every moment together. You know I do. I should not have survived in this business had it not been for your support."

Miss Godwin chuckled, and held her tiny silver horseshoe so that it shone in the lamplight. "You are meant for greater things, Jane, than a dressmaker's shop and your old governess as your only companion. I knew you were meant to have that invitation the minute it was delivered to me. I just knew it."

The Duke of Chandrose sat at the desk where he attended to his daily correspondence, examining his mother's cousin's invitation to a Christmas ball at Prior Park, his mind on Miss Jane Nichol, and the crippled governess she saw fit to support.

A warm fire crackled in the marble-framed fireplace, while a cold rain tapped at the window he kept turning to look out of, watchful for the post. He was expecting a letter.

Behind him, Beth and Celia sat playing cards with his mother while Anne practiced Vivaldi at the pianoforte provided in the fully furnished house.

"Are you sure you will not join us, Edward?" his mother asked for the fifth time. "We are starting a new hand, and could easily deal you in."

"No, thank you, Mother," he murmured. "I've letters to write."

And letters to wait for.

"Letters to whom?" his mother asked as Beth dealt the cards, pasteboard discreetly slapping the tabletop.

"I am responding to Nigel's invitation."

"Mm." She made a pleased noise through her nose. "The ball. The girls are looking forward to it."

"I am looking forward to my new dress," Beth said.

"Oh, yes!" Celia agreed as she arranged her cards. "Thank you so much for the dresses, Edward. Your sisters may well outshine all of the other young women at the ball thanks to Madame Nicolette."

In the process of dipping his quill, his hand froze. He could not help but think of another time, another quill, and Jane Nichol's touch upon his hand.

He had made discreet inquiries—asked for a short history of Nichol and his family. "A matter of business," he had written to his solicitor.

"Is this Madame Nicolette as good as the girls profess, my dear?" his mother asked. "Perhaps I should have a new frock made up for the New Year."

He tapped his quill against the side of the inkwell with a subdued smile. He had even made a point of drawing out the mayor with regard to the local guilds: weavers, drapers, milliners.

He had discovered nothing underhanded in Madame's business practices, nothing stingy in how she dealt with lacemakers or seamstresses. In fact, no one in Bath had anything bad to report of her, other than that she was new to the town, and a foreigner, which in itself was considerable condemnation.

"As you wish, Mother," he said. "Madame is a formidable young woman."

"Young woman?" His mother turned. "Is she young?"

A knock sounded on the door below. Anne stopped in the midst of a refrain.

"Well, is she?"

The unmistakable murmur of the butler carried up the stairs, and then the door shut.

"She is not so very young," Celia said. "But neither is she old."

"That tells me nothing," his mother fussed.

Edward watched the street, watched the lad who came with the mail walk away in the rain. His gaze swung to the doorway that led to the stairs. Dimsdale would be on his way up.

"I think she must be older than Edward. Would you not agree, Edward?" Beth asked. "Certainly she is older than you."

Dimsdale came in quietly, silver salver balanced on the palm of his hand.

"Is she?" his mother insisted.

"Is who what?" he asked, distracted, as Dimsdale displayed the mail for his examination.

"Madame Nicolette?"

He lifted the letters from the tray, sifting through them, searching for the familiar hand. *At last!* He broke the seal.

"Mm?" he murmured as his eyes drifted the length of the page, taking in bits of it, a man's life reduced to phrases.

Thomas Nichol, recently deceased . . . Hackberry Park . . . Basingstoke, Hampshire . . . Attended Eton . . . Cambridge . . . Lincoln's Inn . . . became a barrister . . . married the illegitimate daughter of fifth Duke of Orday . . . assumed the surname Nichol-Powell . . . inherited an estate . . . title, Baron Orday . . . Wife gave him a daughter . . . died in childbirth five years later.

He suffered a pang for four-year-old Jane.

"Is she older or younger, Edward?" his mother interrupted.

He looked up, confused. "What?"

"Bad news, my dear?" she asked with a pointed look at the letter.

He did not want to put it down yet. Not until he had scanned the whole. "Not at all. You asked me something?"

"Madame Nicolette?" Beth said. "Is she older or younger than you are?"

Stupid question. He was already scanning the letter again. "Younger," he murmured absently.

Tory . . . auditor . . . receiver-general of taxes . . . secretary-treasurer under Shelburne . . .

"Do you really think so?" Celia sounded skeptical.

Survived by his daughter Jane.

There it was. Her name!

"I am sure of it," he muttered, his sisters' voices fading as his concentration focused.

Second wife, Jean. Two daughters by a previous marriage.

A footnote. Her name leapt from the page again.

Jane Nichol—currently a runaway. Reportedly last seen in the company of a dance master, a Mr. Davies, recently fired by the baron's widow.

"I would not have thought it to look at her," Beth's voice intruded.

The duke sighed. Neither would he.

"I cannot believe her that young," Celia argued.

Young and foolish, he thought. A dance master, was it?

"For all she makes lovely, tasteful dresses, she has a remarkably heavy hand when it comes to powder and rouge," Beth said.

Anne's fingers stilled on the keys in the middle of a refrain. "Do you think she wears so much of it to hide a pockmarked complexion?"

"Undoubtedly hiding something," he murmured as he carefully penned a single line, to be sent out immediately.

Chapter Ten

The note read:

> *Meet me at the baths tomorrow morning—urgent.*
> *Edward Brydges*

It took Jane a moment to realize that Edward Brydges and the Duke of Chandrose were one and the same when the messenger brought it. She was not accustomed to thinking of the duke by his given name—Edward. Indeed, Edward Brydges sounded like an ordinary man, a man she might fall in love with—a man who might ask her to the baths for a romantic tryst—a man who might ask her to dance at a Christmas ball. The Duke of Chandrose, on the other hand, was a creature of dreams—he asked her to the baths for another reason, an urgent reason. She wondered what it could be.

She had not had time to visit the baths of a morning, as was her habit. Too much to do. Up before dawn, and bent over her worktable until long after the sun had vanished, she did not do anything these days except tend to business, and drop by to see how Miss Godwin fared. She had passed the duke in church and received his nod. She had seen him in Milsom Street and exchanged greetings. She looked up from her sewing table on more than one occasion, looking for his proud profile through the window.

But he did not come to her again with plum cake and promises.

She dared to dream of going to the ball at Prior Park, dared to imagine herself in Fanny's holly green ball gown, dancing—dancing with the duke—but for the most part she kept her head down, her mind focused on the next stitch, the next cut of the scissors, the next delivery to be made.

This morning, in studying the single line upon paper, she wondered what a duke considered an urgent matter.

It felt oddly decadent slipping from her clothes into her bathing costume in the chill, stone changing room of the baths, knowing she had come for no more reason than to meet a man—a man who had summoned her.

The steaming baths were empty; the colonnade echoed with the coo of the doves who took flight at her approach. She was the first this morning but for the birds. There was a familiar loneliness to the steaming green stillness of the water, to the undisturbed reflection of a brightening sky, to the echo of her footsteps on stone.

Urgent business. What was this urgent business? The duke's business would not seem urgent enough to get him here on time. It made her nervous, wondering what he had in mind as she waited.

Setting aside her linen toweling, she stepped into the moist warmth that shrouded the pool's side, the blissful heat drawing her deeper.

The hot bath was just what she needed, its warmth seeping through her every pore, relaxing tired muscles: her back, her shoulders, all of the knots in her neck, unwinding the tangled string she had become.

Urgent business.

She sat on the stone bench that ran underwater along the side of the bath, and leaned her head back, water drenching her hair, heat sending fingers of relaxation around her scalp. What would this duke need urgently of a dressmaker?

The mineral stink hung as strong as curiosity in her nostrils, a smell she had grown accustomed to, even looked forward to. It was worth a little odd smell to submerse oneself so completely. She had no more than a hip bath in her little room above the shop, a luxury at that. It took five steaming kettles to fill it, the water to be brought in from the pump downstairs. Her fingers tingled with the abundant warmth of a bath so large one could walk about in it. The muscles of her arms and fingers relaxed, no stitches to take, no fabric to measure, or cut, or trim.

Just urgent business with a duke.

She must sew buttons on Mrs. Carmicheal's pearl gray day dress today. That was urgent. The ruby ball gown needed trimming. The fabric for the Simpson morning gown had arrived and must be cut. But for the moment she shut her eyes and listened to the birds chitter. Peace and contentment filled her. She needed this. A few moments to quiet body and mind, to be warm and calm. It did not matter if the duke came or not.

Footsteps, heels clicking on stone. A shadow loomed above her, stirring the air. Urgent business arrived, and yet so deep was her contentment she did not open her eyes until he asked, voice gentle, a mere murmur, "Are you with child, Miss Nichol?"

Startled, convinced she had misheard, that the water had distorted his words or lapped into her ears, she opened her eyes, her shoulders springing up out of the water. "What?"

So sharp her voice, and shocked. A trio of alarmed doves took wing, gray shadows above the damp heat that rose from the water.

He stood above her in that silvered mist, clad in street clothes, an elegant black beaver, a dark plum-colored wool coat with a black velvet collar, a figured silk waistcoat, silver-stitched gray smallclothes, and silver buckled shoes.

He had no intention of getting into the water!

She felt at an immediate disadvantage—improperly dressed, her hair drenched, every aspect of her belittled before such a fine, towering figure.

"Are you in trouble?" the duke asked. He looked very solemn in doing so, no hint of amusement in glance or expression. His eyes coolly reflected the blue of the sky, his tone condescendingly concerned, his lips pressed together in a flat line. "I know it is inappropriate to ask, perhaps even unseemly. But this is too serious a matter to let the question go unvoiced."

She burst out laughing, a nervous, self-conscious laugh that echoed uncomfortably. Unwilling to continue craning up at him, she stood up off the stone bench, an arm's length away from him, her neck and shoulders suddenly cold in their dampened state.

"Whatever gave you such a ludicrous notion? Do I look as though I am with child?"

Shivering, she stared down at her drenched clothing rather than look at him. What must he think of her? Why? Pressing pockets of air out of the inflated folds of the bathing suit, she wondered, do I look fat?

"No. You look . . ." He did not seem to know what to say.

She stole a glance at him. Lord, he seemed so very tall standing above her, so very much above her touch, diamond stickpin winking in the perfect folds of his neck cloth.

"Why in the world would you ask me such a thing?"

He looked down, frowning, the frown deepening as his gaze faltered and fell away.

Realizing her nipples stood pert in the cold air, she clasped her arms across her chest. "I am offended, indeed, affronted that a gentleman, a complete stranger to me, should dare to suggest . . ."

He looked upward at the clouds that drifted across the face of the sun. He could not look her in the eyes. She did not want him to. She was shaking now, with the cold, with a growing anger.

"The dancing master," he said lamely.

"Dancing master?"

"I thought perhaps . . ."

"Do you mean Mr. Davies?" She spoke crisply, forcing her teeth to stop chattering, wishing herself dry, wishing herself absent from such a confusing, indeed annoying, interrogation.

"Come, come." He looked angry now as he dared meet her eyes again, as though he were entirely justified in making demeaning suggestions.

She headed for the steps, for her towel. She need not stand shivering, need not answer any more ludicrous questions.

"How would you even know his name unless you had been spying on me!"

He paralleled her progress, thrusting forth his hand to assist her leaving the bath. She might have ignored that gloved hand had the drenched and steaming skirt of the bathing suit been any less cumbersome.

But she could not, lest she further embarrass herself by tripping. She placed her wet hand in immaculate gray kid, at once struck by the butter-soft warmth of the leather as her touch soaked it. She steamed, the heat of her visible, and yet he was warmer. Sparks of heat seemed to shoot from his fingers to hers, the tingling sensation searing its way through her veins all the way to her elbow. His clasp was unflinching—as strong as the delving way he looked into her eyes.

"I demand an explanation," she said, low-voiced, disarmed by that heat, struggling under the weight of yards of drenched fabric. She did not want to depend upon his hand, distrusting his strength. As a result she teetered on the step, so that he reached out to steady her, kid-gloved heat searing both sides of her body, the look in his eyes as startled as she felt.

For a moment she swayed, fear rising like the steam that surrounded them. Water dripped from her elbow, splashing the high sheen of his right shoe. His gaze never wavered. He did not step away.

The fear within her grew, would not allow her to forget her anger, made her shiver in the sudden cold. "Sending me urgent messages—" She sneered, wrenching away from his troubling warmth. "Insinuating that I might be with child." She bent to wring water from her skirt with angry vigor. "I've better things to do than to be so insulted."

She rose to find him holding her toweling ready. Like a shawl he draped it about her shoulders. The gentlemanly gesture softened her heart. She felt herself uncivil, even childish as she bent to wrap her head. She diverted her anger to her hair, vigorously toweling the dripping strands. She twisted the linen about her head in a turban, and rose, flushed, to ask, "Why do you think . . ." She stopped, then shook her head. The turban teetered. "Who planted such an idea in your head?"

His gaze locked on hers, blue eyes searching, his tone insistent. "What of Davies? Where is he now?"

The turban could not withstand the fresh jerk of her head. It toppled forward.

He caught it as it fell.

She reached for it, smoothing back damp and tousled hair, feeling at a distinct disadvantage again. "I've no idea where Davies is."

"He has abandoned you?" He seemed disinclined to release the towel. "Well, did he?"

"No, but . . ."

"He was fired from Hackberry Park shortly before you ran away with him." So grim his mouth in spitting out the words, so concerned the look in his eyes.

She stared at him in outraged indignation. "*With* him?"

"Did he say he loved you?" Righteous contempt burned in his voice; a delving need to know fired the blue of his eyes as he grabbed her shoulder and gave it a wet shake. "Did he say he loved you, and then abandon you?"

"No," she said firmly, looking about them, panicked. He must not be seen speaking to her thus. "You do not understand."

He let go of her abruptly.

"He is here? With you?" Pain narrowed his eyes—a wounded look.

As she had feared, voices intruded on their privacy. He stepped back, his gaze gone hard as glass. "I beg your pardon."

"Wait. You do not—"

"I should not have intruded upon your private business," he said briskly, then walked away.

Chapter Eleven

She hoped to see him outside again, waiting to speak to her as he had the last time, but by the time she toweled herself off and changed into dry clothing the colonnade was empty, no sign of him in the walk to the shop, nor in the bakery along the way.

Frustrating. Disappointing. She was sure he misunderstood. She wanted to explain. But what was a young woman, a dressmaker, to do when a duke misunderstood? She could not go chasing after him; could not go pounding on his door to demand a moment of his time, of his understanding.

She went on with her day, with Madame's responsibilities, hoping, expecting him to walk into the shop. Surely he did not mean to leave things as they stood—unfinished and confused?

She looked up every time the bell rang, every time a knock sounded on the door in the alleyway. She could not stop thinking of the one who had set this flood of success in motion—the Duke of Chandrose.

He did not come.

Each time she was disappointed. Each time it was a customer, customers she had gained by way of the duke—by way of his sisters' patronage.

His sisters!

Of course.

"Marie. Can you manage the shop for a half hour or so?

"*Oui,* Madame."

But even as Jane turned to go, a shadow darkened

the doorway. The bell rang again, lifting her hopes, turning her in her tracks, heart full of hope.

Oh, Lord!

Not the duke who stood silhouetted against the light from the street. No. She would recognize that proud profile anywhere. Her stepmother stood in the doorway, and at her heels, Rose and Lily, blinking as their eyes adjusted to the change in light! The last people on earth she wished to encounter in that moment, and no avoiding them.

"Such a pity he is leaving," Rose was saying.

"Such a pity he will not be attending the Christmas festivities," her stepmother agreed. "I had counted on him dancing with each of you at least once."

Lady Nichol's head turned. Her gaze fell briefly on Madame Nicolette.

Jane's heart stopped.

"Que voulez-vous?" she said by rote. She greeted anyone who walked through the door with the same question voiced in the same bright tone. "How may I help you, ladies?"

In her heart she panicked. How in heavens could she hope to fool those who had known her for years?

Like an automaton, Jane took a deep breath, plastered a welcoming smile on her powdered face, and went into Madame's normal routine of bowing and scraping, hands fluttering, eyes never settling too long on anyone, her French accent at its heaviest. *"S'il vous plaît."*

Could they be fooled? she wondered.

"Something for a Christmas fete, perhaps?"

Would they know her in an instant?

"On you, *demoiselle.*" She whirled about Rose with a figured muslin swatch. "Pale rose-colored satin, with a filmy white gauze overskirt, *oui?*"

Rose smiled, delighted, fond of the color that bore her name. "Oh, Mother, may I?"

Lady Nichol frowned ever so slightly, and said in that dreaded silken tone, "Rose, my dear, you've no need for a dress if you insist on resisting the baron's attentions. You know it is your sister who requires clothing."

"Ah, oui!" Jane could not believe they did not cry out her name and point their fingers at her accusingly. She whirled, light-headed, turning her attention to Lily. She cocked her head a moment, tapping at her lips with her pointer finger—a habit of Madame Nicolette's. Never Jane's habit. She must forget all of Jane's habits.

"Lilac. You are liking the color, *non*?"

She had been unable to fool the duke. The perfume had given her away.

"For you, lilac *gros de Naples* with the small lace tucker, here, *mais oui*?" She pointed, then swept her hands outward along Lily's skirt. "The twisted rolls of embroidered ribbon here, yes? Something *bleu*— Prussian *bleu*. And for the sleeve, I think something short, and poofed. *Très bien*?"

She had changed perfumes. She would not make that mistake again.

Lily sighed. "Sounds heavenly."

It would be. Jane knew exactly what suited her sisters best. Had she not sewn most everything they had worn in the years she had lived with them? Her stepmother's idea of economizing.

It brought her some joy to think they would be paying through the nose for her efforts this time—if they did not recognize her.

Rose pouted.

Jane wondered how long it would take her to talk Lady Nichol into purchasing the rose silk. How long before Rose capitulated with regard to her mother's wishes, and the baron's attentions. She wondered how long it would take one of them to recognize her.

Rose was too busy being spiteful to Lily—her favorite preoccupation—to look too closely at a dressmaker. "A pity the duke will not be here to see you in it, Lily dear," she said sarcastically.

Duke? Did she mean the Duke of Chandrose?

"It is a pity. A very great pity he should be called

away before you have danced with him." Lily's voice was equally biting. "We all know how well you have learned to dance."

A most unfortunate topic—dancing, the dance master—an explosive subject.

"And for *madame*?" Jane interrupted what promised to be a sulky response. The baroness was looking at fabric swatches.

"French gray, perhaps? Understated and *sophistiqué*?"

The baroness made a face. "I think not."

Of course she would never wear gray. Jane knew her stepmother hated dull colors. She also knew Lady Nichol loved contradicting and belittling those beneath her. She made the suggestion with every expectation of its being refused.

Lady Nichol fingered a bolt of amaranth-colored watered silk. "Something more festive."

Of course. Red. The baroness liked to upstage her daughters.

"Sarcenet, or brocaded gauze?" Jane suggested, of which she had neither. Marie sent a troubled look her way.

"This silk pleases me. You will do bullion trim at the neck and shoulder? And saffron insets?"

"But of course."

"And three gathered, scalloped flounces lined with quilling, also bullion trimmed."

"Excellent choice," Jane said unctuously.

As if Jane were invisible now that the business of choosing a dress style was done, the baroness said, "We must be thankful the duke's sisters do not go away with the duke, my dears. I should like you both to get to know them better—much better."

They did mean Chandrose! Jane realized. None of the other dukes presently in Bath had brought their sisters with them.

"Marie will take your measurements," Jane said faintly, panic rising, her disappointment intense. He planned to go away? Before she had had a chance to explain?

"How soon are the frocks to be ready?" Jane asked.

Marie shot her an anxious look. They had agreed only that morning that it would be wise to refuse any more Christmas orders. There simply would not be time, or ready hands to sew them unless they found more seamstresses to work for them.

"Christmas Eve, if you please."

"But of course," Jane said, knowing they would find someone to sew for them. They had yet to tap into resources in Widcombe. Her stepmother and sisters were preparing to go to a Christmas Eve ball, and she needed the income too much to refuse the making of their dresses. There was no knowing if her business would continue so briskly once the Season was ended.

Was her life now so very different from before?

Yes, she scolded herself, entirely different. Before there had been no choice. Now everything was choice—and necessity. Entirely different. And now she chose to follow through with her plan. She turned to leave.

"Jane Nichol," the baroness said.

Jane stopped dead. The hair at the base of her neck rose. Her breath caught in her throat.

"Qui?" she asked with forced calm.

"I remember now . . ." Her stepmother cocked her head, her voice smooth, dangerous.

Jane took a deep breath, preparing herself for the worst.

"Someone told me you are her seamstress?"

Jane gave herself a mental shake and said with Madame Nicolette's customary nonchalance as she took up the ledger on which she had been jotting dress details, "But of course. Charming *demoiselle.*"

"I wonder if you would be so good as to give me her direction? I had no idea we might run into her here, and should hate to have the holidays pass without calling on her."

Trying not to let that dangerous silken tone rattle her, Jane focused on her pencil. She must not look at her aunt, must not fall back into the abandoned role of supplicant. "I shall be happy to give Miss Nichol your address."

"Oh, but I was hoping you would give me hers."

Jane smiled her brightest smile, showing teeth, as Madame was wont to do—as Jane herself never did. "I am sure you will appreciate my desire to keep private the business of all of my customers."

"Oh, but of course."

"I will tell Miss Nichol of your kind inquiry."

With that, Madame swept away into the back room, leaving Marie to deal with a woman Jane hoped never to encounter again.

She hired a hack to carry her to Great Pulteney Street, the signs of Christmas's rapid approach everywhere. Garlands, swags, and wreaths of greenery brightened almost every door. Mistletoe and ribbons made lampposts cheerful.

The duke's town house was an oasis of light, music, Christmas greenery, and Christmas carols. A wreath decked in bright red ribbon graced the doorway, and candles brightened almost every window.

Madame Nicolette was given entry by the underbutler, who took her cloak and the dresses she brought with her, and led her to a chair outside the music room, where she was asked to wait. Anne and Celia were singing "Hark the Herald Angels Sing," Beth accompanying on the pianoforte. When they had finished the song and been informed who called, they rushed out to greet her, all smiles, anxious to see the dresses.

Laughing and chattering, they drew her into the warmth by the fire and sent for hot chocolate.

"My brother will be sorry to have missed this," Beth said.

"Yes," Anne agreed. "He leaves for home in the morning."

Jane's heart and hopes sank. "I regret to have missed him."

"Oh, but you must meet Mama," Anne said and ran from the room to fetch her.

Celia and Beth led Jane up the sweeping staircase to a bedchamber, where the dresses had been laid out upon the counterpane, and the tray of hot chocolate and biscuits had been arranged on a side table.

With a pleased exclamation, Beth begged Jane to unfasten her, to lend her a hand in stepping out of the dress she was wearing before she assisted her in stepping into the new ball gown. How intimate the scene, Jane thought. How welcome she felt. How trusted.

Guilt pinched her most in such moments. She was a liar, a fraud. These dear young women ought not trust so easily. Not that she meant them any ill, not that she used the lie to their detriment in any way. And yet, it went against the warp and woof of the very fabric of her character, to go on, day after day, living a charade.

"Mama has heard us speak of you often, Madame." Celia bit into a biscuit, little knowing she bit just as deeply into Jane's feelings of duplicity. She turned to have her dress unfastened. "Indeed, your name came up while we were playing cards not two days ago."

Jane wondered what had been said as she helped Celia don her new dress, as she busied herself pinning the hem to a perfect length. Had the duke been party to that discussion? She tried to picture it, tried to imagine him uttering her name without a sneer.

"Madame Nicolette. At last we meet!" The dowager duchess swept into the room, dominating it at once, her hands outstretched as though they were old friends as Jane rose from her task. "My children speak highly of you."

Feeling guilty, as she always did in taking praise as Madame Nicolette, Jane cordially greeted the duke's mother in French, surprised to have her hands grasped warmly, her gaze met with inquisitive interest. The duchess had a mouth very much like her son's, a knowing mouth, a mouth that verged on amusement without ever crossing the line into laughter. She examined Jane most keenly with eyes of a familiar robin's egg blue before releasing her hands, saying, "But I keep you from your work."

"My pleasure," Jane said, hating the French accent, hating the lie of it.

"I must come to your shop myself—the girls are so pleased with your taste." The duchess gave her arm a motherly squeeze. "A new dress for the new year."

"But of course. I would be most happy to oblige," Jane said, and could not help wondering what it would be like to have such a mother, such a warm and loving family.

The duchess smiled and studied the stitching on her daughters' dresses, then commented favorably on the colors and fabrics chosen while she joined them in a cup of chocolate, and without rushing or appearing in the least annoyed in having been lured away from the day's business, went away again, leaving Jane and her daughters to finish marking hems.

Jane conscientiously pinned and tucked, took an occasional basting stitch to mark a seam change, and listened to the girls' talk of the upcoming Christmas entertainments with enviable anticipation. Not much younger than she, the lot of them, and no real idea how fortunate they were. They were nice girls. She chatted companionably enough with them whenever the words of a dressmaker would not intrude, but the whole time her mind was elsewhere, her ears tuned to listen for the sounds of an arrival, his arrival, her ears hungry for sound of his voice.

Her measuring was all done, the half-finished dresses carefully bundled for transport back to the shop, and still he had not arrived, nor was there any expectation among the duke's sisters that he might soon return.

Pleased with her progress, Jane yet felt her afternoon had not met its full potential. She kept framing words in her mind that she might deliver to His Grace by way of his sisters, a message in which she might convey some sense of what she meant to tell him, some sense of the misunderstanding between them.

Not finding the words, she said only, "Please convey my appreciation to the duke," when the butler came to lead her to the rear entrance.

And then she was on her way out, down the wide stairs, the butler turning away from the main door, her bundle in his hands. She scanned the frost-touched windows, the cold, rain-swept street beyond, hoping against hope for some sight of him.

Hope dashed, she was led to the rear of the establishment, to the doorway that the servants used.

It opened as they approached. With a cold inward sweep of wind and wet and the smell of horses, a gentleman entered, a riding crop in gloved hands. Greatcoat fighting the cold, wet capes flapping at his shoulders, a diamond stickpin gleamed brightly at his throat.

"Your Grace," Dimsdale said calmly. "Enjoy your ride?"

"Bracing, Dimsdale, bracing." The duke swept his rain-diamonded hat from his head in a glitter of wet and swung the dripping greatcoat from his shoulders in another arc of silvered droplets.

Dimsdale turned to hand the bundle of dresses to Jane. "You will wait here a moment, if you please," he said as he carried away the outerwear.

The duke had not seen her, standing as she was in the butler's shadow. Indeed, he might have sailed right past her, his feet were in motion to do just that, had she not said quietly, "Good day, Your Grace."

His brows rose, the only indication of how much she startled him. "Madame Nicolette."

He meant to keep walking, to turn his back on her as he had before. Right past her he strode, as if she were nothing more than a servant in the way, a tradeswoman on her way out. She could see the determination in the set of his mouth, felt the uninterrupted flow of momentum in his stride.

She could not allow him to walk out of her life—not without telling him—clarifying the misunderstanding between them.

"About Mr. Davies," she blurted at his back, silvered light glinting on his button-back coattails.

It took two strides for the words to sink in.

She clutched the bundle of dresses tight to her chest, afraid he might not respond, might not care.

He stopped at last and turned halfway, as though only half interested. "Yes?"

"Rose planned to run away with him."

He turned more fully, with a puzzled look, light winking on the droplets that sprinkled his cheek. "Rose?"

She nodded, almost looked away so intimidating was his piercing gaze—steeled herself instead, and stood up straight, pride lifting her chin, pride and the need to be understood. "The dancing master was dismissed before she could make a fool of herself." She watched over his shoulder for the return of the butler.

"I see."

Did he? She had to be sure.

"I had no wish to leave you thinking . . ." She struggled for words. "With a misunderstanding."

He was looking at the floor, head bent. Drops of rain there, from the passage of his coat and hat, drops of rain in his hair, light gleaming on them to rival the diamond at his throat.

There seemed nothing more to say. She turned to the door. Her hand was on the latch. She could feel the tug of the wind, the impending damp.

"Love does that," he said softly.

She could not believe her ears. She drew a deep breath, waiting for more. There was no more. "Your Grace?"

"Leads one to make a fool of oneself—love."

She looked at him a long moment, the bundle of

dresses crushed to her chest, as if the weight of them might slow the rapid beat of her heart, as if it might muffle the thudding that peltered in her ears. Could he hear it?

"I suppose so." She tried to sound calm. She must not misinterpret his saying such a thing, as he had misinterpreted her. Too dangerous, such confusion, and she was confused at the moment. Did he mean Fanny? He must mean Fanny. No need for a careening heartbeat, for the sudden surge of hope. He could not mean her.

"I understand you intend to leave us," she said, her hand still on the latch.

He nodded. His eyes gleamed, brighter than the rain. "That was my intention."

"A pity," she said.

He took a step in her direction, his expression entirely serious in asking, "Am I pitiable?"

She frowned, confused by the question. "A pity to miss Christmas with your loved ones," she clarified.

He stood a moment, staring at her, his expression unreadable. "Indeed, it would be." His voice was very low in asking quite conversationally, if with a trifle more intensity than before, "Have you ever been in love, Miss Nichol?"

The question left her momentarily speechless, and in that moment, the butler returned.

The duke addressed him smoothly, as though he had been expecting the man, as though he meant all along to ask of him, "You will send for the coach?"

"But, of course, Your Grace. Do you require your coat and hat?"

The duke gave his glossy head a shake, droplets raining down his temples. "It is Madame Nicolette who is leaving," he said. "See to it she is returned safely to her place of business."

"As you wish, Your Grace." The butler hurried away.

In a vaguely uncomfortable silence they faced each other.

He did not press for an answer, merely looked at her, a hint of curiosity, his mouth amused, as it was always amused.

She longed to brush the wet from his face.

Did he still mourn Fanny's loss? she wondered.

"I understand," she said.

"What do you understand?" He cocked his head and looked at her quizzically—the question a challenge, doubt in his eyes. Raindrops starred his lashes.

She did not look away, would not allow her gaze to falter. "I understand making a fool of oneself in love. I understand how dreadful to love deeply without any hope of affection's return."

Interest narrowed his sable-fringed eyes, tugged at his delectable mouth.

"I loved my stepmother once," she said. "When she brought fresh light to my father's eyes, when she made him laugh, and sing, and dance again."

"But she did not love you?" He asked it quietly, gently, as if he already knew the answer, sympathy in his tone.

She shrugged as was Madame's habit, and said matter-of-factly, "She resented my father's deep affection for me. She believed he favored me over my stepsisters, and thus found no room for favor in her own heart."

"I see," he said. He bowed his head—contrite. "I must apologize then, for my most ill-mannered and insulting assumptions. I am rather good at it, you see."

"Are you?"

"Better than you will ever know. Almost as good as you are at skirting questions."

She frowned and might have asked him, "What do you mean?" but the coach arrived to take her away in that instant.

He opened the door for her, brows tilted quizzically, as if he still wondered what her answers might be.

He handed her into the readied carriage, the touch of his hand to gloved fingers, to the cloaked crook of her elbow, stirring a heady flutter of feeling deep in her stomach.

It was then she realized what he had asked her—"Have you ever been in love?" The question lingered still, in the tilt of his head, and the arch of his brows.

She could not look too long into his eyes, could not allow him to search the depths of hers. There might be something there to give away her growing feelings for him. She was decidedly taken with his laughter, unquestionably infatuated by his smile. Was this love? Could it be love? How dreadful to fall in love without hope of affection's return. He was a duke. She was a dressmaker. And he was going away.

"Au revoir," she called to him, treasuring this last glimpse of that incessantly amused curl of lip, assuming it would be the last time they saw each other, the last time her fingers would hum in just such a manner. She forced a smile and reminded herself it was a good thing that he would not go away assuming the worst of her, that he had been exceptionally kind in seeing to it that she was provided warm, dry transport home, that she owed her future, whatever it might hold, to this man above all others.

She would have been surprised had she looked up as the carriage carried her away from the house, to see the duchess standing in a window, watching her departure with keen interest.

Chapter Twelve

Jane's shoulders ached, her back ached, her fingers were swollen with abuse. Her eyes felt like sandpaper. She fell into bed as one dead to the world, but never enough of the oblivion of sleep was hers to indulge in. There was always more to be done, and more, and more, and more. Weariness seeped into every pore of her being. The work of sewing, once such a cherished activity, such an expression of her innermost creativity, had become, for the most part, an unending and repetitive chore, no relief in sight. Too much to be done in too little time for the work to be pleasurable, and she had always relied on the pleasure to ameliorate any feelings of self-sacrifice.

The money helped, the feeling that she was providing a whole list of fellow seamstresses additional means to feed their families, and yet she found herself heavy of heart, dissatisfied. Her dreams of a successful business had come true, but it was not enough. She was lonely.

Not even the idea of going to Prior Park for Christmas lifted her spirits. The duke would not be there. She had hoped to dance with him. Hoped . . . oh, but it was foolish to contemplate what she had hoped.

"Promise me you will not allow regret to swallow you whole, Jane." She could hear her mother's voice, see her hand reaching out for the child that she had been. "Cherish what is, not what you've imagined."

The words bolstered her flagging energy daily, gave

her fresh courage, fresh appreciation for the business of her every waking hour. She would survive, given the fruits of this Christmas bounty. She would thrive. Her mother had not had the choice. She must not squander what she had been given. She must not mope over a man she might never see again.

She did all she could think of to ease the burden of her labors. Her network of seamstresses expanded. She and Marie improved their bookkeeping methods. They had a form printed up by the local stationer for the taking of an order. Another shopgirl and a delivery lad were hired, the latter a well-kempt fellow with a disarming smile, a polite tongue, and enough muscle to carry the heaviest of bundles, the former a matronly woman of even temperament, infinite patience, and a deft hand for the displaying of materials and trim in the shop window. Mrs. Bell liked to cut and press fabric, she said, and so they put her to work cutting the majority of the patterns, and she happily took over the arduous task of pressing the finished dresses.

The holidays loomed, with dozens of gowns to be finished for the same three events: the Christmas ball at Prior Park, the Christmas Eve concert at the Assembly rooms, and the Christmas morning services at Bath Abbey. Anybody who was anybody in Bath would be attending, and of course one could not be seen in the same dress on all three occasions. Orders never ceased to flood in.

"No more," Marie said at last. "You must tell them no more orders can be made ready before February. We cannot handle another stitch, Madame. We will be hard-pressed to complete what we have agreed to do."

"It is just so difficult to turn away work." Jane had trouble agreeing to such a strategy.

"Customers will never truly appreciate what it is you are doing for them until they realize it comes in a limited supply," Marie insisted. "You allow them to use you up. You must get to bed at a decent hour, and do something other than work on the Sabbath. It is not healthy, this incessant drive to please everyone but yourself. You lose your looks. You will lose your *vivacité* in creating the dresses."

It was true. When Jane took off Madame Nicolette's wig, glasses, and powder, she no longer recognized herself in the mirror. When she took up her scissors, she no longer felt that uplifting surge of joy.

But no time to think about it. The bell over the door was ringing again, and who should it be but her stepmother and Lily, come to check the progress of their ball gowns. Her stepmother was scolding Lily in the most silken of tones as they came in the door.

Lily retorted petulantly. "It is not my fault Rose did not wish to come, Mama. With no dress to look forward to, and her heart still pining for you-know-who, who can blame her if she has flown into a pet?"

"*I* can blame her. I am her mother. It is my responsibility to point out to both of my daughters when they are being obstinate, peevish, and ill-mannered."

Oh dear, Jane thought. Her stepmother was in one of her moods. And when she was in this sort of mood, nothing pleased her. Nothing. It would be foolish to show her the new gowns today.

With forced enthusiasm, Jane assumed her role and greeted them with Madame Nicolette's boundless enthusiasm. "Madame, *mademoiselle,* I have just sent our lad to tell you the ball gowns will be ready for a final fitting tomorrow."

"Have we wasted our time in coming here today?" her stepmother asked peevishly.

"No, no, Madame." Anticipating her request, Marie swirled out through the curtain to the back room, a ball gown on each arm.

Jane's heart sank.

"There it is!" Lily exclaimed. "Only look how pretty, Mama!"

Lily's dress was charming, if rather predictable, but Jane had been longing to see Lady Nichol's reaction to the red dress. Her stepmother's gown was breathtakingly eye-catching, a triumph of gold bullion and saffron quilling. The sleeves had left Marie speechless in their bold abandon.

"Magnifique!" she had crowed at sight of it, and John, the delivery lad, had agreed.

"A rum go, that, destined to turn heads."

"Dazzling!" Mrs. Bell's eyes had lit up at sight of it. "One of your most courageous, my dear."

Jane had to agree. The dress had surpassed her own expectations.

Thus it was most distressing to see Lady Nichol eye it with brows knit and lips pursed. A full minute passed as Marie held it before her in the mirror. Finally Lady Nichol sighed and, turning to her daughter, said in an irritable voice Jane knew all too well, "Come. We must try them on."

From the dressing room, as Marie assisted them, Jane could not fail to hear her stepmother's complaints. "It is tight—far too tight. Yes. There and here. And do not dare to suggest I have had too much to eat. The measurements must have been taken incorrectly. Added to that, the neckline on my daughter's dress is all wrong. The fashion is far lower this year. Far more provocative. Do not think I have not familiarized myself with the most recent fashion plates."

And then she was speaking to Lily, no effort made to lower her voice. "All Jane's fault, you know. She has set a dreadful precedent—running away as she did. Flouting my will. Now we must depend on Rose to marry well—to bolster the family fortune. Do you think she had captured the duke's eye at all?"

Silence on Lily's part.

"If she has not . . ." Lady Nichol required no answer from her daughters in a great majority of her conversations with them. "She must take Jane's place in marrying the baron."

"But, Mama! Rose hates the old troll."

"You must not call him that in public, Lily, a gentleman who one day shall be brother to you."

"Everyone calls him the troll. Even the parson. And why not? I have never seen an old man with more warts upon his hands and seeping sores about his lips, and his nose and fingers have gone quite amber-colored from all of the snuff he inhales."

"You exaggerate."

No, Jane thought—she did not. None of which had revolted her so much as Baron Gulston's reputation, and the rumor that he suffered those same seeping sores on other parts of his body. *Poor Rose!*

"Rose still pines for Mr. Davies," Lily said, quite foolishly, for of all things to say, this would make her mother more obstinate, not less.

"Nonsense. She could not be so foolish."

Lily did not know when to stop. "Her pillow is wet with fresh tears every night thinking of him."

Her mother's tone slid from silken to snide. "Her obstinancy has cost her a new Christmas dress, and an afternoon locked in her room. Do not let it cost you as well. Who is Mr. Davies compared to either a duke or baron? What sort of life could a dancing master give her? I ask you? Should she insist on marrying a pauper, it will cost her a whole lifetime's worth of dresses. Now let me see how that looks on you. Turn, so I may see the back."

Jane closed her eyes, prepared for the worst.

After a moment's silence the ax fell. "I do not care for the sleeves," her stepmother said. "The neckline must be made lower, and those silly flounces must go at once."

"Oh, Mama, I most particularly like the flounces."

"I think you would look far more sophisticated in something different, my dear. Vandyked edging, perhaps."

Lips pursed, her spirits flagging, Jane dutifully jotted notes in her ledger. Her neck and shoulders felt even more weary than before.

"No, Mama. Please."

Jane shook her head, knowing how little good pleading did when Lady Nichol's mind was made up.

"My mind is made up. No sulking now. It is unbecoming. As for this thing." There was a rustling of silk as the baroness donned the "thing" in question.

"Oh, Mama!" Lily gasped. "How beautiful!"

"Do you think so?" The snide tone was even more pronounced than before. "I am not at all pleased."

Jane's heart sank. This was not at all the reaction she had hoped for. The dress was wonderful—striking—bold, the perfect reflection of her stepmother. She had been so certain it would please her.

"Madame does not want the dress?" Marie sounded completely cowed.

"I do not think the color suits. What do you think, Lily? It is far too harsh for my complexion, do you not agree?"

Lily was not one to contradict her mama. The pleased enthusiasm with which she had first met the dress, faded. "Perhaps it is," she said meekly.

Jane could take no more. She parted the curtains to the dressing area.

"You!" Lady Nichol asked sharply. "What do you think? It is far too distracting a combination of red and gold, is it not?"

Marie shot a stricken look at Jane.

"Madame must decide what best suits Madame," Jane said diplomatically.

"This is not at all what I wanted." Lady Nichol scowled at herself in the mirror.

Jane took a moment to examine her stepmother, knowing the dress was a lost cause, knowing, too, it was the most beautiful gown her stepmother had ever donned.

"It is a magnificent dress," she said quietly. "And Madame looks magnificent in it."

"No." Lady Nichol shook her head decisively as she began to extract herself from it with rough hands. "I have decided I am not at all fond of it. This line of bullion at the neck is too garish—quite unacceptable. I much prefer the rolled embroidery you have done on my daughter's dress. How could you expect me to approve of so bold a dress? It does not resemble anything I have seen on anyone else this Season."

"You do not want the dress?"

"Yes, of course I want the dress, just not in this color, with this trim. Surely that is not so hard to change?"

Jane wanted to laugh and cry all at the same time. The pounding in her head intensified. "And Madame wishes the changes by Christmas?"

"But of course. It is a ball gown, meant for the Christmas ball."

Of course.

"Marie will show you our fabric choices," Jane said with a show of calm.

She stepped out of the dressing area, heart aching, head splitting.

Marie swept out of the dressing room in her wake.

"Madame realizes the magnitude of the task?" she demanded low-voiced, in French. "She has not asked for alterations. She asks for a completely new dress."

"Yes. We must start over." Jane maintained control over her voice. She managed to sound unruffled. This could be done. It would be done. There was nothing for it but to see that another dress was made.

"Tell her it cannot be done." Marie was indignant.

Jane closed her eyes. She must not crumble. She would not. "But it can."

"At what expense? And what are we to do with the wonderful red dress?" Marie's anger only added to Jane's ill feeling.

"I do not know," Jane said. "For now, you may put it away in the back room. We will speak more of this when I return. I must run an errand."

"*Oui*, Madame," Marie said resignedly.

Jane had no errand. There was no purpose to her walk at all other than taking a moment to clear her head, to calm her soul, to get away from her stepmother and the tempestuous calamity that followed inevitably in her wake. She headed south into Bridge

Street, toward the river, the wind crisp, pinching color into her cheeks, nipping the tip of her nose. The cold wintry, river-musky air was refreshing after days bent over her sewing, days with no horizon other than the next stitch, the next twisted roll of trimming, the next row of buttons or quilling or tucks.

A brisk stride soon heated her blood, the tingling stir of life firing warmth in legs and fingertips. She was alive and healthy with a thriving business—doing far better than she might have anticipated. She must not allow her stepmother's pique to throw a pall over her outlook. She must not fall prey to black moods and megrims. She had no time for mawkish weakness. She had not the patience for it.

Ignoring the crowd gathered about the minstrels singing carols to the tune of horn and flute, on the south side of the bridge, she took the steps on the north side. Down to the towpath along the riverside she went, the wind brisker, cooler by the water, tugging at her cloak, at her wig, swooping up under her skirt. Her mobcap flattened against her forehead. The tips of her ears burned with the cold. Her eyes stung.

The cheerful drift of voices caroling above her intensified her loneliness, her sense of despair.

She felt like weeping whenever she thought of the beautiful red dress. Hours wasted, days. Her fingers ached with the work that had been involved in the quilling alone.

She had produced exactly what she had envisioned, every detail exquisite. It was a remarkable gown, a breathtaking creation. She kicked at a tuft of sod. A great pity if no one should ever see it, if the remarkable quilled skirt should never twirl about on a dance floor.

A rowboat was on the river, a little red rowboat, a sturdy, red-nosed fellow in a stocking cap leaning rhythmically into the oars. The oarlocks creaked, the oars plashed as the boatman touched his cap and called "Good day to you," then leaned into the stroke again. The boat glided past, leaving ripples in the river, quiet ripples, and the distant music of the oarlocks.

She must simply keep rowing, she thought, must make this day the good day he had wished upon her. This temporary heartache would glide past if she simply focused on where she was going, instead of the disheartening tug of the undercurrent.

Perhaps she would find another use for the red dress, as she had found use for Fanny's dresses, many of which had been adjusted to fit other customers. There were only the ball gowns left, the gold-and-white one, which she had already worn, the green one she would wear to Prior Park. She loved them too much to part with them, these bits of glittering finery that connected her to her past—to all that was no longer hers to enjoy. She felt the potential for a finer world, a finer future for herself whenever she looked at them.

Surely nothing was wasted that was well done, that nurtured her soul, that brought pleasure and beauty to someone in the world? She would find a use for the red dress.

Cold now, she turned and headed back toward the bridge.

Chapter Thirteen

The duke glanced away from the glittering display cases of the jewelers on Pulteney Bridge for no more than a moment. Just a quick glance through the holly-trimmed window while he pondered which of two necklets to purchase for Anne. But in that moment he spotted a familiar figure. Madame Nicolette, in a fashionable cloak and cheerful green-and-red-ribboned bonnet, passed the shop, walking quickly.

She looked despondent, and it was not the Season for despondency. He was feeling quite cheered by his task of choosing gifts for loved ones. He wanted to share that spirit. And of all the people he had met in Bath, it was this woman he would cheer the most. She had pulled him out of his self-absorbed self-pity over the fiasco with Fanny. She had reminded him of the importance of family and loved ones in the Yuletide Season.

"And have you decided, Your Grace?" the jeweler asked, but with a jingle of the shop's bell Edward was outside and on the bridge, looking for Jane, only to find the street crowded with people bundled against the growing cold, shopping like he was, and none of them Madame Nicolette.

Baffled, he wandered both sides of the bridge, peering into shop windows on the lookout for her bonnet, sending sharp glances between the passing coaches. Had she crossed to the other side when he was not looking? How did she elude him? he wondered. He knew the direction in which she had been headed.

The bridge was cold, the wind a bit stronger, a bit colder with little to block it. The chill breeze smelled of Christmas and the persistent damp of the water passing below. At the west end of the bridge three mittened and capped lads were selling boughs of holly, yew, and mistletoe. At the east end a heavyset man pushed a wheeled brazier, selling hot chestnuts, fresh hot chestnuts. A group of traveling minstrels sang carols and rang a bell on the south side of the bridge where the steps led down to the towpath. The abbey's bells rang in the distance. The river sparkled and winked like a hammered silver ribbon in the welcome sunlight.

Jane Nichol was nowhere to be seen, in any guise. Had she been a figment of his imagination? A bit of wishful thinking? Edward hailed the chestnutmonger, the smell too enticing to resist. He bought a packet of hot nuts and sampled one before turning his back on the carolers to watch a red rowboat pass under the bridge against the silvered sheen of the water. The boatman paused an instant in the rhythm of his rowing to tip his hat to someone on the towpath.

Of course!

Pocketing the nuts, Edward set off down the steps beside the bridge.

Jane stood riverside on the towpath, staring into the water, the dance of light playing on her face, her glasses, on a teardrop sparkling briefly on the apex of her chin. The wind kicked at the hem of her cape, at the ribbons that streamed across care-bowed shoulders. Her curling brown wig looked more tousled than usual. As he watched, she drew up her shoulders, straightening her posture in taking a deep breath, and gave a little nod in the direction of the rowboat's wake before she turned in his direction.

"Good day," he said.

She started, her bleak expression transformed at sight of him. "Your Grace!' she said with a most gratifying smile, as if she were as glad to see him as he was to see her. "What do you do here? I thought you had left Bath."

She spoke, low-voiced, no trace of a French accent.

"I changed my mind, decided it would be a pity to miss spending Christmas with loved ones. I saw you from the bridge," he said. "You looked downcast. Is something the matter?"

She shook her head, dark curls whipping powdered cheeks that bore the damp tracks of her unhappiness. "Nothing that cannot be overcome," she said.

"Where are you going? Do you mind my walking with you?" He hesitated at the bottom of the steps, a sudden gust pushing him toward her.

She tried hard to smile, but failed, gaze dropping. "I am going nowhere," she said. "Nowhere at all."

"Ah." He studied her profile as intently as she regarded the polished tips of his shoes.

"Just needed some air," she said, her forced smile failing in the attempt. She pursed her lips.

"Do you require solitude as well?"

She took a deep breath and moved toward him, toward the stairs, shaking her head, the wig's curls slapping her cheek. "Not really."

"Do you like chestnuts?" He thrust forward the packet from his pocket.

She took a handful, commenting on their warmth, and sliding an amused glance in his direction, said, "Do you always feel compelled to feed me, Your Grace? Have I an ill-fed look?"

He laughed, then fixed her gaze with his own and said, "You do. My guess is you are too pressed by Christmas orders to eat properly. Am I wrong?"

"No. Quite right, in fact. And these are very good."

They munched contentedly a moment.

She tossed empty nut shells in the direction of the river, the sun turning them golden before they disappeared in the quicksilver of the water.

The singing on the bridge fell still. A cloud cast a shadow over the sun.

She shivered. "I'd best be getting back."

"May I offer you the warmth of my carriage?"

"It is only a short walk." She meant to resist further charity. He could see it in the proud tilt of her chin.

"Come, come," he coaxed. "The most sought-after dressmaker in Bath ought not to be seen walking the streets with tear-streaked cheeks and swollen eyes."

One hand flew to her cheek. She looked up at him, light winking on the dreadful glasses, the shadow of the bridge reflected there. How stricken she looked. "Are they so very swollen?"

"Few would notice," he admitted, "if you insist on walking."

She set off up the steps, cloak swaying at her heels. "I shall not insist," she said. "It is very kind of you to offer."

He caught up to her and extended her the crook of his arm, through which she tucked a gloved hand. He reveled in the warm weight of that contact, in the brush of her cloak against his legs as the wind took liberties. The sun warmed his face. What a pleasure it was to stand close enough to a pretty woman to hear the snap of the wind in her bonnet ribbons.

Up the steps and along the crowded walkway they went, the duke and the dressmaker, turning heads, stirring comment, attracting assessing glances. And he, who hated to be the center of attention, wanted to laugh, for they did not know her. Not for what she truly was, this French dressmaker. Only he knew. Only he could truly appreciate their walking arm in arm. It had been he, after all, who had determined to look for a woman honest and true, no dissembling, no lies. And here, he linked arms with the greatest liar of all and did not want to let her go.

Smiling then, that secretive smile that was uniquely his, little knowing it was one of the things she admired in him most, he led her away from the noise of the minstrels' renewed singing, into the confined space, the nearly complete privacy of his carriage.

His coachman, Mr. Goodge, met news of his extra

passenger without dismay, though it was not the duke's practice to take stray tradeswomen into his carriage. He listened to the route requested of him with no more than a nod, a "Yes, Your Grace," and a calm, "Walk on," to the horses as the door snapped shut.

For a moment Edward and Jane were plunged in darkness as their eyes adjusted to the reduced light, as the sway of the coach demanded their attention and good balance. And then her silhouette came clear to him, Jane's silhouette, wearing Madame Nicolette's hair, and the gleam of her gaze caught his as sunlight cut through the windows, bathing her in a moving shaft of flickering light.

She passed a gloved hand over the heavy gray brocade tufting that upholstered the seats. It was a fabric to attract the eye of a dressmaker. A luscious, luxurious fabric in dappled shades of gray, the raised threads depicting castles and coaches, and silver gray horses like his own. He had insisted on nothing but the best. Silvery gray glove leather pouches hung from the doors. The metal trim was silver, to match the team's harness. One could not find better coach springs, nor a smoother ride.

Her gaze roved about him from polished parquet floor to ashen pale silk-lined ceiling. "How lovely!" she said breathlessly, the rumble of the wheels almost drowning out her remark.

"You like it?" he asked as he eyed the slim space that separated their knees with a heightened awareness of just how close the interior of a coach forced one to another.

"Exquisite!" she said softly, her gray-gloved hands stroking each of the fabrics. "It is a marvelous brocade."

"Thank you. I designed it."

The low voice of the coachman as he called to each of the horses by name reminded Edward that their every word was overheard by Goodge and the two tall footmen, who clung to the back.

Jane Nichol seemed as aware as he of their being

overheard. "How *merveilleux* to have a *soupçon* of the sun again after so much rain," she said in Madame Nicolette's thickest accent as they clopped past Milsom Street.

"Yes," he agreed as the coachman turned into Gay, the street that paralleled Milsom. "I find that the sun, too long absent, can have a deleterious effect on my mood."

She frowned in looking out of the window. "But where are we going?" she asked. "Your driver passes Milsom."

"Yes. I asked him to. Do you mind a slight detour? A momentary diversion?"

"Whatever for?"

"Nuts, Madame Nicolette."

"*Merci.* I am no longer hungry."

"Not chestnuts."

"*Non?*"

"Acorns," he said.

"The ones in the Circus?"

"You know of them?"

"*Oui.* I have seen them."

With or without those dreadful glasses, he wondered. Lord, how he longed to snatch them from her nose.

"I have not seen them, and would witness them for myself. Will you indulge me in this minor detour?"

She shrugged with exactly the nonchalant élan a Frenchwoman might possess, and he wanted to tell her to stop it, to rub the dreadful powder from her face, the rouge from her cheeks, to lift the wig from her head. He longed for the straightforward Englishwoman he had met at a ball, met at the baths, the Englishwoman he had shared Bath buns with.

The carriage turned into the impressive circle of curve-fronted houses known as the Circus, Christmas wreaths on every door, red ribbon bows on the street-lamps, and swags of greenery gracing the wrought-iron fences guarding basement entrance steps. The carriage wheels rumbled to a stop.

"Come," he said, and whipped open the door.

She accepted his hand in stepping down. He did not
want to let go of it. There was no trace of Madame
Nicolette in the touch of her gloved hand, only Jane
Nichol. Dear Jane Nichol, who looked after her old
governess, and employed dozens of old women, and
dared to ask him to pay for his mistakes.

"Have you heard the story of the acorns?" he asked
briskly as he led her out of earshot of his servants to
stand beneath oaks clad in tattered brown in the center of the Circus. He turned then, to point at the Portland stone acorns high above them, his eyes on her
rather than the architectural oddities. He looked for
fresh sign of the slender sylph from the Baths, impatient with the heavy silhouette Jane cut as she tipped
back her bewigged and bonneted head to look upward
at the acorn-studded roofline.

The oak trees planted in the center island between
the column-fronted houses threw fingers of light and
shadow upon the tear-streaked powder that spoiled
her cheek. He thought he saw an equal play of light
and shadow in her eyes when he said, "My grandfather told me the story when I was a lad. I thought of
you recently when I heard it retold to my sisters."

She turned her green-eyed gaze on him, glasses
glinting, mirroring the treetops.

"What? The story of King Bladud?"

"You know it then?" He was disappointed. He had
hoped to spin the tale for her—a most fascinating tale.

"I know that he was Roman, had leprosy, and chose
to leave his father's kingdom on the other side of the
river rather than risk giving it to anyone else. He became a swineherd to distance himself farther from
people he might infect. This prompted you to think
of me?"

"Yes."

She was puzzled, but not immediately offended as
so many women might have been. Lord, how he had
come to admire the knit of her brow, the careful consideration with which she met the world, the amused
tilt of her lips.

"I assure you I do not have leprosy," she said conversationally. "And no desire to become a swineherd."

He laughed. It felt good to laugh. "No, of course not, but you left your father's kingdom, which took equal courage, and came to Bath, just as he did, and started a new life."

"There was no Bath in Bladud's day, no more than a muddy spring. I was much more fortunate than he, I dare to say."

He wondered if he was the only one to recognize her insistence on seeing the best of the bleakest situations, if he was the only one privileged to hear Madame Nicolette relinquish her French accent. How taxing was it to pretend every day to be something one was not? Did she pretend her positive outlook, only to come to believe her own imaginings? Far more remarkable than Bladud and his pigs, in her own way.

"Bath offered more than a muddy spring," he reminded her. "It offered the promise of larger acorns as well." He lifted his face to the chill breeze and eyed the houses on their side of the Circus, the row upon row of stately columns, the continuity of architectural detail, the pale acorns thrusting skyward between huge multiflued chimneys.

"The acorns were a lie," she said, the wind catching wisps of her wig's hair, tossing it rudely against her mouth. She brushed impatiently at sun-silvered strands. "The pigs had contracted the leprosy," she said, "and the prince did not wish to take them back to their owner ill."

When he did not respond, she prodded, "I suppose that reminded you of me as well?"

"Not the pig part."

"You are too kind."

His turn to chuckle, to explain. "The baths cured the prince's leprosy. Bladud got a fresh start. As Bath gives you a fresh start."

"Yes, but there the resemblance ends. Bladud was the prodigal son. They killed the fatted calf and welcomed him back. I've no desire to go back. You did not hope to convince me, did you?"

"No."

"I will not go back. Ever."

"I did not . . ."

"Nothing you can say will change that." So belligerent that chin of hers, the glint in her eyes.

"Nor do I try," he said impatiently. "I meant only to compliment you in persevering against what would seem to be insurmountable odds."

"Oh?" she said, and looked into his eyes, quite startled behind the glass wall of those dreadful horn-rimmed glasses.

He reached forward to remove them.

She flinched, caught completely off guard, and indeed, it was rather forward of him to attempt to make free with her person.

"You do not need them, do you?" he asked, a trifle embarrassed.

She blinked at him over the rims, then gaze dropping, shook her head. "Acorns," she said.

"I must say I dislike them."

She slid them lower on her nose and looked at him again.

"Much better," he said. "I can see your eyes now. You have very pretty eyes, Miss Nichol. It is a great shame to hide them."

"No, Your Grace." She slid them smartly back into place. "To hide is entirely the point, and you know it."

"But who is there to hide from here but me?"

She spread her arms. "A whole world lives in the Circus, Your Grace, many with nothing better to do than spend their time looking out at every carriage that goes by."

She was right. Curtains twitched above them even as she spoke, light glinting off the rows of windows as brightly as it shone upon her glasses. The doings of the duke with the dressmaker would be gossip by sundown.

As they walked back to the carriage, he wondered

if he did her reputation damage in bringing her there. Or would his attentions only add luster to a French seamstress's credentials?

As he handed her in, her hand warm and vibrant in his, she turned on the step, looked back at the stone acorns, and said, her musical accent in place again. "Did you hear how Bladud *fini*?"

Her eyes looked so very green in the light, beautiful despite the horn-rimmed glasses, despite their recently tearful state. Even the dark curling wig and heavy cosmetics could not hide entirely the features he began to hold dear. "The prince was welcomed back into his father's court," he said. "The ring his mother had given him made no one dispute his claim to the throne."

"His mother," she mused. "*Oui*. She was there to welcome his return. And after that?"

"It would seem you know this story better than I," he said wryly.

"Bladud thought he could fly." She tilted her head in such a way he thought she meant to challenge him to call her liar as she settled herself by the far window. "He did not know when it was foolish to persevere in the face of insurmountable odds."

"What happened?" he asked as he slid into the seat across from her, his back to the driver. He would look upon her face as she spoke.

"He had a set of feather wings made, and leapt from a cliff. It is said he glided upon the wind like a bird."

"Remarkable," he said, caught up in the story, in the sparkle of her eyes.

"Unrealistic," she contradicted him. "One might even call the prince supremely stupid. A seam among the feathers ripped, and he dashed himself to pieces on the roof of a temple."

He sat in silence a moment, studying her painted features, the faux French lilt of her voice still resonating in his mind. She looked defeated he thought, at the end of her tether, no better than when he had met her—and he had hoped to lift that melancholy air.

"Sounds as if he was in need of a good seamstress," he said quietly.

She laughed. Oh, how he loved the sound of it, the look of her, Madame Nicolette, or plain Jane Nichol. It did not matter. She laughed.

Chapter Fourteen

Jane felt much better by the time he delivered her to the shop, more herself than she had felt in a long time. How good it was to be with someone who knew who she really was. And what a great deal of difference a bit of fresh air, and laughter, and good company could make to the most dreadful of days.

She was, in fact, thinking of the upcoming ball at Prior Park when she whisked in through the doorway, the jingle of the doorbell no longer the bane of her existence, but a bit of music to her ears. She hummed a bit of the Christmas carol the minstrels had sung on the bridge and took a whirl through the empty shop. She would dance with him yet, the duke. He had mentioned the ball, mentioned he meant to be there—no mention at all of leaving Bath anytime soon.

Life was sweet, the sun was shining, a duke took interest in her—Jane Nichol.

She must find a conveyance to take her to Prior Park. She needed a fresh pair of gloves, stockings, and shoes. She needed to try on Fanny's green dress. It would need a bit of taking in through the waist and bodice.

She burst through the curtains to the back room, sure she would find Marie and Mrs. Bell, ready to set to work again, a smile on her lips—a smile that faded as shock set in.

Marie and Mrs. Bell sat together at the cutting table, carefully picking apart seams. The fabric was a familiar green. *Fanny's green ball gown!* Her gaze flew to the gap on the rack where it had so long hung waiting, waiting for her, waiting for the ball.

The sleeves and bodice were already in pieces, the length of the gown was split asunder.

"What's this?" The words came out weakly. She swept up one of the ripped-away sleeves.

Marie looked up with a brilliant smile. *"Problème* solved!" she said with enthusiasm.

"Problem? What problem?" Jane could not believe her eyes. She could not really take in the dreadful truth that the dress was ruined—no wearing it to the ball now—and yet she had a sinking feeling she knew the answer before it was given.

"Lady Nichol saw the dress, liked the color," Mrs. Bell explained. "We've only to add a panel of embroidered trim down the front, love, to make it wide enough to fit her, and of course the sleeves need to be recut, reset."

"Of course," Jane said with a slightly hysterical laugh, as she allowed the sleeve to fall back to the table, the sleeve she had pictured on her arm, in his arms.

Marie's smile was fading now. Her hand faltered. "You are not pleased? The gown will be *fini* in good time for Christmas."

Jane turned away from the satin and lace carnage. She rubbed her hands together and pressed them to her temples. No use fretting. "How wise of you to suggest such a solution, Marie," she said, though it pained her to utter the words. "Very clever, indeed, to convince Lady Nichol to take the dress."

Marie nodded, confidence returning, her hands destroying the careful stitches with renewed zest.

Mrs. Bell patted the green bodice she was carefully ripping asunder. "It seemed a shame to waste such a pretty dress."

"A shame, indeed," Jane said, and could not help thinking, a shame for Lady Nichol, who always looked sallow in shades of green. And what to wear to Prior Park now? Or must she abandon the dream of dancing with the duke after all?

She turned to the rack where Fanny's gowns had long hung. She could always wear the silver-and-gold-trimmed gown she had worn to the Assembly ball. But the only unclaimed gown that waited there, forlornly, was the red-and-gold gown she had made especially for her stepmother—a gown far too big for her, far too harsh in color for her fair complexion.

"Where is Fanny's other ball gown?" she asked, dreading the answer, her eyes shutting out sight of the red dress.

"Lady Nichol took it," Marie said. "For her daughter Rose, who is to be married soon."

"Oh dear. To the baron?"

"A baron, yes." Mrs. Bell looked surprised. "However did you know?"

The duke went to the White Hart that day for nefarious reasons. He went to fetch a parcel from London—tins of tea he had ordered as Christmas gifts for the patients at St. Joseph's. They were intended as a charitable gesture, of course, a kindness to those less fortunate than himself, but deep in his heart of hearts he saw them as the perfect excuse to approach one patient in particular, that he might find out more of Miss Jane Nichol, who possessed his thoughts since their last encounter, to the point of obsession.

He did not expect to see anyone he knew at the White Hart. Thus, it was with surprise he observed one of Jane's half sisters, Rose, ducking into the posting house ahead of him, a valise in one hand, two bandboxes dangling from the other, her head twitching from side to side as she went through the doorway, as if she was afraid she might be observed.

It was this wary stance, and not at all his aversion for the company of the young woman, that prevented him from calling out to her in greeting. After all, here again was someone who might tell him more of Miss

Jane Nichol, and so he hurried after her with the intention of speaking to her if at all possible.

This intention was thwarted, however, in stepping inside, for though his eyes took a moment to adjust to the darkness, his ears had no trouble at all in hearing, above the clopping hoofbeats and rumbling wheels of the approaching post coach as it pulled into the yard, the breathless squeal of "Mr. Davies!"

The name turned his head. He must see the infamous Mr. Davies.

Rose had dropped her valise and bandboxes and flung herself at a well-built young man who opened his arms to receive her with an ardent cry of "My love! Are you ready for Gretna?"

An elopement, was it? Not the most opportune time for a friendly little chat with Rose Nichol.

But was it his business to intervene? To stop this runaway marriage?

Certainly if he had not informed Lady Nichol of the whereabouts of one runaway daughter, he could not justify informing her of a second daughter doing the same. It would be quite hypocritical of him, would it not?

Rose looked exquisitely happy in the arms of this Mr. Davies. And Davies? He, too, looked happy in the moment. What had he to gain by this Gretna union other than a cast-off Rose?

Edward walked past the couple, his mind not yet made up on his responsibilities to Miss Nichol's stepmother and stepsisters, none of whom he held in very high regard. He stepped into the yard, where the post coach divulged its passengers and parcels, still puzzling the matter.

The yardman, recognizing him at once, called out, "Your Grace! Parcel's come."

"Splendid!" he said, only to find himself accosted by one of the passengers, a well-dressed, if rotund, hunchbacked man with balding pate, bad teeth, and a scarlet carbuncle on the tip of his nose.

"Chandrose?" he asked, as if quite sure Edward would respond in the affirmative.

"You have the advantage of me, sir," Edward said.

"Name's Bagshott. Horace Bagshott. Knew your father, lad," the old man said with a sepia-tone smile.

"Baron Blomefield?" Edward held out his hand, and while he gave the old fellow's fingers a vigorous shake, he was at once glad of his gloves in doing so. The man had a horrendously bewarted hand gone as snuff yellow as his teeth.

"That I am! You have heard of me from your grandfather?" The old man's face lit up.

"I have heard your name mentioned, my lord." By a certain Miss Nichol, he thought, not my grandfather, and while he knew how little regard Miss Nichol had for marriage to the fellow, she had mentioned no specific ills to detract from his character. He wondered just how his grandfather had felt about the man. "What brings you to Bath for Christmas?"

The old man waggled bushy salt-and-pepper eyebrows. "Same thing brought you here, lad. Hopes of a Christmas wedding, my boy. Though I hear your union has been canceled, and offer all due condolences. I shall take a bride home for Christmas if it is the last thing I do. Shall I send you an invitation once the date is set?"

"Very kind of you, I'm sure. And who is the lucky bride? If I may be so bold as to ask?"

"She bears the name of Nichol. One of old Baron Nichol's stepdaughters."

"Can it be Rose or Lily Nichol you mean, my lord?"

Baron Blomefield, in the midst of taking snuff, sneezed explosively, a most distinctive sneeze. Edward could be relatively certain anyone standing inside the posting house must have heard such a sneeze.

"Indeed, Your Grace. You have met them?"

"I have met all of Nichol's daughters."

The old baron squinted at him cannily as he wiped his nose with a much used handkerchief. "I'll warrant you only think you have met all of them, Your Grace, for one has run off with a dancing master, the silly puss, and up to me and my fortune to restore the family's good name."

"Ah, I had heard tale of such a rumor and wondered at its source. You refer to Rose Nichol, perhaps?"

"Aye, that's the one I mean to wed." The baron's smile was even more unpleasant than before.

"But how can this be, my lord!" Edward looked at him in mock surprise.

Blomefield's smile faded. "You would question, perhaps, the difference in our ages, Your Grace?"

Edward paused a moment, studying the man, wondering what possessed him to consider marrying a chit half his age other than lascivious intent. And then, as Blomefield's face began to take on the same scarlet hue as the carbuncle at the end of his pockmarked nose, he said in the most soothing of tones, "Not at all, my lord. I am sure you have given such a serious matter careful consideration."

The Baron looked at him with gimlet eye, as if not quite sure how to take the remark.

"Indeed, how very good of you, my lord," Edward said with no hint of the sarcasm that stirred such compliments. "To concern yourself so intimately with the fortune and futures of Nichol's fatherless daughters. I question only your choice with regard to that which we have already discussed."

"What's that then?" Blomefield blustered, the vein in his forehead pulsing plum color.

"Is not Rose the daughter who has run away with the dancing master?"

"No," Blomefield huffed with a bark of a laugh. "That was Jane."

"Was it really?" Edward bit back his own amusement.

The baron gave an airy wave. "Of that I am absolutely certain, Your Grace."

Chapter Fifteen

Jane got busy with her work, convinced the worst had befallen her. That was the silver surprise in dreadful events. When life could not get worse, it must get better.

Besides, she had Christmas gifts to make, and no time for moping. She and Marie were stitching red flannel nightgowns and cozy white flannel caps for all of the seamstresses who had helped them. The list of names grew longer and longer, the stack of finished gowns higher and higher. Their labor of love seemed unending, perhaps because they added to the count some forty gowns and caps to go to St. Joseph's, and a dozen or more to each of three almshouses. They had plenty of flannel and crimson dye, and the results so cheerful and warm and useful, their spirits were lifted immeasurably in doing the work.

Jane might almost have begun to forget the upcoming ball, she might have content herself with not going, had it not been for the constant reminder of dozens of ball dresses in every shape, size, and hue that passed through her fingers, none of them hers, the world of waltzes no longer hers.

She was not a lady of leisure. She must work for her supper. And she was fortunate indeed business blossomed. Thanks to the duke.

She might not find opportunity to dance with him, as she had hoped, but she must in some way repay him. She wondered if there was any sort of Christmas gift she could give him without appearing too forward. She pondered the matter for several days.

And at last—it was so obvious once she had thought of it—she knew what she must give him, and a little box to put it in. That was what she needed, a little silver box.

"But, my dear, you must go!" Miss Godwin railed on one of Jane's many visits, as she set aside the teapot and offered Jane sugar. "You must find something to wear. I have promised the duke I mean to be there, and you with me."

"What? You have spoken to the duke?" Jane clattered cup against saucer in her surprise.

Miss Godwin nodded proudly. "He means to send his spare carriage to fetch me."

Jane's hand trembled in taking up the sugar tongs. "When did you have opportunity to speak to the duke?"

Miss Godwin smiled through the steam on her cup, a mischievous smile. "He brought me a present."

Jane stared at her, openmouthed.

"Well, if you must know." Miss Godwin looked a little sheepish. "He brought all of us presents. That tea you are drinking, and the little walnut tea caddy to store it in, and the silver strainer, and lemon fork."

Jane turned to admire the tea caddy. She held the silver strainer to the light. "How very kind of the duke, Miss Godwin! A most appropriate and thoughtful gift, as is the use of his coach. Whatever did you say?"

"Well, I might have mentioned that I was coming in the company of one of my old pupils, and that we were looking for proper conveyance to go such a distance."

"You didn't!"

"I did."

It was not Miss Godwin's habit to defend her actions, but no denying the defensiveness of her tone in this instance.

"And why not?" she insisted. "I had a feeling he

might suggest something, and quite right I was. Without the slightest hint of condescension he suggested that I would be needing conveyance, and that as he had two it would give him the greatest pleasure to provide me with it."

"And so it does, Miss Nichol."

The duke spoke from the doorway. No mistaking his now familiar voice.

Both women looked up in dismay.

He was wearing that self-assured, slightly amused look that Jane had begun to relish, for beneath it now she always saw a hint of vulnerability, perhaps even affection.

"Indeed, I hope you intend to accompany her to Prior Park, Miss Nichol?" he said, voice gentle, his manner still amused, one might even say playful. His eyes looked so very blue today, his gaze fathomless. Perhaps it was the color of his coat. "Indeed"—his gaze faltered a moment, his voice fell—"I look forward to a dance."

"Yes," Jane said at once. She could not meet the vulnerability in this gentleman's eyes with any other answer, though Miss Godwin's brows rose, and she felt a bit of the fool for responding with too much haste when he bid them both adieu after a moment's small talk.

She sat stunned, amazed that he cared to know if she came, that he wished her to have use of the coach, that he wanted to dance with her.

Miss Godwin said, "So you do mean to come, after all?"

"Yes," she said, still dazed. "I suppose I meant to go all along."

"And what of a dress?" Miss Godwin asked archly.

"I do not know," Jane said. "In fact, I cannot see how it can be done without the borrowing of a garment, which is not something I am at all inclined to do with any of my customers. But I will give it thought. I must come up with some sort of solution."

* * *

Work gave Jane no time to give the matter of a ball dress much consideration. In a great flurry all of the parts and pieces of the ball dresses that had been jobbed out, began to return to the shop. In a rush of renewed activity these sleeves and bodices, skirts and flounces, must find their mates and be put together, which meant a great deal of work for her and Marie, and the basters, who loosely assembled the pieces for the final fittings. And with those fittings came a steady stream of women into the shop and in and out of the dressing rooms, each of them to be measured again for the fitness of every seam, and the measuring for hems, or changes. There were always those who wanted changes.

A sprinkling of new customers arrived as well, for Madame Nicolette's fame continued to spread as satisfied customers carried away their finished creations, and so it was no great surprise that the duke's mother, who had mentioned the making of a dress upon their last meeting, should step through the doorway.

When the bell rang, and Jane turned with Madame Nicolette's most polite welcome ready upon her lips, she could not help feeling a deep-seated flutter of anxiety that anyone connected with the duke should come to her. Because he had been so very kind to her, Jane felt every inclination to be helpful and kind to his mother. And because she liked the duke and his sisters and had enjoyed their brief chat when they last met at the duke's house in Great Pulteney, she expected to like the duchess as well.

The arrangements for the purchase of a dress went as well as could be expected.

Like her daughters, the dowager duchess had a decided sense of style, and distinct preferences in color. The details of what she wanted were soon carefully noted in Madame Nicolette's ledger. There was only the matter of which trims the duchess wanted. She and Madame Nicolette sat in a corner, thumbing through a set of cards that held sample snippets. These always proved most helpful in the making of such decisions.

They had talked of the weather and of the upcoming holiday celebrations, and the duchess had mentioned how very pleased her daughters were with their dresses, and Jane had begun to wonder if the duchess meant to mention her son at all when she said, quite unexpectedly, "I wonder if I might ask you something very personal, Madame Nicolette."

Personal? Jane had no idea what to expect. Madame Nicolette was not a character to divulge much that was personal to any customer. After all, an imaginary woman had nothing much to offer in the way of truth. That it might have something to do with the duke sprang at once to mind. That he might have revealed something of who she really was to his mother made her terribly nervous. "*Allez en avant,*" she said with forced conviviality. "I cannot promise to answer."

"My son," the duchess began very quietly, unwilling to be overheard.

Jane leaned forward, breath held.

"Has been seen in public, in the company of a woman . . ." She paused, choosing her words carefully, "far beneath his station."

Jane blinked, surprised. *What was this?* And why would the duchess confide such a thing in her?

The duchess glanced about to be sure she was not overheard, her face a picture of motherly concern. "This troubles me no end, as I am sure you will understand. I am averse to so much as a suggestion of scandal, you will understand, so hard on the heels of Edward's jilting of Fanny. A dreadful business, the gossip and speculation." She sighed, and set aside the embroidered ribbon she had been examining. "If it were only Edward's reputation to think about, only his chances of making a good match, I should not worry, but a mother must be concerned where her daughters' reputations may be affected as well. You do understand?"

"Indeed, I do, far better than you may believe, and

I wish I could help, Madame, but on my honor, I have heard nothing *dérogatoire*."

The duchess sighed, shoulders sinking. Her voice dropped lower still. "There is no mistake," she said delicately. "And the reason I come to you in particular with such a question, is that I am told she is a dressmaker. I thought perhaps you might know who. That you might warn her against indiscretion."

Jane's brows rose. "But, Madame, I do not know . . ."

The duchess patted the back of her hand, her manner more urgent. "He has been seen with her in his carriage. Standing in the Circus. Walking by the river."

Of course! The duchess meant her! Madame Nicolette.

"*Vraiment!* But, Your Grace. That was *moi!*"

"You?"

"*Oui.* Your son was kind enough to . . ."

"Oh, my dear woman, I am relieved." The duchess's voice shook with emotion. "And here I thought I really had something to worry about. A dangerous liaison." She exhaled heavily and found it within her to smile tremulously as she patted Jane's hand again, quite triumphantly. "Here I knew you would be able to help me. I am so glad I chose to confide in you."

"*Oui,*" Jane said with a small nod, reminded quite firmly of her lowered status in the world. Perhaps it was best, indeed, that the duchess had seen fit to confide in her before she puffed herself up too much in response to the duke's suggestion he hoped to dance with her. What chance, after all, had a dressmaker and a duke, even when the dressmaker was daughter of a baron? She was disgraced—a runaway—suspected of the worst sort of behavior by the society of her peers, unwanted by her stepmother for anything other than the money she might bring by way of marriage. What had she to offer this reserved and highly respected gentleman, and his reserved and highly respected family? What expectation had she of being welcomed by the duchess into that family?

Jane's heart sank as she looked into the eyes of the worthy duchess.

None. She found no true hope there.

Dreaming. She had been dreaming.

Chapter Sixteen

The duke was in a quandary.

How did a gentleman go about calling upon a dressmaker? How did one find moments alone with a woman it would not be wise to be seen alone with? There were eyes everywhere. Tongues to wag. Ears bent on listening—servants, his sisters, his mother, complete strangers. Everyone watched the business of a duke. It was a price that came with title.

His mother had laughed about her conversation with Madame Nicolette. Laughed over her foolish concern. He could not tell her she had every right to suspect him of a *tendre* for the dressmaker she was now convinced he offered no more than courtesy. He could not tell her he was irresistibly drawn to Jane Nichol. Drawn, but not head over heels into idiocy.

He knew society would frown upon such a match. He knew his mother would question the soundness of such an attachment—such a linking with scandal—especially after Fanny. He knew Jane's stepmother and stepsisters would prove socially embarrassing, indeed an annoyance, emotionally and financially if he pursued his desires, affections, his very curiosity. He knew that for the present he ought not divulge his interest, his concerns, or her true identity. And yet, he must know more, must speak to her again, must untangle the raveling fabric of her life, and the feelings that welled in him whenever she was near.

He could not keep going to the dress shop. His

attentiveness in such a female-dominated sphere would be noticed and commented upon without fail.

His habit of going to the baths in the morning had been noticed already by his mother.

"Take your sisters," she instructed him. "If bathing is good for them, then let them bathe. But take care they are not bothered by riffraff."

There was no riffraff, only the elderly and lame. No Miss Nichol either, much to his chagrin. She did not show herself again on any of the mornings he and his sisters went for a plunge. Perhaps best—he would not have felt comfortable trying to get to know her there with Anne and Beth and Celia looking on, trying to intrude upon their conversation.

No, he was not yet ready to share her with his family. And not for merely negative reasons. There was something magical in the privacy of their shared moments, in the secret of who she was, known at present only to him.

His sisters would compare her to Fanny. They would most assuredly report his attentions to the duchess. And what his mother would have to say about a baron's daughter become dressmaker he preferred not to think about. Not yet. He must be clear first as to his own feelings, and in order to sort out those feelings, he must see Jane Nichol again, alone, if it could be arranged.

A challenging task—she was not to be seen at any of the normal gathering places in Bath; the Assemblies, concerts, and breakfasts where the *ton* met and mingled were not the haunt of a dressmaker who hid her connections from the world she had abandoned.

How did one make better acquaintance with a woman who worked to the exclusion of all else? She did not make a practice of taking the waters in the pump room, in either of her guises—a wise move, as her stepmother, Lily, and now Baron Blomefield made a habit of frequenting the place at all hours.

The baron was convinced the waters were going to carry away the lesions on his lips, he confided in the duke. "Only see how they have reduced the size of the carbuncle on my nose!"

Edward had duly examined the pockmarked nose and resolved again as he did so with all the conviction in his soul that Jane Nichol must never fall prey to this fellow, come what may.

Lily looked quite despondent of late, and the baron rather possessive of his clutch on her arm. Rose Nichol might just as well have fallen off the end of the earth for all the mention that was made of her—of her sudden absence—of a troublesome dancing master named Davies. The baron seemed constant in his affections in only one regard, and that was to the family name of Nichol.

Jane seemed to do little other than labor, day in, day out. And while Edward Brydges, as Duke of Chandrose, was a gentleman who took great responsibilities upon his own shoulders and handled investments and properties, a great deal of paperwork, and the overseeing demanded of both, he had always been one to find moments of leisure. He enjoyed the finer things in life that his efforts provided him. He could not imagine shutting himself away from the world for weeks on end.

The only time and place that he could count on seeing Miss Nichol was on Sunday at Bath Abbey. She was faithful in attendance, if a trifle too timely in her arrival and departure. She was not one to linger after the service, chatting, nor did she come early for the same reason. He was afforded no more than an occasional exchange of glances, and never knew in what guise she might come, only that she chose to sit in the same spot near the back where he could gaze upon the nape of her neck as he walked in with his sisters if he troubled himself to arrive after she was settled.

It took careful timing on his part, very careful timing. His sisters complained of his sudden need to be perfectly prompt, of his unwillingness to arrive early.

He wondered if his behavior bordered on obsession. It worried him a little.

He envied Miss Nichol in a way, for no one, other than he, took notice of her arrival or departure, while his family's passage was always regarded with a great deal of neck craning and whispered comment. And thus, he could not turn to try to catch her eye, or look her way too often or too long as he walked in. He must be careful, circumspect, discreet.

There was only one other place where they might meet without comment, as Miss Jane Nichol and Edward Brydges rather than the dressmaker and the duke, and that was at St. Joseph's Hospital, where she still came every other evening to look in on her governess, as herself, the unobjectionable Miss Nichol.

He thus made a point of timing his own excursions there to coincide with hers, and haunted the hallway where Miss Godwin was lodged, hoping for a glimpse, a smile, a "Good evening."

On the first day they encountered each other thus, she bid him good day and smiled. The second day they chatted briefly of the weather, and how much Miss Godwin enjoyed his gift of tea. The third day he lingered late, just outside the doors of the hospital, determined to share more than a few words, a few moments.

"Miss Nichol," he said with a tip of his hat as she stepped into the lamplight, looking rather waiflike and lithe without Madame's padding.

She looked up at him, surprised, the lamplight gleaming golden on wisps of smoothed-back ashen fair hair, no glasses to hide her sparkling green eyes from him tonight. "Your Grace."

How different she looked without Madame's powder and rouge. How youthful and sweet.

"Might I offer you escort in walking home?"

A flash of pleasure swept her eyes, her lips, and yet she hesitated. Her brows knit in the manner he found so captivating, and with a frown at her shoes she said, very quietly, "I do not know that it is wise of you to be seen in my company, Your Grace."

He smiled. "Wise? No."

Lamplight flickered on her rose-flushed cheek. Her expression was one of solemnity as she nodded and walked past him down the steps.

He longed to bring another smile to those lips.

He fell into step beside her with that goal in mind. "I do not think it wise of you to walk home alone in the dark."

She wore an understated blue wool pelisse on these evenings to St. Joseph's, a plain blue-ribboned chip bonnet. Plain Jane Nichol did not look as prepared to defend herself as Madame Nicolette might have— nowhere near so formidable.

"It is not so very far," she said quietly, no trace of a French accent, quiet and demure. And yet he knew the boisterous dressmaker lurked just beneath the surface—part of her personality allowed voice only in costume.

Was there such a character lurking inside of him? he wondered.

"Bath is a quiet place," she said. "These neighborhoods offer no dangers to me. I know better than to walk in Avon Street, and have never so much as seen Holloway."

She referred to a haunt of prostitutes and a den of thieves on the far side of the river. He took a deep breath and said, "It is not your safety alone that prompts my asking to accompany you."

"No?"

"No. I find myself . . ." He frowned, struggling for the right words. "I . . . miss you. I find myself seeking you out as often as I may without attracting too much attention."

"Oh."

"I cannot imagine . . . going another day without . . . conversation with you. I do enjoy our conversations."

"As do I, and yet . . ."

Finger to his lips, he said gently, "Please, do not add to the reasons why we ought not do this. There are too many already."

She took a deep breath, looked about her at the

almost unearthly still of the street, and nodded. "All right."

The darkness held its breath as they walked into it. Cold, and crisp as an apple, it caught at Edward's throat and sent his gaze skyward toward the brilliant twinkle of winter stars. The faced medallion of the moon carried a silver halo. A spectacular sight, and it seemed they two were the only ones abroad that evening to witness it. Edward was pleased to share such silence, such beauty with Jane.

In the distance a dog barked, and the bells of Bath Abbey rang. A horse and carriage clopped by, bells jingling on harness, the horses blowing clouds. The smell of coal fires and roasting meat prompted him to ask, "Hungry?"

She chuckled, a warm sound that puffed into the air a silvery cloud. "Ready to feed me again, are you, Your Grace? Have you hot jacket potatoes stuffed in your pockets?"

He had to laugh. It was a common enough practice among the lower classes. "No. But there is a pieman ahead."

"I have eaten," she said. "But do not hesitate to purchase something if you have not."

"It is not pie I hunger for," he said, the words surprising him, for they hinted at his true desires, a far baser hunger, and he had never intended that this should be a topic of conversation between them.

"Doubtless you are accustomed to finer fare than a pieman's wares." She seemed oblivious to his unwitting suggestion.

I am lonely, he wanted to admit, *and Fanny's father brought suit against me today—and all I want is a glimpse of your face, the touch of your hand, some sense that there is more to life than that which I daily delve.* The words would not come. "How goes your work?" was all that he managed to ask.

"An endless circle of stitches," she said. "And you to thank for the vast majority of them."

"Me?"

"Yes." She stared at the man in the moon a moment before admitting quietly, "I am quite beholden to you, Your Grace. Obligated to a degree I cannot repay." She gave him a worried look, as if afraid he expected something in return.

And in that instant he saw his request for a private walk in the dark from her perspective, and understood her fears. She felt obligated to him! She must wonder if he meant to take advantage of that obligation.

He rushed to say, "I would not have you think I mean to put you in my debt."

"No. Of course not. And yet I am. The favor of a gentleman so well respected."

"Is not so great a thing." He hurried to stop her praise. "Please, Miss Nichol."

She would not be quieted. "The honor of serving your sisters, your mother—such patronage cannot but bring in other customers."

Ah! He knew now from whence this sudden sense of obligation, of reserve, sprang.

"My mother mentioned coming to see you." He tested his theory.

Her voice quieted. "Yes, Your Grace."

She looked away. What had his mother said?

"Will you do me a very great favor, Miss Nichol?"

Her steps slowed. "That would depend upon the favor, Your Grace."

"There are limits, then, to your gratitude?" He meant the remark to test his suspicions.

Her chin went up. Her jaw stiffened. "Yes, Your Grace."

And to think he had once suspected her of attempting to compromise him. It would seem the shoe was on the other foot this evening.

"What is this favor?"

"No more compliments. No more expressions of gratitude or obligation, and most of all, please, will you not stop 'Your Gracing' me, Miss Nichol—Jane."

Her mouth fell open a moment before she pressed her lips together with a puzzled frown. "How would you have me address you, Your Grace? I am sorry to disregard your wishes at once, but surely anything else would be considered inappropriate, given our circumstances."

He was not really prepared to answer. He could not ask her to call him Edward, could he? Not on such short acquaintance.

Matching her frown, he said irritably, "I do not know. It is just . . . you seem determined today to throw my title between us."

"Does it not stand between us always?"

So very troubled, her dear face, he thought.

"I am a dressmaker. You are a duke. I have only to be seen with you on the street to become a matter for gossip."

He watched the movement of their feet a moment, the moonlight silvering the Portland stone pavement, their shadows following them like dark ghosts. His gaze rose to study the windows they passed, lamplight glowing from some, moonlight winking in those where darkness held sway.

"My life has always been an object of scrutiny, of speculation," he admitted.

"And mine must not," she said firmly.

That brought him up sharp. He had no answer for it. They stood a moment in awkward silence.

"I can make my own way home, Your Grace." Her stride was straight-backed and proud. Her voice held the same strength of purpose he had begun to expect of Madame Nicolette.

This was not working out as he had planned. Frustration rose in him like a wave. "Can you, Miss Nichol? That would depend upon your definition of home, would it not?"

She stopped beneath a streetlamp and turned, the light glazing her golden, her tone defiant. "Home is where the heart is, is it not, Your Grace?"

Something in the tilt of her head, in the brilliant sparkle of her eyes, prompted him to action, when he had never intended to act.

He closed the space between them, stopping so close to her she took a startled step backward.

"Look up, Miss Nichol," he suggested wryly, pointing.

She glanced upward warily, the line of her chin, her throat enticing, gilded by the light. "Oh dear," she said, closing her eyes to the sight of the cluster of pearl-berried mistletoe dangling from the lamppost.

Her lashes were golden moths, fluttering as she opened her eyes to look at him again, fear hovering, fear and expectation, as she moved to step away, and he gently caught her arm and asked, "Where is your heart, Jane?"

Before she could answer, he leaned forward to kiss her cheek, swift and soft, and as he pulled away, his mouth hovering above hers, their lips almost touching, he whispered, "Where *is* your home?"

He did not expect a reply, certainly did not expect what happened next. She turned her head, cheek brushing his, soft as down, and she whispered, the noise more an exhalation of breath than spoken word, her lower lip grazing his earlobe, "Here."

She broke away then.

Stunned, unsure of her meaning, he let her go. Did she mean here in Bath, or here in his arms?

She ran, heels making music on the paving stones, the upward sweep of her hair catching the light as her neck scarf, ill attended, billowed out behind her, ghosting her passage for several strides before it broke free, and sank to the pavement in a pale gray puddle of silk.

He picked it up and held its soft, jasmine and roses warmth to his cheek for a moment, and imagined her voice in his ear once again.

"Here."

Heart peltering, nerves jangling, Jane ran the rest of the way home. Cold air filled her chest, warm, cedar-scented memories her head. Her cheek tingled from his kiss. She could still feel the brush of his earlobe against her lip. What had she done? What had she done? What must he think of her? And yet her heart beat a happy tattoo. Her feet had wings.

He had kissed her! He had kissed her! He had said he could not imagine another day without conversation with her. Could it be he felt for her the same rush of anticipation and unnerved glee she experienced whenever she saw him? Did his pulse race?

She did not quite know what to do with herself, with this frothing rush of feeling. It raced through her veins like spirits, left her giddy and nervous, happy and invigorated to do something—anything!

She could not go to sleep feeling thus. She could not lay head upon the pillow and be calm. Neither could she pick up needle and thread and work. This moment, this night, was extraordinary. It required an extraordinary outlet for her energies.

She unlocked the door to the shop and muted the bell with her hand as she walked in, the place different in darkness, or was it she—she who was different?

Lighting a lamp, she carried it to the back room, the glow of it glittering in the foxed mirror as she closed the door. She lit a second lamp, the mirror doubling the light again.

She knew what she must do as soon as her eyes settled on the red dress. It hung in the shadows, the darkness turning it plum-colored. And in that very lack of light lay her answer.

He followed her home at a distance, for two reasons. First, he wanted to be sure no ill befell her, and second, he felt cheated that he had not had the chance to say good night. He could not let her go just yet, must lock the moonlit silhouette of her in his mind—another facet of this gem of a woman he could not dismiss from his thoughts, his dreams, his desires.

He watched from the corner as she unlocked the door to the dress shop. He watched the golden bloom of lamplight and stood waiting, watching the upstairs windows, expecting the light, expecting Miss Nichol to climb to bed.

It did not come, and that concerned him, for the light was extinguished now in the shop as well. He walked to the alley as he had once before, and there light shone brightly in the ground-floor window, and he knew she set to work again.

Marveling again at her tenacity, her perseverance, her strength, he went away at last, to walk the quiet streets to his own bed, where he found little comfort and less sleep, knowing she still labored.

Chapter Seventeen

Jane woke to the tune of the street vendors and traffic in the street, as a shaft of silvered sunlight cut across her bed, illuminating her hands, faintly blue, the nails rimmed in darker blue.

Indigo dye.

Oh dear! she thought. It would never come out before the ball. She would need gloves, pearl gray gloves, and she must take care no one saw her hands bared. The ball was tonight, and so much to do!

Into Madame's costume, into Madame's wig, a dash of powder and rouge, and down the stairs she raced, to check on the dress, to see if it was dry yet, to see if it looked right in the harsh light of day.

It hung waiting in the back room, the red and saffron dress now deep plum color, indigo still dripping from the heavy quilled hemline. The dye had turned the saffron insets dark green.

She had taken the dress in before she dipped it, a nip here, a tuck there. The gold bullion had been carefully removed. When the dress had dried, she would replace the gold with silver bullion, and filmy silver gauze.

She would have a ball dress after all—a wonderful dress, a magical dress! She envisioned it completely finished in her mind. It would be done. It could be done. It brought her mother to mind.

Just looking at her plum-colored creation swelled her heart with joy of the Season, with anticipation for the Prior Park ball, for the moment when he would

take her in his arms again. Smiling, she grabbed up
bonnet and cloak and flew out the door, headed for
the baker's shop.

A morning at the baths, contemplating memories of
the evening before, anticipating the evening to come
at Prior Park had warmed Edward to the heart.

"You are in a cheery mood," Anne said as he stood
in the colonnade, whistling "Good King Wenceslas,"
waiting for her and Beth to finish dressing.

"Indeed, I am," he said. "For I have just had a
wonderful idea."

She smiled. "It is good to see you recovering so
nicely from . . . well, from . . ."

"Fanny?"

"Yes. I hope I do not stir bad memories in so
saying."

"No." It surprised him to realize it was true. No
bad feelings, despite the breach-of-promise suit. He
would pay Fanny, pay her father, and be done with
it, no regrets—indeed he had to admit a sense of gratitude. "We were not meant for each other, Fanny and
I, I know that now," he said.

Anne's eyes widened. "I thought you were in love
with her."

"So did I. Dear Fanny. I think she knew. Lord
knows she was clear enough as to her own feelings."

"Which were?"

He shrugged like a certain French dressmaker he
knew, considering how to put it. "She was in love with
the advantages of marriage, not me in particular."

"Oh, Edward. I am sorry."

"No need to be," he protested in good spirits, his
mind on a young woman toiling deep into the night.
"I must be thankful Fanny was good enough to be
honest."

Beth joined them. "Honest about what?"

Edward had no intention of repeating himself. He
caught up Beth's hand, and whirled with her through
the colonnade in a lively jig, humming the tune he

had been whistling. Before long he was singing, and Beth with him.

". . . Therefore Christian men be sure, wealth or rank possessing, Ye who now will bless the poor, shall yourselves find blessing."

Breathless and laughing, they reached the end of the row of columns, where Edward said, "I have decided we must visit butchers and bakers this morning."

"What has Fanny to do with butchers and bakers?" Anne insisted, catching up to them.

Beth laughed and looked from one to the other of them as if they had both gone mad. "What! No candlestick maker? Why must we visit these tradesmen, if you please?"

"Blessings," Edward said. "I am in need of them."

New gloves purchased, Jane hurried next to the baker in Bond Street. Sight of a familiar coach standing at the curb slowed her steps and set her heart racing, fixing her thoughts on a mistletoe kiss in the dark. The duke stood at the open door, handing paper-wrapped parcels to his sister Anne.

Such a handsome profile he cut, such a well-dressed, wealthy profile in his gleaming beaver top hat and sable-trimmed coat. Jane wondered how he would react to her today in the company of his sisters—after the kiss—after what she had said. She considered turning in her tracks and walking away.

But then Anne looked up and saw her. "Madame Nicolette!" she cried out with a smile. "How are you today?"

The baker's doorbell jingled, and out stepped a rosy-cheeked Beth, more parcels in hand. "Madame Nicolette!" she called with equal enthusiasm. "Good day to you!"

"*Bonjour!*" Jane stepped closer, stealing glances at the duke, furtive little glances, less comfortable than ever in her disguise.

He wore his amused look, his gaze fixed unwaveringly on her. She might have thought he laughed inwardly at her pretense, at her French gesture, French accent. But there was heat in that gaze. A heat that swept through her every time their eyes met.

"So many parcels!" she said. "What do you do with so many parcels?" She smiled nervously at all three of them. She must not appear to single him out.

"Christmas gifts." Beth laughed. "My brother is in a mood to feed everyone in Bath this year."

"A noble goal," she said, smiling at him in earnest. Such a good-hearted individual he was. So generous. "And what would you feed them? Cake?"

"Ham and goose, plum pudding and Bath buns," Anne said.

"We have taken all the local butcher and baker have to offer." Beth beamed at her cheerfully, happy in the morning's task.

"Now off to make deliveries," Anne said, handing the last of the parcels to her brother.

"A pleasure to see you," the duke said smoothly, the only words he had uttered, though his eyes had proven quite eloquent in his regard of her. "Do you come to Prior Park tonight?"

She thrilled to hear him ask it, to think he cared. *"Non,"* she said, and observed the beginnings of a disappointed frown take possession of his brow. "But all of my clientele go to *la fête de Noël.*"

"Miss Nichol. Will she be there?" he persisted.

His sisters looked at one another, brows raised.

Jane supressed a smile, supressed the swell of happiness that threatened to have her grinning like an idiot. "I believe it is her intention," she said.

He was smiling now, pleased, and she must smile in return. "She has a ball gown in any event."

"Good," he said. "I should like very much to see her again. Our last conversation was interrupted. A good day to you, Madame, and a Merry Christmas."

"Merci. Joyeux Noël, to you."

They climbed into the coach, and she turned to the baker's door, and as she opened it, the wonderful smells from within reaching out to her, she heard Beth

ask him, "Which Miss Nichol do you hope to see?
Rose or Lily?"

"Neither," he said with that enigmatic smile she had
grown to love, and with one last meaningful glance in
her direction, he tipped his hat to her reflection and
stepped into the coach himself.

She watched the coach windows through the baker's
window as the horses were set in motion. She could
not deny she hoped for one last glance.

She was not disappointed. He turned to look out,
his gaze locking on hers, his gloved hand rising to
press palm to the pane—and thus it remained until
the carriage turned the corner.

Chapter Eighteen

The warmth of her encounter with the duke heated Jane's cheeks more than the baker's ovens. A bit absently she studied the baker's near empty bins, her mind on the sight of Edward Brydges's hand pressed to carriage window, her own reflection in the baker's glass case, reminding her she was Madame Nicolette today, not plain Jane Nichol.

"How may I help you?" the baker asked. "Fresh out of Bath buns and plum pudding, but I've some good rye bread here, and plenty of fresh wheat rolls."

"I wonder will you sell me a box of the trinkets that go into plum puddings?" she asked in her best French accent.

"Be happy to, had I any," he said. "But they've all just walked out the door along with my plum puddings."

"All of them?" She was stunned.

"I shall have more for Christmas, of course."

"*Vraiment!* But I need them today!"

"Sorry, love. Can't help you."

Disappointed, even disbelieving, Jane stepped into the now empty street. Once again her careful plans went dreadfully awry.

She had to laugh.

What else could she do? It seemed the height of irony, after all, that no silver surprises were to be found when she needed them most, and that the duke, of all people, had carried them away!

The duke felt fortunate, as he chose what he would wear that evening, as he received the attentions of barber, manicurist, and valet. Delivering food to the halt, the lame, the poor, had reminded him of all the ways in which he and his family were blessed. It reminded him, too, of all that Miss Jane Nichol had cheerfully given up for a life of uncertain independence rather than marry a man she could not love.

It astounded him afresh. It moved him to a renewed level of respect for what she had done.

It reminded him of Fanny, of how different this evening would have been had she not chosen to speak openly to him of her feelings, her expectations—or perhaps it was more accurate to say, the lack of them.

He imagined the upcoming evening, imagined sweeping Jane into his arms. He wanted to sweep her off her feet, into his care, away from her struggle to survive. He wondered if she would be willing.

Never had he admired a female so much, her ingenuity, her talents, her resistance to settling into the life that was expected of most young women of fortune and breeding. Security, title, money, lands, then love. That was what most young women looked for in a match. Not she. Never had he seen a woman give up security for independence, for creative expression. What courage that took, what drive and sacrifice!

He considered, as he sent his second carriage to St. Joseph's, how best to verify his feelings, how best to determine hers. He would not have a repeat of a Fanny sort of fiasco. In addition, he considered how his pursuit of such a young woman, a runaway from her family, an imposter on society, might affect his reputation, his sister's prospects, his mother's pride.

Church bells rang in the distance, reminding him of the time.

"And so you managed to find a ball dress after all?" Miss Godwin met Jane's arrival at St. Joseph's early that evening cheerfully.

Jane twirled before her in the late afternoon light

cascading through the window. "Yes, though it is not quite what I had envisioned."

"How so?" Mrs. Roe, the old woman with gout who occupied the neighboring room, had hobbled to the door for a look. "You are a pleasant sight to these old eyes, let me assure you."

"The color is quite lovely," Miss Godwin said.

"Plum." Jane fingered the charms she had taken from the plum pudding the duke had given her. They dangled from a little silver chain at her throat, glinting in the sunlight, in the light of the candles Miss Godwin was lighting.

"Suits you."

"Does it? Thank you."

"And why is it not what you envisioned?" Mrs. Roe pressed.

"Perhaps it is silly of me, but I meant to sprinkle charms across all of the quilling along the hem."

"Like a plum pudding?" Mrs. Roe clapped her hands together. "What a lovely idea. Did you change your mind?"

"No." Jane smiled ruefully. "The baker was temporarily out of charms due to the Duke of Chandrose's largesse. He had bought every plum cake the baker had in the shop, and with them all of the silver trinkets."

"And we know just what he did with them, do we not, Miss Godwin? Brought everyone housed in Saint Joseph's a feast, didn't he? Plum pudding and mincemeat pie and a smoked goose," Mrs. Roe said. "You are welcome to the charm I took from the pudding. I shall just go and get it."

"Oh, no, my dear Mrs. Roe. It is too late for sewing them on now."

"Nonsense," Mrs. Roe called back over her shoulder. "It will only take a moment."

Miss Godwin seemed pleased to have a moment alone with Jane. "I've plum cake charms as well, my dear. We have all eaten very well today, thanks to your good duke."

"He is not mine, but I must agree I find him very good."

"Yes." Miss Godwin winked at her. "Mayhap the best I have ever had the good fortune to meet. Come help me with the charms."

"It really is silly to destroy a perfectly good plum pudding for no more reason than the charms," Jane objected as they cut into it.

Miss Godwin leaned forward with a glance toward the door. "Never mind the pudding. The duke also made a point of assuring me the coach was coming, and then, very carefully, he tried to ascertain if I was sure you meant to come."

"Did he really? He asked me much the same thing at the baker's shop."

Miss Godwin smiled at her, as if she were in no way surprised. "Anxious, is he?"

"Here we are." Mrs. Roe hobbled in the door. "I have obtained some gray thread from Mrs. Willet, and she is busy plucking charms from her plum pudding as well."

Jane was moved. "How very kind you are," she said. "But you really need not . . ."

From the doorway a querulous voice said, "I've a pig here."

A woman with fluffy white hair and sparkling gray eyes peered in at them as if they should know at once why she brought them a pig.

"Mrs. Pritkin?" Miss Godwin beckoned. "Please come and meet my former student, Miss Nichol."

"Do you want the pig?" Mrs. Pritkin squinted at Jane. "Mrs. Willet says the young lady is in need of charms. I've another one here, but cannot make out what it is. My eyes are not what they once were, as you well know."

"That's a crown and scepter you have there." Mrs. Roe plucked up the silver trinket and held it to the light. "Power and wealth. A very good charm. Thank you, my dear. And is this an owl with plum pudding still stuck to it?"

"Rub it off, love." Miss Godwin handed over a napkin, and Mrs. Pritkin set to work polishing at the little charm.

"Here I come," another voice called from the doorway, as a woman with silvery gray hair and a hunched back came in, her hands full of charms, her eyes sparkling with good cheer. "I 'ave been at Mr. White's plum pudding. Crumbs everywhere. You should 'ave 'eard the old fellow complain. 'Only look at all the good luck you give 'er,' says I. And what do you think? Stopped grousing at once, 'e did."

"Splendid, Mrs. Willet." Mrs. Roe handed her the bobbin of thread. "Pitch in now, love. You can see better than Mrs. Pritkin. See how I am sewing them along the skirt trim here?"

"Oh, yes, very pretty."

Jane felt a distinct draft, as her skirt was lifted by yet a second pair of tugging hands. She had no control of the situation, and when she looked to Miss Godwin, her old governess was threading needles.

"Here, Jane." She handed one over. "You work the front, we'll do the back."

No sooner had Jane set to work than another gray head popped in the door. "Is this where the silver charms are needed? Oh, my, I can see that it is."

The old man covered his eyes rather inadequately with one hand, for he peeped through his fingers with a broad grin.

"Come in. Come in, Mr. Smythe," Mrs. Roe beckoned. "And don't be an old fussbudget about a little raised skirt. I am sure you have seen your share of petticoats in your day, haven't you now? What have you brought us?"

"Sewing luck into her hem, are you? Very clever. Very clever indeed. Here's a silver punchinello so you may always have laughter, young lady, and a silver elephant to bless you with long life and a good memory. Elephants never forget, my dear. Did you know that?"

"I know I shall never forget your generosity in giving me these."

"Do you need thread, my dear?" he asked Mrs. Pritkin. "Hand the needle over. My eyes are better than yours."

"What's this?" One of the nurses stood in the doorway.

"Sewing luck into Miss Nichol's hem," Mr. Smythe said. "Have you any to spare, Patrick?"

"Half a tick. We've a plate full down at the desk. Very good, that plum pudding. Had ours with our afternoon coffee."

And so it went. A flurry of helping hands brought an outpouring of silver trinkets: horses and foxes, rings and crowns, elephants and horseshoes. Miss Godwin's room soon filled to bursting with people glad to assist, everyone passing about slices of Christmas pudding, smoked duck, cups of tea, and little glasses of brandy or port. And all of the silver heads were turned to gold by the late afternoon light that poured in through the window like warm cider. The talk was of younger days, of powder and patches, and ball gowns with panniers, and how they had kicked up their heels.

Oh, how their faces lit up to remember! Oh, how the dim-sighted eyes gleamed. Ghosts of youth and beauty flitted across their features, a hint of the flirtatious here, a glimpse of the coy there. Suggestion and innuendo fired laughter and a mock scold or two.

And all the while a handful of the most industrious little old ladies bent gossamered heads to sew the trinkets, the memories, the cheerful spirit of Christmas into the hem of Jane's plum-colored dress, chattering and fussing, thrilled to be part, no matter how distant, of the upcoming ball. Silver needles flashed, thread tugged. They murmured among themselves like a cooing flock of pigeons. Their gentle touch, their open-hearted gift of time and tokens brought tears welling to Jane's eyes.

"Now, none of that, lass," Mrs. Roe scolded. "You'll turn your eyes all bloodshot and red."

"There she is." Mrs. Pritkin stood back. "All sparkles now."

"A plum cake surprise," Mr. Smythe announced.

The results were wonderful, touching—perfect—exactly as Jane had visualized the dress should look.

"Rather fun, really," she said, smoothing her skirts down over her petticoats, turning that she might see, her skirt jingling festively with every move. "To be covered in so much silvery good fortune."

"Imagine yourself the beneficiary of so much good luck," Mrs. Roe suggested expansively. "Horses for travel, foxes that you may be clever, owls for wisdom."

"The pig that you might never go 'ungry," Mrs. Willet said.

"Stars for wishes come true," Mr. Smythe went on. "Hearts for love, and rings for marriage."

"We have sewn all the baby booties at the back of the dress," Mrs. Pritkin confided. "A young lady certainly does not want babies to come before marriage. Is that not right, dearie?"

Jane nodded, blushing.

"And here," Miss Godwin said with a knowing smile "are silver thimbles for a useful life."

"Your coach has arrived," Nurse Patrick called from the doorway.

"Oh, goodness. And just in time," the little old ladies cried, smoothing her dress, patting her shoulders, tugging at her skirts that they might hear them jingle one last time.

They fell back to make a pathway to the door, all except Mr. Smythe, who stepped forward, very straight-backed, to ask, "May I have this dance, my dear?"

Jane curtseyed deeply, her skirt making music, her heart light. "I would be honored, sir."

Together they danced stately steps across the room and out the door, where more had gathered outside the room and along the landing to share in the celebration.

Another old gent stepped into Smythe's place, and so she was passed from hand to hand, laughing, while her cloak was carried in her wake, and Miss Godwin was lifted in her sedan chair by two brawny footmen in the duke's livery and carried in state down to the waiting coach.

Happy and breathless, Jane climbed in beside her old governess once she was settled, and asked if she were comfortable.

"What fun!" Miss Godwin said as the footmen leapt aboard the back of the coach and the coachman slapped the reins. "I cannot remember when I have had such fun."

"Father would have laughed to see so many needles flashing," Jane said. "Would that he had lived to be here."

"Your mother would have loved it, too," Miss Godwin said. "Only look. They are not yet done."

From the doorway a ring of gray heads poked, and merry voices called, "Have a lovely time."

"Take a turn for me."

"Come tell us all about it."

"Take advantage of the mistletoe."

Jane smiled and leaned out the window to wave, then turned at last to Miss Godwin to say, "I wish Mother could have lived to see this day—so much generosity."

Miss Godwin nodded. "She loved Christmas, she did. Always made a big to-do of it."

Unexpected tears scalded Jane's eyes. "I begin to forget her face, you know."

"Oh, but Jane, her acts are far more important than her face, my dear. Do you not remember how she went about the house humming, sometimes bursting into song. Christmas carols. All the old favorites."

Jane nodded. "She would join in when the servants came a-wassailing."

"And food. She had Cook bake so much that the whole house smelled of . . ."

"Cinnamon and nutmeg, and cloves."

"That's right. Fed the whole neighborhood, she did, with enough left over for Boxing Day."

Jane nodded. "I shall never forget her gingerbread

men, her mincemeat pies, her plum pudding." Tears
sprang to her eyes.

"I remember." Miss Godwin patted her hand, her
voice soothing and calm. "I recall as well she was
always sewing or knitting or embroidering something
useful at Christmas—hats, gloves, mittens, lace tuck-
ers. I am sure it is her gift with a needle you have
inherited."

The sun, briefly trapped in cloud cover, suddenly
shed its fading light into the duke's coach. The silvered
brocade upholstery glowed. Jane's gray-gloved hand
traced the horse and carriage pattern in the fabric.

"She seems so close at Christmas. I think it is the
light. Generally so muted this time of year. Turns everything silver and gold."

"Well, and perhaps that's because she cannot stay
away at this time of year. Perhaps it is her light shines
down on you."

Jane smiled. "What a lovely thought," she said as
the duke's dappled gray horses carried the coach into
a silver-edged twilight.

Chapter Nineteen

The coach took them through Bath, its crested panels and matched horses drawing many an eye. Jane thought of another day in the duke's coach as they clopped past the baths, the cathedral, across the Pulteney Bridge, the Avon glowing golden, doubling the brilliance of the setting sun. These places she now associated with the duke, with his kindness—his interest in her.

"Your mother would have liked the duke," Miss Godwin said.

"Father, too." Jane had to nod. They could not have helped but like him.

The coach turned onto the new road to Widcombe at Sidney Gardens, past the cultivated area that ran beside the Avon Canal, past the new terraces being built along the curve in the river, into the road that ran through Coomb's Down to Prior Park.

The sun had not yet given up the day when the well-sprung coach topped a rise in the downs, carrying them past the sunlit silhouette of a castle wall, light shimmering through the crenelated toothwork at the tops of two tall, rounded towers, two shorter square ones, through the gothic archway. The arched windows, the Roman cross archer's slots, were dark. The impressive facade wore a deserted, abandoned air.

"How pretty! Whose castle?" Jane exclaimed.

"It is a sham," Miss Godwin said with a chuckle. "A builder's folly. Not a castle at all, only the facade of one, with nothing to back it, constructed for no more reason than to improve the prospect."

"Stop the coach!" Jane called, that they might better view it as the sun sank, a breathtaking sight. She said nothing as the fading light stained the stone facade first gold, then copper, then soot color.

" 'Tis lovely," Miss Godwin said with a sigh.

"But all that loveliness is a lie," Jane murmured. "No substance to back it up. A bit like me." And before Miss Godwin could contradict her, she urged the coachman gruffly, "Drive on!"

The duke stood with his cousin, Nigel, at the base of the flambeaux-lit stairs, one of four flights that led to the elegant, Palladian-style entrance to the house called Prior Park. Lamplight glowed golden in the windows, a welcome sight as darkness settled about them like a dusky cloak. The dowager duchess and his sisters had gone on before him. They did not care for the brisk night air, for the darkness. They wore new gowns, and new gowns were best seen in a candlelit ballroom.

The sound of music drifted from the house as the doors opened to welcome a steady stream of guests. Edward had gotten a good look at Prior Park as the sun set. It wore an elegant, orderly Christmas cheer in the form of fresh garlands and fat red ribbons decorating the ten enormous Corinthian columns that supported the portico. Lamps and garlands and more cheerful red bows ran the length of the colonnade that connected the main house to its equally proportionate wings, the whole grand edifice curving the crest of a downhill slope that looked out over the treed park. At the foot of said slope more flambeaux led the way to a beautiful Palladian-style bridge that spanned the stream.

"A pretty penny to lease the place," Nigel said as he lit his second cheroot, the match briefly illuminating his face. He shook it out, puffed an aromatic cloud, and said, "Worth it. Would you not agree? Quite stunning for a Christmas ball, is it not?"

"Perfect," Edward said. "I have heard much of Prior Park's grand old days. Oh, to have been a fly upon the wall when Allen was master here."

"The quarryman?" Nigel asked in surprise, the plume of smoke he exhaled with the words' silvered contrast to the growing darkness.

"How can you sneer? He made a fortune from that quarry."

Nigel studied the glowing end of his cheroot.

Edward pressed the point. "If not his money, or his postal system, surely you admire the brilliant company he kept?"

After a moment's smoky thought, Nigel said, "Pitt and the Earl of Chatham I will grant you. And Gainsborough's portraiture I have always admired. But Pope was an uncharitable ingrate, Fielding a worn-out, gouty rake, and Garrick nothing more than a common actor."

Edward laughed. "Nothing common about any of them, Nigel. I am surprised at you, cousin."

Nigel squinted through the cloud of his own making at an arriving carriage. "I prefer never to mix with rabble if it can be helped. Next thing you will be telling me the rumors are true."

"Rumors?"

"French dressmaker rumors." Nigel waggled his brows. "I dismissed the tales for patent falsehoods, of course. I was not in error in so doing, now was I? Or are you merely recovering from Fanny? What was that business all about? Would she not have you? Or was it the other way around?"

Nigel sucked fresh brightness into his cheroot and blew smoke rings in the pointed silence that hung between them before he went on, "Do assure me I was not cajoled into inviting a common dressmaker to the ball."

Edward frowned—at the moon, at the line of questioning, at his cousin's assumptions.

"What was her name? Goodwin? Certainly does not sound French."

Edward watched Nigel's smoke rise to dim the bright face of the moon, reminded afresh of the viewpoint both friends and family were likely to take should he pursue in earnest a young lady turned dressmaker. "Never fear." His voice sounded strained. "Miss Godwin is English, a governess, and in her dotage."

"What?" Nigel sounded surprised.

"She arrives even as we speak."

"In your coach?" Nigel chuckled knowingly, as if he understood far more than he did. "You must be smitten."

"Really, Nigel. The woman is crippled. Would you have me insist she walk?"

"From the look of things, she walks just fine." Nigel pointed his cheroot like a smoking finger—at Jane, who stepped down from the coach first, the light from the flambeaux glittering on the ribbons in her hair, throwing her cheek, the arch of her neck, into temporary highlight.

Such a slender silhouette she cut in the darkness, so graceful her every movement. Edward found himself suddenly jealous that Nigel should see her, that he should speak of her with anything but reverence and respect. He felt a pang, personally offended in advance by what he knew must be his cousin's opinion of this young woman he began to hold so dear.

"That is Miss Nichol."

"Miss Nichol? And why do you lend her the use of your carriage?"

So snide Nigel's tone—so unnecessarily suggestive.

"She is the governess's former pupil."

"Oh ho! Here lies the true reason for the invitation, then. Do not scruple to tell me she is not. I know all too well how a lonely man's mind works, cousin."

Edward could not deny the assumption. It startled him that he could not. It placed him quite suddenly in a league with Nigel, and that bothered him far more than he liked to admit. And so he made no attempt at reply, simply stepped forward to help Miss Godwin into the sedan chair that would carry her to the house.

Nigel cast aside the last of his cheroot, and Edward made polite introductions.

"Miss Nichol, is it?" Nigel bowed low over Jane's hand. "I know I have heard that name before."

Jane curtseyed prettily.

Nigel snapped his fingers in recollection, his face lighting up as they set off up the steps. "Daughter to Baron Orday?"

"You knew my father, my lord?" She sounded pleased, and Edward would not have Jane pleased with Nigel.

His cousin had heard the rumors, Edward surmised with growing alarm. Nigel was always one to keep his ears filled with the latest gossip.

"I regret to say I did not know the baron," Nigel said contritely. He was adept at adopting just the right tone—always had been. "I do beg pardon for asking so forward a question," he said with an endearing grin that set Edward's teeth on edge. "But are felicitations in order?"

Jane looked at Nigel, then Edward, bewildered, unaware the wolf wore lamb's wool. "I do not take your meaning, my lord."

Nigel tilted his head, teeth gleaming, ready to take the next bite.

Edward stepped between the two. "To what do you refer, Nigel?"

His cousin smiled knowingly and wagged a finger at Jane. "I have heard that Baron Blomefield is in Bath. That he is to be married to a Miss Nichol, daughter to Baron Orday. I would wish you happiness if you are the daughter in question."

Jane took a deep breath.

"No." Edward answered for her. "Miss Nichol has run away."

Nigel's brows rose.

Jane opened her mouth abruptly, as if to speak, as if amazed he should announce her secret so readily.

Edward went on, leaving no room for interruption. "Miss Jane Nichol's half sister, Rose, was promised to Blomefield, cousin, but Rose has run away rather than marry the baron."

Jane's jaw dropped.

Miss Godwin's eyes widened.

Nigel wrinkled his nose. "Has she really? I had not heard. How delicious! Cannot blame her. Nasty piece of work, Blomefield."

"Rose has run away?" Jane rubbed at her forehead, as if to help the news sink in.

"How do you know?" Miss Godwin asked, low-voiced, as the footmen paused at the second landing with her sedan chair.

"Forgive me." Edward felt as if his hand had been forced—as if he had blurted out something far too private to be rashly voiced, as thoughtlessly as the basest of gossips. He had been indiscreet. And discretion was one of the characteristics in which he prided himself. "I . . . I had intended to inform you both privately. It pains me to tell you I saw Rose step aboard the northbound post on the selfsame day that Blomefield arrived."

"You did not stop her?" Jane sounded amazed.

"How could I?" Edward said levelly. "You know it is not my habit to stop a woman from fleeing certain unhappiness."

She gave him a thoughtful look, a half smile of understanding in the growing darkness. "No. It is not, is it?"

Nigel was tapping at his teeth with his forefinger, watching and listening to their exchange far too keenly. "Rose. Rose. I knew it was a flower I had heard mentioned, but thought it was the lily and not the rose. Blomefield himself said he was bringing her."

"Bringing her?" Edward said.

"Yes." Nigel nodded jovially.

"Do you mean here?" Edward insisted. "Tonight?"

Jane stopped in the middle of the last flight of steps, concern written on her features.

"Yes." Nigel seemed to enjoy their consternation.

"Oh dear," Miss Godwin murmured from her lofty perch. "Shall we turn around and go home, Jane?"

Jane backed away from the doors ahead of them, away from the music and laughter. "Nonsense. You must stay. Enjoy the ball, but I . . ."

"Lord. Have I done something wrong?" Nigel stepped between her and the stairs.

"I really should go," Jane said.

"But you've only just arrived," Edward protested.

"No wish to cross paths with Blomefield, have you?" Nigel guessed. "Well, do stay a bit. I am told he makes a habit of late arrivals."

"Yes. Don't go," Edward coaxed for completely selfish reasons. "You must stay for at least one dance."

Jane's head was shaking no. She opened her mouth on a refusal.

"You will warn us of his arrival, Nigel?" Edward was determined to have, at the very least, one dance.

"But of course." Nigel winked at him. "I shall inform all of the footmen to have a lookout for him. And I do apologize." He bowed over Jane's hand. "Had no idea the baron would be scaring away my loveliest guest. Would have made a point of not inviting the man had I known."

"Should have mentioned it," Edward agreed.

Nigel took Miss Godwin's hand and urged the footmen to carry her onward.

"Come along, my dear. No worries. We shall get you settled in a comfortable corner with a plateful of food and half a dozen dear old souls I know would love to talk to you, and let these two have a whirl about the dance floor, yes?"

Jane had yet to be convinced. "I still do not think . . ."

Edward gave her a steadying look, a bracing look. "Just one dance. Come now."

She lifted her chin, straightened her shoulders, and took his arm.

Skirts twirled and coattails flew to the tune of a small orchestra set up at one end of the main hall on the ground floor, a grand, vaulted echoing space decorated with Corinthian pilasters, carved festoons, carved heads protruding between the capitals, and beautifully framed wainscot panels of oak gleaming in the candlelight.

Edward was not interested in viewing the house, though he had never seen it before. He was not inclined to greet his hostess, to mingle with the other guests, to introduce Miss Nichol to his mother, to see to the partnering of his sisters—all of his usual, dutiful tasks at balls. All he wanted at that moment was to take Jane in his arms and forget for a moment the approach of danger.

He wanted to dance—to dance with Miss Nichol and no other—to dance without delay. Their time together was short.

And so he simply handed his overcoat to the first footman he encountered, helped Miss Nichol from her cloak, and whirled her into the waltz that had almost everyone present in a spin of satin, velvet, and lace.

She made no demur, in fact she fell into step as though they had planned the whole, as though she, too, knew the evening was meant for dancing, for the clasp of his hand to her waist, her skirt belling, jingling faintly, his tails whipping out behind him—their breath coming faster and faster, the music spinning away all problems, all conflict.

Around and around they went, nothing in the moment but the lithe bend and stretch of her waist, the gentle weight of her grip on his shoulder, the stars of a hundred chandeliered candles reflected in her eyes.

They caused talk, of course.

"Who is the young woman the duke dances with?"

"What an unusual dress she wears."

"They seem to know each other well enough. Is she family?"

"I have seen her before. Was it at the Assembly rooms?"

He did not care what they said. They danced on, oblivious, their bodies perfectly suited, perfectly synchronistic—as though they had been dancing for years, her moves a mirror echo of his own—one might almost call it magical.

His mother turned to watch. His sisters eyed him discreetly over the shoulders of their dancing partners. He gave them no more than a glance. His eyes were for Miss Nichol. He had imagined this moment, this joining of gaze to gaze and body to body. He would not be cheated of it—not one moment of the pleased curve of her lips, the direct look from gleaming eyes, the sway of her waist beneath his hand.

Without words they danced, the look in her eyes supplanting conversation, the touch of hand to waist and shoulder all the speech that was necessary. The moment seemed a bit of forever, perfect.

The music wound down.

"You are beautiful," he said, gaze traveling head to toe. "Your hair shimmers in this light. Such a pity to hide it beneath that dreadful wig."

"It is a very expensive wig," she said staunchly. "From some poor shorn nag's tail." She smiled. "But I thank you. I do prefer my own."

Her skirt jingled faintly with her every move, a Christmas sort of sound. At her throat more silver charms winked in the light. Could they be the very charms he had given her? "Your dress is very clever," he said.

"A mistake. A lucky mistake." She laughed, green eyes sparkling.

He must smile to see such joy. "How so?"

"It's a long story," she warned.

"I like long stories, but it will have to wait. Nigel is waving at us."

"Oh dear. What to do?" She stiffened in his arms, her gaze lost to him as she sought out the door.

"Are you ready to face them?"

The shake of her head was vehement. "No." The word was a whisper.

"Shall we make a run for it, then?"

"Please." Like a lost child, she looked.

Everything protective and brotherly in him surfaced. Nigel was pointing.

"This way." Edward guided her away from the dance floor, past the worried wave of Miss Godwin into a room lined with more gleaming wood wainscoting and linen-draped tables. A sideboard had been loaded to the groaning point with punch and grog, cider and wine bottles, a carved roast of venison, and silver trays full of soft white rolls.

Edward was not hungry for anything but her, had no thirst but for her lips.

"Care for something? Might be your last chance." He nodded toward the tables, shooting carefully nonchalant glances over his shoulder, avoiding falling into conversation with several who called out to him. He acknowledged the greetings with quick nods and an unstoppable stride.

With swift grace he scooped up two crystal punch cups and filled them from the bowl.

She plucked up napkins, briefly eyed the rolls, the venison.

Behind the table a painting hung—the fable of the fowls plucking the crow of his borrowed feathers. She stopped to examine it more closely, napkins clutched, her stance suddenly rigid, resistant.

"Hisst!" Nigel was at the doorway, head tilting in a come-hither gesture, a look of sparkling deviltry in his eyes.

"Miss Nichol." Edward beckoned.

She did not budge, seemingly mesmerized.

"Jane!"

She turned, her gaze faintly melancholy, definitely fearful as it strayed beyond him to the doorway.

"Shall we go?" he asked, careful of what he said. His every move was watched, his every word attended to.

She nodded and seemed aware of their audience in saying, "I am not particularly hungry."

"No sense in hanging about the chickens, then." He tipped his head in the direction of the painting.

Amusement sparkled in her eyes. "In no mood for a plucking?"

He smiled, knowing she meant her own plucking, then shook his head.

They joined Nigel in the doorway. His cousin stood observing the activity in the hall. "Your mother holds court between here and the front door," he said conversationally. "And the blue parlor, where card tables have been set up, currently keeps the baron and his guests entertained. Might I recommend the view from the upstairs gallery? I must go and greet my guests."

"How long do you think the baron will keep you occupied, cousin?"

"One never knows," Nigel said airily. "I shall do my best to keep him belowstairs, but should you hear us coming, there are five bedrooms, and any number of dressing rooms and closets in which to lose yourselves."

"I am not the sort who gets lost," Edward said briskly. "Nor is Miss Nichol."

Jane followed their exchanges without interruption, a puzzled pucker knitting her brow.

Nigel shrugged. "If that's the case, there is the chapel balcony to see, or you could take a stroll in the garden if you find the house overcrowded." He pursed his lips on a smile. "The bridge is very pretty in the moonlight."

"Thank you, Nigel. Are there back stairs?"

"But of course," Nigel said playfully, "at the back."

"I must apologize," Edward said as he and Jane set off up the stairs. "Nigel can be . . ."

"A tease," she said.

He had meant to say, "Too suggestive."

"I like him," she said. "It is clear to see he cares for you, would do anything for you, and he is a rather amusing sort of fellow."

He studied the crown of her head, the smooth, upward sweep of her hair. He did not want her to find any other fellow but himself, amusing and likable. But was it a trace of envy he heard in her voice?

"I am glad you like him," he said, and tried to believe his own words. He wondered what it would be like to have no one in the way of family who cared for one and would do anything for one. He took such things for granted.

They were not alone in their climb. Many of the guests would view the gallery. The second floor was well lit, and yet Edward felt they engaged in illicit wanderings, his cousin's wink, his words too provocative, his own private thoughts too close to such suggestiveness for comfort.

One could not help but consider the potential of what lay behind the doors they passed—bedchambers in which they might find privacy—as Nigel had suggested—perhaps too much privacy. Even were he to whisk a willing Miss Nichol into such a liaison, his attentions to her would not go long unnoticed. There were no secrets for a duke. There were always eyes watching, servant or peer. Their climb was observed by several. Their passage into the gallery did not go unnoticed.

He did not want to be watched so closely, wanted only some time with her—alone, for plain conversation—not the criminal kind. Such options were not open to him, unwise to so much as consider them.

The gallery was enormous, far longer than the hall with equally soaring ceilings. It had to be close to a hundred feet that it stretched across the face of the house, the inner walls lined with bookshelves, the outer walls with windows that looked down over the park.

The bookshelves bore painted doors, famous philosophers guarding their wisdom in painted effigy. Marble busts graced every niche, and paintings occupied the spaces above the bookcases.

"A marvelous room," she said, and he longed to promise her more marvelous rooms, the beauties of

Candon Manor, his home. She must see it. He must show her. And yet, he held silent, struck for the first time by the full impact of what a serious commitment to this young woman—this runaway baron's daughter turned dressmaker—would mean.

An incredibly long Turkey carpet muffled their footsteps, and two steel stoves, coal fed, warmed the room. A pleasant space. Welcoming despite its enormity. Chairs and stools offered weary feet a rest, but they were both too nervous to settle, too ready to move on should the need arise. The windows drew them, the twinkling, starlike lamplight of Widcombe and Bath in the distance, the dark, moonlit wink of the stream that ran across the park, the darker velvet of the Avon.

Would such a union win him anything but disapproval from his peers? Would it prove an unending source of unwanted attention and gossip? Did he risk his mother's well-being, his sister's reputations? What if he were wrong again—as he had been with Fanny?

It was terrible to contemplate, and too early to make promises.

"Do you miss the views from your home?" he asked suddenly, to stop his thoughts, to pierce again the fabric of hers. He must know her better to know if the feelings within him, the undeniable draw, was real or imagined.

"The views? Yes." Her eyes took on a distant look, as if she pictured them clearly in her mind's eye. "The rooms of Hackberry Park, the country surrounding it, hold many fond memories. The only memories, in fact, of my mother."

"Did your father love her?"

"I am told he did."

"I am told . . ." He hesitated, pursed his lips, and thought better of saying it.

"What? That she was illegitimate?"

She would seem to harbor no feelings of shame for her mother's history. How level her regard, how open. In all the time he had known Fanny he had never looked so deeply into her eyes. Neither had he questioned Fanny's parentage. Her lineage was impeccable.

"I had heard . . . your father . . ." He shook his head and made a low noise of disgust with himself. "No. I will not say it. I feel it is inappropriate to question such things."

She pressed her lips together, those lips he longed to kiss, then dampened her lower lip with the tip of her tongue—more tempting than ever. "Perhaps I can guess why you hesitate," she said. "You have heard that my father married my illegitimate mother for money, land—a title."

He looked for condemnation in her eyes, but found none.

"Precisely." He would not lie to her.

"It is true. He won all of that and more in marrying her."

Again that direct look, such an earnestness of gaze. It reached into the heart of him, and made him question all that he had once held sacred.

"Did he love her, you ask." The distant look was back in her eyes. A trace of melancholy. "If he did not to begin with, he grew into it quite profoundly," she said with certainty.

"And yet, you do not think you could grow to love the baron?" he persisted.

She frowned at the glittering brilliance of the view. "No." The word ended in a bitter chuckle. "Never."

"You would give up all that your father won for you by way of marriage in refusing a like marriage?"

She laughed. How he loved to hear her laugh, to see the curl of her lips.

"I have never looked at it with such clarity," she said.

"Clarity or crudity?"

She smiled. "You must not put words in my mouth. I do not refuse *any* marriage, merely *that* marriage— much as you did."

He darted an uneasy glance toward the doorway

through which they had come. He hated the feeling of impending discovery hanging over them, spurring his pulse, affecting their conversation. He took her arm and led her deeper into the room.

"What went wrong with you and Fanny?" she asked.

"Wrong?" He steered her away from a group of gossiping matrons. Her reflection paralleled his progress in the row of windows.

They looked right together, the duke and the dressmaker.

Had he and Fanny looked right?

He stopped in a quiet spot and looked through his reflection, into darkness. He could see the two of them now in his mind's eye. Fanny had looked good on his arm, good—but not right.

"Thinking back on it," he mused, "I would have to say, it never went right."

So serious her reflection looked, so intent on his every word. "I do not understand."

"Neither did I," he admitted.

It pleased him, her intensity. Fanny had looked at him intently, but never with a need to know the inner depths of him—as Jane did. Fanny had always felt a need to fill silence—Jane simply waited for him to voice his mind, the silence between them comfortable, the only tension their common fear of discovery.

He turned to face her, his every desire to touch her, and yet he refrained. The room had eyes. His own were drawn to the wink of silver at her throat, four silver charms linked together on a silver chain. A star for wishes come true, a crown and scepter for wealth and prosperity, an owl for wisdom, and a silver punchinello, that she might always have laughter. They were the charms he had given her in the little plum cake. Only the horseshoe was missing.

Good luck gone missing. He wondered what had become of it.

"I thought I was in love with Fanny," he tried to

explain. "I thought she loved me. I wanted to marry her."

Jane nodded, her gaze dropping. "What changed your mind?"

"Fanny . . ." He shook his head, searching for words. "Something Fanny said."

Jane nodded. Her reflection nodded in tandem. "She came to the dress shop that day, in tears. Said she had told you the truth. That she might have lied." So quiet her voice, so deliberate and sure—straightforward and unflinching—no dancing around a difficult topic. She simply said the thing, direct and unvarnished. No pretense when they talked like this. No coy disguise. "I have always wondered," she said, "what truth she told to so alienate you."

He sighed. "She said—"

He was stopped by the approach of a footman, the footman's gaze meeting his in such a way it was clear he wished a word.

"Your Grace," he whispered, "the baron is taking a tour. His lordship said you were to be informed."

"Indeed. I thank you. Are they on their way up?" Edward tried not to sound alarmed.

"Yes, Your Grace. His lordship also mentioned you might wish to walk to the bridge rather than join the party."

Edward nodded.

"This way, then, if you please. The back stairs are the most direct route, and I've a man waiting with your coats."

Nigel was very good at subterfuge, Edward thought, perhaps too good. Nigel's servants were very good at subterfuge as well. It felt in some way unseemly to be led along one of the corridors that led from the gallery. They went without undue haste, attracting little attention, as best suited him, and the footman kept his face carefully expressionless, yet Edward could not ignore the feeling that they seemed to work in collusion at something illicit and disgraceful. It bothered him.

He was a gentleman used to living his life openly—no secrets, no lies. Down the stairs to a side door the first footman directed them, where, as promised, a second footman waited with their coats—two who knew of their escape—two who stood watching as the duke helped a young lady don her cloak that they might slip out a side door.

Jane's dress jingled as she turned. She glanced over his shoulder at the silent servants as he slipped them each a coin. Could one buy silence? Edward wondered. Could one truly keep secret something so many were privy to?

Then they were outside, just the two of them, no more pretense, no reason to skulk about like thieves, and yet there was still the edge of the illicit in their being alone in the darkness, just the two of them.

"A shame to hide your dress so soon," he said as they stepped onto the fog-shrouded pathway that led through the deeper darkness of the trees to the river. His breath came fast, his blood pumped with the excitement inherent in secrets, in the possibility they still might be discovered.

The trees cut dark silhouettes against a cloud-veiled moon. The air smelled of leaf mold, the cold, and a damp so heavy it beaded upon the collars of their cloaks and in the tendrils of their hair. When she turned to look back at him, she looked as if she were beaded in brilliants—not a real woman at all—certainly not a dressmaker—the runaway baron's daughter. She was, for the moment, wood sprite, garden sylph, or Christmas angel conjured from the mists.

Like distant fairy bells she rang as she walked.

"However did you think of such a thing?" he asked, drinking in a deep breath of air, catching wind of the perfume he began to associate with her and no other—jasmine and roses—a summer scent in this winter garden. "A plum pudding dress."

She jingled across the fallen leaves beside him, her face silvered by the moonlight, their footsteps rustling.

"I have never thanked you for the plum pudding you gave me not so long ago."

So earnest she looked, so appreciative, so beautiful. The look in her eyes, the set of her mouth, held magic.

"It was nothing."

"You are wrong." Her hand rose to play with the glinting silver trinkets that dangled from the chain at her throat. "I have a special place in my heart for plum pudding."

The path took them beneath trees that rustled in the slightest breeze and flung their remaining leaves at them like starched lace handkerchiefs. The moon, silver trinket tossed high, seemed caught in the clasped hands of the branches.

"Tell me why plum pudding is so fortunate as to gain a place in your heart."

She said nothing for so long he began to wonder if she had heard him. Then she took a deep breath and said, "A plum pudding was part of my mother's last Christmas gift to me."

"You were . . . was it . . . four?" he asked gently.

"You remember." She seemed surprised and pleased.

He smiled up at the man in the moon. "I've a rather good memory for things important to me, Jane."

"Oh."

Again she fell quiet, a sweet smile playing about her lips.

"You were saying—about the plum pudding?"

"Yes," she sighed, and then seemed in no hurry to speak. "Mother knew she was dying. Complications after a stillbirth."

He blew out his pent breath in a sudden rush, the mist of it temporarily blurring the moon. "I'm so very sorry."

Too dark beneath the trees to see her face, to see if she shed tears.

"Ah, well." Sadness hung heavy in her voice, and resignation. "It was long ago. The only reason I bring you such a sad tale is its importance in understanding the significance of plum pudding."

He made no attempt to interrupt, to hurry her. His steps slowed to match hers.

"She called for me." Her voice was small—the injured child. "Last words."

He remembered going to his father's bedside for last words as a young man, fully aware of the gravity of the moment. But as a child? Would he have grasped it?

The moon chiseled her features as if in marble. "I shall never forget what she said."

The pained pull of her mouth was so beautiful it made him ache with the need to hold her, to comfort her.

"Three things she told me."

A wisp of hair blew about her puckered brow, a bit of golden gossamer.

"One: 'Life never unfolds as one expects.' Hers certainly did not."

He longed to capture the errant strand in his hand, to still its silvered dance.

"Two: 'Cherish what is, not what you imagined.' "

He cherished this moment, imprinted it upon his memory—the misted night, the silvered moon, the cavorting strands of hair—but most of all, these shared intimacies.

"Third: she begged me promise her, not to allow regret to swallow me whole."

It hadn't, he thought. She did not live a life of regret. "Wise words," he murmured.

A tinkling sound, and looking down he saw one of the silver trinkets from her hem had fallen at his feet. A silver heart. He knelt to pick it up. And as he rose, her heart cradled in the palm of his glove, he said, "What has all this to do with plum pudding?"

She tilted her head, the better to see what he held, and rather than take it from his palm, her face underwent a sad transformation, brow knitting, her hand rising to clamp over her mouth, a sudden sob stifled, tears upon her cheek now, bright as silver.

"Tell me," he begged, the little heart forgotten as

he fumbled for his kerchief, hands rising to cradle her face, to wipe away the tears. "Please, Jane. Tell me why you weep."

She put the handkerchief to good use, took a deep breath, stood straight, and forced a smile. "I do apologize. I was telling you about the plum pudding."

"You need not go on if it grieves you."

"Actually it brings me great joy every year at this time. You see, as I was carried away to bed, never to see her again, she called out to me." She stared past him into the night. " 'Look for the silver surprises in the plum pudding at Christmas,' she said to me, 'and know that I put them there for you.' "

For a moment he said nothing, and then she smiled, a smile quite genuine, and her eyes gleamed brighter than before as she faced him. "Every Christmas I have the feeling she brings me"—she tugged at the strand of tokens about her neck, his tokens—"silver surprises."

He could see the misted moon reflected in her eyes. Silver surprises, he thought, and leaning closer, breathing deep jasmine and roses, he kissed her. Words were insufficient to express his feelings. He must kiss her.

She let him. In fact, she responded quite warmly, her lips gone soft and yielding, her body swaying into his.

"My dear Jane," he whispered, and kissed her again there in the moonlight.

Her lips were like silk, her arms stealing up to clasp his neck, her breath sighing into his mouth. He pulled her closer, chest pressing chest, their breath coming fast.

"Your Grace." She looked deep into his eyes, took a deep breath, and moved to step back, away from him.

He would have none of that. He would not allow her to put cold, unwelcome space between them. He drew her closer, and breathed his name against her mouth. "Edward," he insisted. "You must call me Edward now."

"Edward," she whispered with a smile, with a heart-warming glow in her eyes that must be met with an answering smile.

And then she lifted her chin that he might more easily kiss her once again. His heart soared to new heights as he gladly obliged.

"Edward."

Oh, to hear her voice utter his name.

She looked up shyly through her lashes. "You never finished telling me what Fanny said that day."

He laughed. "You would hear that now?"

She made a little noise of embarrassment. "Yes. For I would not similarly offend you."

He caressed her cheek and pinched her chin. "Do you mean to break my heart by telling me you do not love me?"

So shocked she looked, as if what he suggested were unthinkable. "She did not love you?"

"She said . . ." he sighed, not wanting to remember, "said she would understand once we were married"—he closed his eyes, the pain still there, deep within—"that if I chose to have affairs, as some men are wont to do . . ."

Jane gasped.

"That while she would make no objection, she expected discretion. And reciprocity."

"What?" She stared at him in blessedly outraged disbelief. "She wanted to be able to discreetly have affairs?"

"So it would seem."

She blinked and shook her head. "How awful!"

It had been awful—devastating—more to his ego, he realized now, than to his heart. "You would not ask that of a husband?"

"I would like to think not."

He stood back in mock horror. "What kind of an answer is that?"

She sighed and walked toward the bridge.

Curious, and a little wounded, he fell into step beside her.

"I only mean that had I married the baron—"

"Heaven forbid."

"Yes, well, I might own to being far more sympathetic to such a stance had I made different choices." She stopped again, to face him. "But you loved her, and in such circumstances such a request was . . . is untenable."

"Yes," he agreed.

She set off walking again. They reached the edge of the pretty covered bridge before he spoke.

"Do you see yourself a married woman someday, Miss Nichol?"

She smiled as she stepped into the darkness beneath the first arch. Her voice echoed in responding, "I do."

Moonlight found her again as she passed a matching archway that opened onto the river.

He followed, the rush of the water whispering wetly beneath them, the mist hanging thicker there, so thick it seemed she might get lost in it if he were not careful. "And if you discovered the one you loved did not love you?" He voiced the question so softly it was almost lost in the water's rush.

She stopped in the center of the bridge to lean against one of a row of columns, looking down into the dark ribbon of purling water. "I should hope to do so before making the mistake of marriage."

He stopped beside her and glanced down to find the two of them reflected against starlit water, the moon dancing just out of reach.

"And whom do you see yourself marrying?" he dared ask.

She looked at him by way of their wavering reflection. "Do you mean what sort of cloth would he be cut from?"

That was not at all what he meant, and yet he said, "Yes."

She laughed, a gentle rippling sound, echo of the stream. "He would have to be understanding." The words came slowly, as though she considered and reconsidered each requirement before voicing it. "Forgiving. Strong. Kind. Generous. Thoughtful."

He laughed. "Is that all?"

"No. Also wise and loving."

"A tall order. I have never met such a man."

"I have." How calm her voice, her gaze—content, assured.

"You have?" He was stunned. Could she mean him? "Are you in love, then?"

Her reflection nodded. "Completely."

"Ah."

"And you?"

"What of me?"

"Do you think you will fall in love again?"

No longer content to look at her by way of her reflection, he turned, waiting until she turned to face him, and then he stepped closer and took her in his arms again and whispered, "Undoubtedly," against her cheek before he sought the comforting sweetness of her lips once more.

Chapter Twenty

Distant voices made the duke's back go suddenly rigid, made his lips part from hers. The arms that wrapped Jane stiffened.

"Cousin!" someone called. *Could it be Nigel?* Jane roused from a state of warm and glowing bliss to that of heart-pounding alarm. She must not allow herself to be too caught up in the duke's—no—in Edward's kisses. She must not forget how close she stood to discovery.

"I should go," she whispered, and withdrew from the warm heaven of his embrace, her nerves on edge.

Leaves stirred and crackled upon the path. A woman laughed.

"Come." Hand pressed to the small of her back, Edward directed her away from the bridge toward the cover of the trees. The clouds above proved their ally, scudding across the sky to douse the moon.

A party of people came their way, not just Nigel. There were at least four who laughed and talked. Edward pressed finger to lips and guided Jane off the path beneath the trees, into the shadows of a holly.

The tinkling hem of her skirt proved a danger. They could not keep moving. It made too much noise. Encircling her with his arms, Edward pressed Jane so close to his heart she could feel it race.

They let the party pass, trying not to laugh as the ghost of a breeze brought faint jingling from her hem.

A female voice said, "What a pretty bridge."

Lily. She turned her head to whisper against the warmth of his cheek. "My stepsister."

He turned his head as well, to kiss her.

Forgetting for the moment their peril, careless of the charms that tinkled musically with their every move, and yet unwilling to relinquish too soon the wonder of his honeyed lips to hers, Jane responded as warmly as before.

It was he, at last, who nuzzled her ear and laced his fingers through hers, then said, "We must go."

They took no more than a single step. The hem of her skirt jangled. He flung up his hand to halt her.

The leaves on the path gave additional warning, a single set of footsteps approaching. He stood chest pressed to her back, his hands upon her shoulders. Together they watched a hooded figure pass, a female wearing a tasseled cloak. She crept cautiously, wanting to be seen no more than they.

"Anne," he murmured against her hair.

His sister? What did she do here?

Jane's skirt jingled. All it took was the slightest of movements.

Anne stopped, peering beneath the trees. Jane was sure they must be spotted.

But the voices on the bridge, louder now, in exclamation, reclaimed Anne's attention. She went on her way.

Once she was past, Edward exhaled heavily against Jane's neck and with a silent nudge urged her onto the path again, toward the stables.

Her dress jingled in earnest as they hastened away. Jane had to smile, then giggle, finally to laugh. There was no suppressing it. "Not the best of garments for secrecy," she said.

"Decidedly not designed for stealth." He chuckled, and swept her into his arms and kissed her again quite thoroughly.

They laughed against each other's lips as they were kissing, then stifled their mutual hilarity only when she said, "No laughing matter if I am caught."

"No," he agreed, sobered, but unwilling to let her go just yet. "Time to summon a coach," he suggested.

"And Miss Godwin," she reminded him.

He kissed the tip of her nose. "Do you mind if she is carried home later?" he asked. "Safer that way."

"Fine."

"Wait here while I summon the coach?"

Wait here, she thought as he left her. Her mind could not help but continue the thought. Wait here, in the dark, in the cold, all alone, where no one will see you, not even the coachman.

She shivered, feeling the fugitive, wondering if she was completely foolish to have allowed a duke to kiss her not once but many times. And then she laughed and heard her mother's voice. *Do not allow regret to swallow you whole, Jane.*

She could not regret his kisses, would not. Wonderful kisses, such a wonderful feeling to be clasped in his arms. She would cherish it always, that feeling, no matter what happened next.

She was chuckling when he emerged from the stables. Joining in her laughter without knowing its source, he swept her into his arms, skirt jingling festively, and whirled her into a waltz right there on the drive. "Why do you laugh, Jane? Is it our circumstances you find amusing?"

She nodded. "That and the feeling within me."

He smiled, his eyes very bright, a look of understanding in them even as he asked, "What feeling is that, my dear?"

"Like too much champagne," she said.

"Spirits gone to your head?" he asked, and when she nodded, he pulled her closer and said, "I know you have gone to mine." He closed his eyes and leaned in close to breathe the scent of her and said, as he opened his eyes to look deep into hers, "I cannot get enough of you, my dear. You are a hunger within me, a thirst that nothing but this will quench." And again he was kissing her, deep, tender kisses that set her head and heart to whirling for the next few moments, or was it longer? All she knew was that the stable doors were thrust open, light intruding on their friend, the darkness, and the team, jingling harness, showed their readiness.

She felt warm and glowing and loved and guilty all at the same time as he greeted the coachman, directing him where to go, helping her into the body of the coach.

He leaned against the door as he closed it, to speak to her through the window. "I do not like to send you home alone."

"No sense in tearing Miss Godwin away from the fun."

"You know it is not Miss Godwin I refer to, Jane, my love. Shall I ride with you? See you to your door?"

"I do not think it wise."

He smiled, an endearing smile, a tempting smile. "I am not yet ready to say good night."

"Neither am I." She smiled back at him and ran a finger along his cheek, marveling in the idea that she had any right to do such a thing. "Hence prudent we say our adieus."

He sighed and nodded reluctantly, then clasped her hand to his cheek. "Until tomorrow?" He kissed her fingertips with such fervency her toes tingled, and she thought twice about his offer to accompany her—just the two of them alone in the dark coach—another grand bout of kissing. The idea was very tempting. She thrust her hands in her pockets, determined to be strong. That was when her hand bumped the box.

"Your gift!" she cried.

"What?"

"I almost forgot." She pulled it forth, the silver box wrapped in tissue, and shyly thrust it out the door of the coach. "Merry Christmas!"

He hesitated in taking it, and shook his head. "You ought not . . ."

"Go on." She gave the package a shake. "It is but a trifle. After all you have done for me. You must take it."

He tore away the tissue, trying to ignore the glances of the footmen, the thump of the team's hooves as they grew restless. She knew they risked being seen in this exchange, and yet she was too anxious to see his reaction to wait for better timing.

The silver box emerged—a small, lidded thing, etched with oak leaves. It was pretty, Jane thought. She had been so very pleased to find it. It had seemed the perfect box for the purpose, and yet now, looking at it in the duke's manicured hands, it looked small and inadequate as an expression of all that she felt for him.

"It's lovely." His thumb caressed the gleaming surface, his expression one of surprised pleasure.

"Open it," she coaxed, hoping he really did like the thing, that he did not find her gift wanting, as she did.

He nudged the lid open, revealing the deep plum velvet lining. She had asked the silversmith especially for the change in color. Perched in the velvety softness was the silver stickpin.

"An acorn," he crowed. "Bladud would be proud."

"I hoped you would like it."

"Like it? I am very much of the opinion I should jump into this coach and demonstrate how very deeply pleased I am. But I fear my behavior might bring to mind another part of Bladud's tale. May I call on you tomorrow to express my gratitude?"

She smiled and nodded. "Please do."

"Until tomorrow, then." He tapped the side of the coach and called to the coachman, "Walk on."

She leaned out the window to wave. He stood waiting in the drive, watching, hand raised, the silver box winking in the moonlight. As the coach rounded a bend, she leaned back and settled against the luxurious silver squabs, suddenly bereft, the glow of his presence cooling, doubt washing over her like icy water.

She wondered if she would ever see him again, wondered if he meant to do right by her, wondered if Miss Godwin would forgive her for abandoning her. There was such a dreamlike feeling to the night, to the memory of his touch, his kisses, his voice whispering in her ear. Such a sense of the magical. His affections for her, while welcome and cherished, did not feel as if they could be real.

"Are these but silver surprises?" she asked the memory of her mother. "Is it back to plum pudding now?"

The night's adventures seemed over, the heady magic of it winding down, the rest of the evening safely contained in the rattling bubble of the coach, in the confines of her bed. It would seem there was nothing but a savoring of memories of ardent kisses left to her.

She leaned back, eyes closed, fingering the uneven texture of fine brocade, completely unprepared for a cry of "Wait! Stop the coach!"

A man's voice. Was it he who called out so spiritedly?

The coachman reined in the team.

Jane leaned out of the window.

Not Edward, but his cousin, Nigel, approached, breathless and smiling. "You must not be sent away alone, my dear Miss Nichol," he said. "I shall see you safely escorted."

His suggestion unsettled her. She had been prepared for a lonely ride, not sharing a coach with a gentleman she barely knew. "It is not necessary," she assured him.

"My pleasure." He reached for the door latch.

"Really." His insistence alarmed her. "I am quite happy to go alone."

He flung open the door. "Ah, but my cousin did not wish it."

"No, but he has duties. I understand completely."

"Ah, yes, duty. The duchess is a stickler for that." Up he climbed.

She backed away as the darkness of him filled the doorway.

"You leave your guests unattended."

"I do," he said dryly, and sank down across from her. "But perhaps you have noticed, I am not so dutiful as dear Edward."

"Oh?"

"Have you met my aunt?" He banged on the side of the carriage, calling brashly, "Onward ho!" then settled himself comfortably in the seat, and leaned forward with a cheeky wink. "The dowager? I would imagine Edward keeps you a bit of a secret."

"We have met," she said, "on several occasions."

"Have you?" He leaned back with a grin. "Sly dog. I would not have guessed my cousin would go so far. She will be furious, of course, should she ever discover how he has deceived her. Big plans for our boy, has the duchess. She introduced him to Fanny, of course. Imagine her chagrin when that fell through."

"I cannot help but feel to discuss such matters is highly inappropriate," she chided.

"You would lecture me on inappropriate?" He laughed. "You amaze me, Miss Runaway Nichol, and believe me I am difficult to amaze."

His words took her breath away, and yet she managed to feign composure. "The duke did not suggest you accompany me, did he?"

"No. He would be quite put out if he knew I had run away with you tonight. Entirely my idea. Tell me, does my cousin put you up?"

"Does he what?"

"Pay for your room and board?"

"No!"

"Oh? However do you survive? Have you other benefactors?"

"I am deeply offended by your suggestion, sir. I support myself by honest means."

"Not my intention to offend, my dear Miss Nichol. In fact, the only reason I chased after you was in order to express my profound admiration, and to let you know that should you fall out of favor, or should he lose interest, you must come to me."

"You misunderstand our relationship."

"Do I?"

She banged briskly against the wall of the coach, crying, "Stop! Stop the coach!"

The horses slowed.

"You will leave at once," she said firmly.

His brows rose. "Loyal to him, are you?"

"And you to no one it would seem." She flung the words at him even as she flung open the door.

"*Au contraire.* It is a favor I would offer both of you, don't you see. When he tires of you, I would relieve him of the dreadful business of a lengthy, acrimonious fare-thee-well. You, my sweet, I would offer protection, passion, and no loss of pride."

"Get out," she ordered. "At once! Do you hear?"

"I will go." He gave what little bow he could, still seated. "No matter how reluctantly. And I would have you know I hold you in no contempt for leaving me stranded, but rather appreciate the respect you evidence my cousin."

"How is it you know signs of respect when you show him none? Good evening, my lord," she bit out.

He paused as he climbed down. "I wish you good evening, as well, Miss Nichol. I hope you enjoyed my little party—and your walk in the gardens. I must admit it was a pleasure to watch my cousin sneak about, keeping secrets from my aunt, whom he has never before, at least in my recollection, shown the slightest hint of disrespect." He took another step, then paused again, one foot on the ground. "Oh, and lest you think otherwise, my offer still stands. When you discover at some later date my cousin no longer indulges you in good evenings, do come to me at once, that I might demonstrate what respect I am capable of."

Chapter Twenty-one

Edward returned to the ballroom, pulse throbbing, as if he had run a race, as if he held close to his heart and soul a deep and wonderful secret. Which of course he did, for his feelings were secret to everyone but him and Jane. He smiled, enjoying the private nature of his joy. He was not yet ready to share it with anyone, not yet ready to feel the pinpricks of doubt and judgment inherent with sharing.

And yet, surely everyone must recognize this new level of joy in him, a happiness so vibrant it seemed to wrap him like a blanket, to well within his chest like the hot springs of Bath, to twitch his lips in uncontrollable smiles. The night was beautiful, the stars never brighter, the moon a silver medallion to light his way, and yet none of it so beautiful as his memory of Jane clasped in his arms, Jane lifting her lips to his, Jane smiling into his eyes with a warmth he had never uncovered in a woman's eyes before.

His step was light, his heart leaping. He wanted to dance and sing, and most of all to rush after her, to tell her by way of word and touch and gesture that he was a changed man, a rejuvenated man, a man prepared to give her anything if only she would agree to remain clasped in his arms, her lips to his as long as this feeling lasted.

Christmas. He felt like Christmas embodied—all bright and warm, glittering and glowing, magical and miraculous! She was his new beginning, his life changed—his love, his love, his love, who felt so right in his arms, who met his kisses with such enthusiasm he wanted to shout his happiness from the chandelier in the middle of the ballroom.

Light-headed, wearing an inane grin, he returned to the glittering whirl of the dance floor, completely in tune with its movement, its music. There he encountered his sister Beth, and sweeping her into his arms, led her a merry, breathtaking jig around the room, laughing when she asked him what in the world he was doing.

"Dancing," he said. "I am dancing. Can you not see I am dancing?"

"But of course," she said, "but why must you do so, wearing that fatuous smile? My shoes are pinching."

"Are they?" he asked. "Do they? What a pity, Beth, for it is a night for dancing. A wonderful, beautiful night for dancing."

"You must find someone else for waltzing, Edward. And partake a little less freely of the spirits."

"You think me drunk?" he asked as he led her from the floor. "Well, and perhaps I am. That is very much what it feels like."

"Take me to a chair," she begged.

"Indeed, I shall, if you promise not to ask me to give up these Christmas spirits. I cannot, you see, will not. I am not yet completely carried away by them."

They encountered Anne as Beth sank into the promised chair. Still invigorated, his blood rushing with happiness, Edward fell into step beside his youngest sister, and knowing full well the answer, asked, "Where have you been, Anne, my dear?"

She turned to him with a suspicious expression, something bitter about her mouth, even betrayed. "I had just as soon ask you the same question."

"Skulking about the woods without escort," he murmured. "You must be careful, Anne, not to place yourself in too vulnerable a position."

"Is that so, brother?" She glared at him, and he in

no mood for anything but smiles. "Must I do as you say? Not as you do?"

That wiped the grin from his lips and doused the carefree light in his heart. "What do you mean by that?"

"Come, come, Edward." Her voice was biting. "I saw you."

The cold finger of concern stilled the racing heat of his blood. His smile slipped. "Saw me what?"

"What do you think?" she demanded.

Kissing? Had she seen him kissing?

"I saw you dance with that pretty young creature in the jingly dress. I saw the way you looked at her, as if you knew her quite well, as if"—she hissed the final words—"well, as if you meant to gobble her up with a spoon."

"Anne!" He was shocked to hear her speak so, shocked to think he had been so closely observed.

She looked about her and snapped, "Is she the reason you discarded Fanny, Edward? Is she a common trollop dressed in her finest, and invited here, of all places? I know it is Nigel's habit to pull such tricks, but you! I thought you were above such behavior. Especially as you knew we were to be here—your sisters, your mother."

"Anne. What are you saying? She is not a woman of ill repute."

"I do not believe you." She shook her head, a picture of petulance.

"Why not?"

"You do not behave as if she were a decent woman. You made no attempt to introduce us. Indeed, I saw you whisk her away upstairs, and Nigel in on it, so very hush-hush as he is with all of his strumpets, trying to avoid prying eyes, trying to avoid the Nichols. I followed them down to the bridge, knowing they followed you. Did you really think no one would notice? Did you really think you could stand hidden in the woods with her dress making all that noise?"

"Oh, God, Anne! It is not what you think. She is not . . ." In looking up, he noticed Miss Godwin, trapped in her wheeled chair, from which she could not rise to walk away from the unwanted attentions of Lady Nichol and her daughter Lily, who towered over her, both of them talking, Lady Nichol wagging her finger in a forceful manner.

Nigel, who would have helped, was nowhere to be seen.

"Not what, Edward?"

"Not fit discussion here, at a party. There is something I must take care of, someone I must attend to. We shall speak of this later."

Anne sighed, with such a look of disappointment in him it cut him to the quick.

But he could not leave Miss Godwin abandoned to the Nichols any longer. She wore an even more pained expression than his sister.

"I have seen Jane," Miss Godwin was saying with a much beleaguered air. "Yes, I have seen Jane."

"When?" Lady Nichol's voice was as insiduously silken as ever. "What has become of my dear husband's cherished little girl?"

"Where have you seen Jane?" Lily had not so practiced an air. Her interest was undeniable. "Was Mr. Davies with her?"

Miss Godwin rubbed at her forehead as if it pained her, as if they pained her. "My memory is not what it used to be, you know. Who is Mr. Davies?"

It was not Edward's habit to interrupt conversation, and yet he could not resist. "Do you mean Davies, the dance master?"

Lily Nichol whirled about in alarm. Her mother turned her head in narrow-eyed curiosity, a predatory expression aging her features. Miss Godwin's brows rose, her mouth opened in an expression of relief.

The baron, just arrived, punch cups balanced in each hand, asked with some surprise, "You know the rogue, Your Grace?"

Rogue? Edward thought. The greatest rogue he had

ever encountered dared to label another so, without so much as blinking.

"I do not know Mr. Davies at all," he said coolly. "We have never been so much as introduced, but I ran into your daughter recently, Lady Nichol."

The baroness came very close to spilling the punch she was handed. "My daughter Jane?" she asked, lips pressed thin. Her usually silken voice held a torn edge of irritability. "She spoke to you of Davies?"

"Not Jane."

"Rose?" Lily breathed the word, as if afraid to voice it any louder.

"Yes, Rose."

"Rose spoke to you of Davies?" Lady Nichol asked in disbelief.

"No." The duke shook his head regretfully. He pinned the baroness with a look of contempt. "We exchanged no words, but she was in the company of a young man she called Davies."

Lady Nichol looked for a moment as if he had slapped her. "Where?" The strength of her voice faded. "When did you see them?"

"Punch?" The baron, oblivious to the growing tension, extended the last cup toward Edward.

"No. I thank you, my lord." Edward did not so much as glance in his direction. He wished to observe every nuance of the baroness's reaction, this woman to whom he considered offering a branch of his family tree. "It was the very day the baron arrived, Lady Nichol."

She blinked, her eyes glittering with tightly contained emotion.

Was it rage? Sorrow? Regret?

"Do you remember that day?" he pressed.

"Indeed, I do," the baron said jovially, as if he were the one addressed. "Ran into you at the posting house."

"Posting house?" Lady Nichol echoed the words faintly.

"Rose was at the posting house with Davies?" Lily

caught on fast. "I told you she had run away with him!" she chided her mother uncharitably.

Edward said nothing. There was no need.

"Bound for where?" Lady Nichol asked, trying to recover a veneer of control.

"That I do not know," he said with a sudden feeling of sorrow for her. It must be difficult for a mother, even a bad one, to have not one, but two daughters run away.

"Miss Godwin." He returned his attention to Jane's old governess. "How do you fare? Shall we go?"

"If you please, Your Grace," she said quietly.

Edward saw to it Miss Godwin was carried to the carriage, tucked gently within, and offered a lap blanket. She accepted his every assistance with quietly voiced and completely gracious aplomb. She seemed pleased that he wished to accompany her, and waited discreetly until the horses were set to, the wheels rumbling, before she inquired, "May I ask where Jane is, Your Grace?"

"Sent home," he said. "Away from . . . unwanted attention."

Miss Godwin had no doubt as to his meaning. "Dreadful woman," she grumbled, and then apologized. "Forgive me."

Edward inclined his head. "Not at all."

"I do not make a habit . . ."

"Of course not."

"It is the governess in me," she said.

Brows raised, he turned from the window.

"I have a great aversion to the sight of a young woman's future ruined."

Her face was hidden from him in the darkness. Only her arthritic, knobby-jointed hands were caught now and again in the moonlight. Gray-gloved, they knit the fabric of her gown into an agitated pucker above a motionless knee. He wondered what it would be like to no longer have the use of one's legs—to be at the mercy of others' kindness. That she dared to address him as plainspokenly as she always did he considered an act of great courage—of indomitable spirit.

"I have an even greater aversion," she said, "to the deplorable circumstance of three young women so ill used."

He nodded. "Of course."

"It is due to this strong aversion that I take courage in hand and ask your intentions, Your Grace, where Jane in concerned. She has had the strength of character and purpose to extricate herself from certain unhappiness. I would not see her—"

"No." He reached out to grasp those nervous hands, to clasp them in his own.

The moonlight caught the gleam of her eyes, the hopeful tilt of her head. "You understand then, my concerns?"

"Yes."

"Are you in love with her?"

He was startled she came right out and asked so directly.

"I must know your intentions, Your Grace. For, if they are not honorable, I will advise Jane to return home, to marry the baron, who would honor her with marriage if nothing else. She is a good girl, Your Grace, a hard-working, intelligent young woman, deserving—"

He patted the back of her hand. "You need not detail her qualities. I am well aware."

"Are they qualities worthy of a duchess? Can you see her in that role?"

He had put off considering the matter—delayed standing Jane in Fanny's shoes. His feelings had mattered most to him, sorting them out, not deciding what to do with them. He met her questions with a frowning silence. It was not a retired governess's place to question such matters.

"If you cannot . . ." she persisted, grasping at his hands now as he sat back, "if you've no intention of offering marriage, it would be better for her if you went away."

As much as he might have wanted to argue the point, he held his tongue, for there was harsh truth in what she said, and he with harder decisions to make, for if he did ask Jane Nichol to be a part of his family, he must accept, as well, her connections, great and small.

Chapter Twenty-two

Jane went to the baths the following morning, happy of heart, with a deep-seated desire to see the duke again, and every expectation that he would be there.

He must be there. Surely he would want to see her as much as she wanted to see him again.

She arrived early, as was her habit, and changed in a great rush into her bathing costume, heart beating with anticipation, her expectations high. As she was walking out of the changing room, the duke's sister Anne walked in. Anne, who had stood on the pathway the night before, staring into the darkness at them. Anne, who might have seen Jane held in her brother's embrace.

Their gazes met briefly with a spark of realization, of recognition, then fell apart awkwardly. They had met as Madame Nicolette and her client, the duke's sister, never as Miss Nichol and Anne Brydges. And though they had never received a formal introduction, Jane could not ignore the encounter.

"Good morning," she said as cheerfully as she would offer greeting to any stranger, pleased to think that this, his sister, might soon be hers.

Anne glanced at her again, an unhappy look, then away, chin raised—as if she were not there, as if she had said nothing, were nothing.

The cut direct.

Jane's confidence faltered. Her sunny mood dimmed.

Shaken, she walked from the cold, inhospitable dressing area into the windswept chill of the baths.

The steam above the pools wavered, gusting and eddying in the sharp breeze.

The birds had deserted the place. No one soaked in the baths. Too cold, perhaps, for less hardy souls.

Shivering, the wind cutting through her bathing costume, Jane hurried to step into the King's pool, the water almost too hot in contrast to the cold. Her feet, her legs tingled, the warm grasp of the water taking her breath away. She stepped deeper, sank her shoulders, sighing in the enveloping clutch of warmth, her gaze alternating in its attention to the two openings that led to the dressing areas, male and female.

Would he come out first, or his sister? Surely a gentleman would finish faster than a woman in changing clothes? What would he say to her? How would he react with his sister present? Would he introduce her? Surely he would introduce her. Would his sister ignore her again?

He did not come.

She moved from one end of the pool to the other, rehearsing in her mind what she would say to him. How she would react to his sister's chill, should she prove unfriendly. It still rankled that she had been so cold, so dismissive, as if she were unworthy of so much as a good day.

He did not come.

No stir of life from the women's dressing area, either.

It seemed to take them an eternity of waiting, of worrying. Jane leaned her head back and listened to the cracking sound at the top of her shoulders and wondered how wilted her hair was, then studied the scudding clouds and wondered if her nose was turning red with the cold.

The sound of footsteps turned her head. A woman with a limp leaned into the arm of one of the attendants, shivering and complaining on her way to the Queen's Bath.

Where were they? Jane wondered. Could it be they were not coming? Could it be Miss Brydges had taken one look at her, and turning around, summoned her brother and left the place? Surely that was a most overanxious scenario. Surely she exaggerated the young woman's distaste of her.

She waited until the old woman got out of the Queen's Bath, waited until there was no more hope in waiting. Then Jane ran shivering to the cold dressing room to confirm her fears.

She was not mistaken. No sign of the duke's sister. No evidence of the duke. She had been snubbed completely.

The morning's outing cut short, Edward returned Anne to the house in Great Pulteney through streets teeming with Christmas trade. The street hawkers were offering their greenery and mistletoe at a discount in the last few days before Christmas. The butcher's, the baker's, and the greengrocer's were crowded with shoppers readying their larders for a Christmas feast.

"Are you sure you are all right?" he kept asking Anne in the carriage. She had looked so pale when he had responded to her summons from the changing room by way of the bathing attendant—so insistent that they must leave at once, that she did not feel at all well.

She did not seem to want to look him in the eyes now that they were on their way. Perhaps her monthly complaint, he surmised. It always left her a trifle sullen.

She sighed, her breath steaming the windowpane. "It is simply too cold, too windy this morning for me to feel like bathing. Really, you make too much of it, Edward. I am sorry to have dragged you away."

"Quite all right," he said. "No sense in your coming down with a cold for Christmas. Besides, this gives us a moment alone to discuss last night."

"Last . . . ?" She turned at that, cheeks pink. "Oh, yes!"

"I mean Miss Nichol."

"She is a Nichol?" Anne leaned forward, her expression most intent, her hands clasped in her lap. "But Edward, not connected to those dreadful women?" She shook her head as if to shake them from her memory.

"She is Baron Orday's natural daughter," he explained, feeling strange to discuss Jane thus, as if she were an abstract object, not his beloved. "The Nichols you know are her stepmother and stepsisters."

"She is the one who ran away, then?"

He heard a trace of derision in the question, which made his heart sink, for it hinted at the depth of misunderstanding and resistance he was likely to encounter in everyone who loved him where Miss Nichol was concerned.

"Yes," he agreed quietly. "You have heard of her."

She nodded, lips pursed. "Lady Nichol."

"Ah. Speaks ill of her, no doubt?"

"Most harshly. But I am disinclined to trust any word that woman utters. Is this Jane the reason you abandoned Fanny?"

"No, Anne. I did not meet her until after I had sent Fanny packing."

"Why did you send her packing? Is it something you still cannot tell me?"

"I would prefer not to. It is personal."

"You would not give me example of what not to do or say if I found myself in similar circumstances?"

Edward closed his eyes and considered the matter. With a deep breath he opened them and said, "Be true to yourself, Anne. True to your heart. You could never do or say what Fanny did if you are."

"What about *your* heart? Have you given it away to this runaway?"

He smiled, exhaled a gusty breath, and rubbed at the bridge of his nose. "I have, Anne." He laughed to hear the words voiced. "I must say I care for Jane more than ever I cared for Fanny."

"Really?" She seemed momentarily spellbound by

the revelation. Then her brow puckered. "But is she not disgraced, this Jane Nichol?"

He ran his hand along the back of his neck and remembered what it felt like to run his hand about Jane's waist, along her rib cage. He remembered the urgent rise and fall of her breast against his chest as he kissed her. "Is it a disgrace to refuse to marry someone you cannot love, Anne?"

She frowned, unsure of her answer.

"Do you think me disgraced for refusing to marry Fanny?"

"Of course not," she responded at once, her answer born out of loyalty rather than experience.

"Would you marry Baron Blomefield?"

She made a face. "Never! Dreadful man. Mother has warned me to stay away from him, warned me what the sores about his mouth may mean. She would never ask such an inappropriate commitment of me."

"And if Mother were not so considerate?"

She fell to thinking, lips pursed.

"Or if she asked you to marry a young man with no sores about his mouth, who came of good family, but you did not love? What then?"

Again she studied the matter, very serious of expression. "You pose difficult questions, Edward. I do not know what I would do in such circumstances. I have to admit I do not think I could run away. Surely you do not condone such an action? How does a young woman alone support herself under such circumstances? Surely she is ruined forever in the eyes of society?"

"How is a woman ruined if she takes up an honorable profession and supports herself?" he asked simply, knowing full well it was not a simple matter at all.

"By what means does Miss Nichol support herself?"

She had yet to make the connection of Miss Nichol and her dressmaker, and he was not yet ready to reveal so much. "Honorable means."

Anne made an impatient noise. "You do not wish to tell me, do you?"

"No."

"Why?"

"She would, I think, prefer I did not."

"Would Mother approve?"

"I doubt it. She will likely try to dissuade me from all contact with Jane. Perhaps almost as much as the baroness tried to persuade Jane to marry Blomefield."

"Two sides of the same coin." Anne sounded offended. "Do you in any way mean to compare Mama to the baroness?"

"Only in that they are both mothers, and mothers are wont to meddle when it comes to the marriages of their offspring."

"And siblings? Are we wont to meddle as well?"

He smiled. "Are you?"

She frowned, pouting. "I wish you happiness, Edward. I wish you love. I wish you a woman worthy of you. If this Miss Nichol will make you happy, and love you as you ought to be, and proves worthy in your most discerning estimation, I would not stand in the way. I do not think so, in any event."

He pursed his lips. "Even if your own reputation, your very name, is sullied by her actions, her connections?"

Her brow knit. She shook her head. *Dear Anne.* "Anyone who questions my reputation on so flimsy an excuse is not worth my worry. Are they?"

"Dear Anne, you could not offer me a greater gift than in saying that, but I beg you will not address Mother on this issue. I must decide for myself how best to deal with the matter, with the most appropriate timing."

"As you wish, Edward. But, oh dear! Edward, I must apologize."

"Must you?"

Anne wrung her hands, expression and gestures distraught. "She was there! At the baths!"

"What?"

"I made a point of ignoring her, thinking it the proper thing to do."

"Do you mean Jane?"

"Yes. At the baths. In the dressing room."

"Dear God!"

He thumped the carriage top with his walking stick and called to the driver, "Turn about. Turn about. We are going back, do you hear?"

Jane hurriedly dressed as Madame Nicolette and set off for the shop, striding very quickly, the wind kicking rudely at the hem of her pelisse, at her bonnet ribbons. Her heart raced. Her hopes from the ball were dashed, her spirit crushed.

He avoided her! After their evening of kisses. After the revelation of their passion for each other. There was no other explanation. His sisters disapproved of her, and he must now avoid her! It was a terrible blow, heartbreaking in the extreme.

She felt very much like crying, and yet she must not, would not. She could not ruin her powder and rouge, could not arrive at the shop weeping. There was too much to do, too many people depending on her to be strong, to keep things going.

The sight of Christmas wreaths and greenery and cheerful red ribbon seemed a mockery to her own state of despair. The sounds of an organ grinder making merry Christmas music was almost more than she could bear.

That a gentleman she had grown to love should trifle with her, that she had dreamed and hoped otherwise, made her feel at first pitiful, and then sad, and finally angry—very angry—with him—with herself. She was a fool to have hoped for more. A silly, naive fool.

The walk to the shop, which had begun as flight from the baths, ended in a most purposeful stride. She would not wallow in despair. The day was young. It was possible she was wrong. And if she was right—well, she must simply live with the reality she had chosen. She was a dressmaker now, not a baron's daughter.

At the shop, Marie had seen to it a hired cart had been loaded, as they had discussed, with the stacks and stacks of wrapped flannel gowns they had spent the last two weeks preparing for their seamstresses.

Marie had said she would deliver them, but today Marie had the sniffles.

"Can you send Mrs. Bell and the boy?" she suggested, patting at her nose with her handkerchief.

"I shall deliver them myself," Jane said.

"But, madame! It is frightfully windy today. Are you sure?"

"It is a trifle brisk," Jane agreed. "But I am in the mood to personally thank those who have helped us make this Christmas a bright one."

"*Oui*, madame. As you wish." Marie resorted to her handkerchief again.

"And you," Jane said, "must go home early and eat chicken soup and bundle into bed."

"*Oui*, madame." Marie gave no argument.

And so Jane set out with the cart, alone, into neighborhoods she frequented often enough, where women born without money or station struggled to stretch their pennies by way of needle and thread.

These women and their children, and the parents or siblings they lived with, greeted her warmly, welcoming her into their tidy little homes or rented rooms, each of them offering her of what little they had in the way of food or drink as they turned over to her their latest piecework, pride taken in every stitch. She was humbled by their joy in her flannel gown gifts to them, reminded over and over again of her own good fortune in possessing the means to support herself and proud to provide these women with the handful of silver she doled out to each. The amounts were carefully ticked off in the ledger she carried with her.

The deliveries took all of the morning and into the afternoon. Jane returned to the shop feeling invigorated, her hope restored, for she had been reminded of how much she owed the duke, whether he ever acknowledged her again or not. He had given her the gifts of a good business and an evening's passion. For that she must always thank him.

Returning the cart and horse to the stables from which they had been rented, she set out on foot along the decorated streets with an entirely different outlook. The windows sporting mistletoe bunches and wreaths and bows cheered her further, and the ringing of the abbey's bells, marking two o'clock, reminded her of the true meaning of Christmas. She would take joy in it. She would.

So improved were her spirits it seemed only appropriate as she turned into Milsome, that the duke's carriage should be standing outside the shop.

He had come after all—just as he had promised at their parting. Jane laughed at her own foolishness in believing otherwise, in believing herself spurned by him and his family.

She burst into the shop, heart full of the Christmas spirit, heart racing with anticipation, her thoughts consumed by the image of a bright future. She was brought up short to discover not the duke in attendance, but the duke's mother come for a fitting, his sisters Beth and Celia with her.

"My dear Madame Nicolette!" the duchess said. "How well you time your return. Another two minutes and we would have walked out the door. Your assistant has kindly seen to my fitting, and we are on our way shopping, the girls and I. I hear you have been delivering Christmas gifts to the seamstresses you employ for piecework."

The perfection of Jane's timing was debatable, Jane thought later, for had her arrival been a few moments sooner, a few more minutes delayed, her life might not have so roughly turned upside down.

Before she could open her mouth on a reply, the doorbell jingled again behind her, and she turned to step out of the way, the light through the window, a bright gold band of it, momentarily blinding her.

As she blinked the world back into focus, she expected to see the duke. She was not at all prepared to face her stepmother and Lily.

"*Bonjour!*" she managed to stutter.

"*Bonjour!*" Her stepmother's voice was as silken as always as she swept past her and into the shop. She brightened a bit in saying, "My dear Duchess, what a pleasure to see you."

Lily, who followed her into the shop, paused in the doorway, staring at Jane, uncharacteristically disinterested in the duchess or her daughters. A strange expression possessed her features, a puzzled pucker at her brow.

"In this light, Madame Nicolette," she said, "you look just like . . . just like . . ." And then her eyes flew wide, and she clapped a hand to her mouth before blurting, "It is you! Oh, Lord, is it really you?"

Lady Nichol turned to her with a disappointed pinch to her lips. "Do you mean to be rude to the duchess, Lily? Apologize at once."

"But, Mama, it is Jane!"

"What?" The baroness ran to the window and pressed her face to the pane. "Have you seen her pass? The naughty girl. We must see if we can catch her."

"Not outside, Mama. She is here—wearing a wig and glasses and all that dreadful makeup, but can you not see, Mama? Madame Nicolette is Jane!"

The baroness turned about in disgruntled dismay.

The duchess and her daughters, Beth and Celia, stared at the three of them.

Mrs. Bell came from behind the fabric display with a look of confusion painted on her wholesome features.

Jane felt caught between the vise of their examination. She wanted to run for the door, but Lily blocked her way. Besides, it was pointless to run. She had nowhere to go, no place to hide. Her secret was out. She must face the consequences.

"So you would hide behind a wig and a pair of

glasses!" Lady Nichol's voice was not at all silken in her dismay. Her complexion mottled with anger, her eyes narrowing to slits, she plucked the wig from Jane's head and the glasses from her nose. "Right underfoot, were you? Very clever, my dear Jane, but not clever enough. Not clever enough, by far."

Jane stood revealed, her reflection, she thought with chagrin, looking rather like a pale, plucked chicken. For an embarrassed moment she felt as if she would like nothing better than to sink into the floor.

"Madame!" Mrs. Bell cried, dropping an armful of fabric.

No sinking. No rescue. The light from the window glinted in her stepmother's eyes like silver arrows.

Jane straightened her back and shoulders. She lifted her chin. She would not cringe, would not grovel in this, her moment of shame. She had chosen this path, this moment. She had believed it for the best. She had succeeded beyond her wildest imaginings. She had believed the duke would fulfill his promise, that he would transform her life as much today as he had in first bringing to her his business.

And in a way he had. By not arriving, by leaving her to face the music, and her stepmother, as well as his mother and sisters—alone, he brought her as low today by way of his absence, as he had helped her to transcend heights by way of his lips the day before.

She had believed in him. She had counted on him. *Foolish girl.* She was, as her stepmother was so fond of telling her—a most foolish girl.

The duchess swept past with a look of utter disdain, and whisked out the door, her equally appalled daughters—his sisters—hard on her heels. With them went Jane's hopes that they ever might accept her— that she ever might find a place in the duke's world.

The bell over the door tolled the death of her dreams.

Chapter Twenty-three

In the dreadful silence that followed the echo of that bell, Lily blurted, "You will make her marry the baron, Mama, now that she is found. Will you not?"

"You cannot make me marry the baron," Jane protested.

"I think I can." Her stepmother spoke languidly as she took comfort in a chair, nonchalantly fingering Jane's wig, peering through the lenses of her glasses.

Jane turned her back on both of them and stalked into the back room, scaring Mrs. Bell away from the part in the curtain where she had taken cover and stood observing the whole. "You are not French, Madame?" she whispered, shocked.

"English," Jane said with a sigh. "I am sorry to have deceived you."

She flung aside the curtain to reveal Marie, sitting at the cutting table, her nose red, eyes watering, handkerchief clutched to her mouth, flatiron poised above one of the finished Christmas dresses. She had heard the whole.

"Mon dieu!" she murmured, gaze traveling over Jane's bared head in amazement.

Jane shot a look in the mirror behind the door. She looked a fright, but far more frightful was the biting guilt she suffered for the lies she had told these honest women, her faithful assistants.

The baroness called after her, "You will come along nicely, Jane, and marry the baron, or I shall make a point of reporting you to the mayor, as a menace to the public—perpetrating a fraud on Bath's finest."

Jane went to the pitcher and basin to wash the powder and rouge from her face, wishing she might as easily wash her stepmother from her life. As she toweled her cheeks dry, she could see the shocked faces of Marie and Mrs. Bell regarding her every move in the mirror.

"A baron? *Se marier* a baron?" Marie asked.

"Not if I can avoid it."

"Such a young thing you are," Mrs. Bell said in dismay. "How can we have been so deceived, Marie?"

Jane wanted to cringe in facing them. "I am sorry," she said ardently, her back stiff as a poker, braced for rejection, recrimination. "Terribly sorry."

The baroness darkened the doorway, where she stood regarding the three of them with undisguised contempt. Lily stood on tiptoe, peering over her shoulder.

"What would your father say, Jane?" the baroness drawled. "To see you in such reduced circumstances? A baron's daughter dirtying her hands in a trade, wearing a trumpery disguise." She whirled the wig on the tips of her fingers. The curls flew about her hand. It looked, for the blink of an eye, like a great, hairy spider.

Jane snatched the precious wig from her. "He would say shame on you, Madame, for trying to force your daughters into a disgraceful alliance with a horrid old man."

Lily stared at her, eyes wide. She had always been surprised when Jane confronted her mother.

The baroness laughed.

Marie and Mrs. Bell exchanged startled glances.

"You shall not get away from me this time, Jane. If you try, make no mistake, I shall have you and your employees arrested—your governess as well, as another accomplice in your plot."

"Plot?" Mrs. Bell sounded worried. "What plot?"

"*Mon dieu*. What does she mean arrested, Madame?" Marie cried.

"Not a madame at all," Lady Nichol corrected her. "Shall I introduce you?" she asked Jane snidely, and then without awaiting an answer, she announced with mock courtesy, "Did you not know, you poor deluded fools? This is the daughter of Baron Orday you work for. She is to be married to the revered Baron Blomefield."

"Is it true, lovie?" Mrs. Bell asked.

"Tell them yes, Jane," the baroness cooed. "And then tell them they are out of their jobs, for you must leave at once to make preparation for a Christmas wedding."

The duke had been hunting for Jane all morning.

She was not at the baths when he and Anne returned there. She was not at the shop when the carriage pulled to a halt at the curb. The delivery boy told him as much without his ever stepping out of the vehicle. "Gone to deliver Christmas gifts to her seamstresses," the lad said.

He had driven at once to St. Joseph's.

"Just missed her," the old ladies told him.

"You will tell her I am looking for her, should she return?" he asked of Miss Godwin.

"But of course. Is anything wrong?" She looked worried.

"No," he said in the same instant Anne responded contritely.

"I have offended her, for which I am very sorry. I would apologize, not only because she is dear to my brother, but because it was very wrong of me. She must not think . . . I would not have her think . . . Edward meant me to be rude."

Mrs. Godwin nodded with a look of dismay. "I shall tell her as much, my dear, should she return before you speak to her."

They went home then, for it was well past midday. They had stopped for nothing to eat or drink in their chase after Miss Nichol, and Anne began to feel quite light-headed.

It was at the house in Great Pulteney, oddly enough, where they happened upon report of Jane Nichol.

"We have been to Madame Nicolette's," his mother snapped as they walked in the door. "And who do you think we discovered there?"

"An imposter!" Beth cried.

"Miss Jane Nichol," he said evenly, knowing at once from their wide-eyed regard that she had been revealed.

Chapter Twenty-four

"I mean to marry her," Edward said calmly an hour later, after much private discussion with his parent, as he swung on his cloak again and strode out of the parlor, where they had been closeted.

"I cannot allow it." His mother rushed to stand between him and the door, her expression one of profound displeasure.

From the stairway his sisters watched and listened.

"I love her," he said, generating gasps from the stairwell, and a moment's silence from his mother.

"You said the same of Fanny," she reminded him. "And she was far more suitable."

"I disagree."

"You cannot argue with me on this point, Edward. Fanny's background was impeccable, her lineage unquestioned."

Edward said nothing. There was no arguing that point. It was true.

"Tell her!" Anne cried from the stairwell, voice echoing.

"Tell what?" his mother insisted.

And when he paused again, grappling with the words, Anne's voice floated down to them again. "Fanny did not love him, Mother."

"Nonsense!" the dowager duchess called to her youngest.

Edward sighed and took her hands in his. "Can you imagine I would have cast her aside for any other reason, Mother?"

"But, Edward . . ." Her defenses were crumbling.

"Come. You must not stand in the way of my happiness now that I have been fortunate enough to find it in earnest." Gently he released her hands and pushed past her to the door.

"And what of my happiness?" she called after him. "And your sisters'?"

"That is entirely up to you," he insisted as he stepped into the rain, into the waiting carriage.

He urged the coachman to hurry as they traversed the streets of Bath to Milsome Street. He had the sinking feeling as he stepped down in front of the dress shop that he arrived too late.

A tearful Marie met him inside. An astounded Mrs. Bell. "She is gone! The shop is to be closed," they told him the minute he stepped in the door.

"Where is Jane?"

They stared at him blankly.

"Madame Nicolette?"

Understanding registered and recrimination. "You knew!" Mrs. Bell surmised.

"Where is she?" He headed for the back stairs that led to the rooms above.

"Not up there."

"*Allé!*" Marie waved her hands toward the door. "Gone. Carried away by that awful baroness."

"Where? Where have they taken her?"

"*De mariage.*" Marie was weeping again.

"What? What marriage?" Edward's blood ran cold.

"To that dreadful baron," Mrs. Bell explained. "Preparations to be made, they said. Close the shop at once, she said, and tell these women they've no longer any positions here."

"She? Do you mean the Baroness Orday?"

"Indeed. Threatened to have Madame Nicolette arrested for defrauding the public. Said she would see to it we were thrown in jail as well if she refused to marry this Baron Blomefield."

"Horrible old man," Marie sobbed. "He has a dreadful reputation. Madame ought not be forced to wed such a rogue."

"She agreed?"

"It was that, or have us all clapped behind bars."
Mrs. Bell handed Marie a fresh handkerchief. "The
old crippled lady as well. What is her name? Good-
min?"

"Godwin."

"Can you believe it?" She shook her head, the lace
on her cap trembling. "Threatening us in such a way?
We'd done nothing wrong, other than being deceived
by the young woman. What is her real name?"

"Jane. Jane Nichol. Do you know where this wedding is to be?"

Marie shrugged and looked to Mrs. Bell.

Mrs. Bell shook her head, the lace cap trembling
more furiously than before. "No idea," she said.

He turned on his heel to go—stunned, his heart in
his boots, his mind in a turmoil. *What to do next?
Which direction to turn?*

"Wait! Wait, Your Grace!" Mrs. Bell came running
after him as he stepped into the carriage, footsteps
slapping the wet pavement, her starched cap going
limp in the rain. "Not in Bath, Your Grace." She stuck
her head in the window.

"What?" He leaned forward, coach springs creaking.

"Leaving Bath at once, they said."

"Thank you very much," he said crisply, his mind
focusing afresh. "Is that all you remember?"

"Yes, Your Grace. I am sorry, Your Grace.
Stunned, we were. You will understand."

"Yes. I am a bit stunned, myself. Tell me, will you
be so good as to keep the shop open, see that all of
the Christmas orders are filled?"

She frowned at him uncertainly, rain dripping from
her eyelashes. "What are we to tell people when they
ask where Madame is?" Terrified, she looked completely at a loss.

"Tell them the truth," he said with an amused twist
of his lips. "That she has gone away to get married.
That their dresses are finished."

"Yes, but . . ."

"I shall see to it you are well compensated."

"Oh, Your Grace!" The clouds cleared from her brow. "Do you mean it? Well, then, of course. As you wish," she said, much astounded, but eager to please, drenched face beaming. "You may count on it. On us."

It was easy enough to discover where the Nichols had been leasing rooms in Bath, not so easy to discover their immediate destination.

The landlord informed him with grumpy discontent, "They took off in a great hurry. Did not tell me where they were off to. Left the premises in a great state of disarray. Something about a wedding."

Edward left, frustrated, but undismayed. He would discover the road they had taken from the stables where they had housed their carriages. Of that, he was certain.

Chapter Twenty-five

Jane thought about making a run for it with every mile that carried her away from Bath. She yearned to throw herself out of the racing coach, to tumble into a hedgerow headfirst, to return at any cost—on foot if she had to.

She would go to the duke. She would beg his assistance. Could he turn her away? After kissing her the way he had? Could he refuse her to her face? Surely a gentleman who professed his love for a woman could not be so cruel as to neglect her in her hour of need?

But each time she thought of the dismissive expression on his sister's features at the bathhouse—of the assumptions his cousin had made in the carriage—of the disdain with which his mother had left the shop, her resolve faltered. She could be sure of nothing, but that her stepmother was not to be trifled with. She would make good her threats, to arrest Marie, Mrs. Bell, Miss Godwin—to humiliate them all with an appearance before a magistrate, public scorn, imprisonment, or fines. No matter that they had done nothing wrong. No matter that she hated the baron and professed again and again her unwillingness to be his wife.

The baroness would have her way. Her mind was made up.

With every mile Jane's hopes withered, her confidence sank. And yet she did not despair entirely. She had composed a hurried letter to the duke in her rooms above the dress shop as she packed to leave. She had wrapped it in another brief missive to Miss

Godwin, and before she stepped into the carriage to abandon Bath, she slipped the letter to their delivery lad and watched him walk away with it.

Perhaps she need not go to the duke. If he really loved her, mayhap he would come to her.

How odd, Jane thought, as the coach pulled up the familiar winding lane to Hackberry Park. Some deep-seated part of her rejoiced in this homecoming despite an almost overwhelming simultaneous sensation of distaste. It was good to pass the tidy tenant farms of the Sandringham and the Beale, good to spot the familiar roofline through the grove of elm and beech, to pass beneath the old lime trees that lined the drive.

The faces of the servants who ran to take the horses' heads were all too heart-wrenchingly familiar, as was that of the butler who opened the bewreathed old oak door.

Even the bark and flurry of the baroness's pug dog as she ran to welcome her mistress tugged at Jane's heart and made her glad to see the house again. Too bad it was not under better circumstances, she thought. Too bad she could not have returned with her future settled in a manner more to her liking.

"Mr. Ash." She tipped her head as she followed her stepmother into the house. "How good to see you again."

"Mistress Jane!" the old man exclaimed in an uncharacteristic show of enthusiasm, his pale cheeks pinking, his rheumy old eyes glittering with sudden moisture. "You are come home to us!"

How glad he sounded. She almost expected him to enfold her in his arthritic old arms, as Cook did, running out from the kitchen in a cloud of cinnamon and cloves.

"Is it our Jane, come home?" she crowed. "Oh dear, Mrs. Delamore, Kitty, Polly, Sue! Only come and see who has come home for Christmas! Can you believe it?"

The housekeeper burst into tears at the sight of her.

"My dear Jane," she murmured as she wiped at her eyes, "I thought never to see you again, my dear."

"All right, all right," her stepmother grumbled over the head of the pug. "Back to work, the lot of you. Get on with it."

"Your room, Miss Jane, is exactly as you left it," Kitty assured her with a curtsey as she turned to the stairs.

"Give us half a minute and we shall have hot water ready for you," Sue said with a wink.

How welcome they made her feel. How intense the sudden rush of emotion at the sight of them.

"I shall be right up," she promised. "But first a look around."

Polly smiled and said, "The old place has not changed much since last you saw it, marm."

It was true. The wooden flooring creaked as it always had. The smell of gingerbread and mincemeat wafted from the kitchens, as it did every year at Christmas.

The carved lion newel post still grinned at her hungrily. She smiled and playfully slid her hand between its carved teeth, as she had as a child, daring it to bite down. An imaginary danger. A lukewarm sort of courage. It had taken far more courage to walk away from the familiar smell of beeswax and rosemary, the luster of sideboard and dining table, the glitter of freshly polished brass and silver in the great Hall, the chime of the mantel clock in the drawing room.

She would never forget that day—how her heart had pounded. Risen before the servants, all that she meant to take with her had been packed into a single valise. A change of clothes. The jewelry she had long ago pawned: her mother's diamond ring, her father's diamond stickpin, her own set of garnets, the ruby her aunt had given her. Like a thief in her own house, she had crept out as the coming light tinged the morning sky a fainter gray. Bound for Bath—for a new life. So strong her resolve had been—not to marry the baron—not to succumb to her stepmother's wheedling.

And here they were, back where they had started, and she with no more jewelry to pawn. No Bath to run to without discovery. Even London would not be safe to her if she got away. They would know to look for her in the garment district. They would know her gift for disguise.

Could she make a new life in Scotland? The Americas? And yet, how to pay for the fare to take her to either destination?

Mind working furiously, she drifted into the haven of many a youthful quandary—her father's study. It looked much as it had on the day of her leaving. The same wall of bookcases, the same tidy desk, the same portrait of her father, from his younger days, above the crackling fire in the stone-framed fireplace. How quickly the sight of his face brought tears. How weak her knees went. How much she longed that he should be there to take her in his arms, to stroke the crown of her head as he murmured, "There, there, my pretty. This, too, shall pass."

She sank into the welled-out bottom of his leather chair, and closing her eyes, marveled at the lingering odor of pipe tobacco, pomade, sandalwood cologne, and aging leather.

This was what had passed—this fleeting sense of comfort, of well-being, of a father's care. She rose and passed from the study to the drawing room.

She had dreamed of coming back, an independent woman, with money enough to buy the place. Dreams, she thought, as dormant as the hidden promise of the rose garden her mother had planted as a newlywed. She stood staring at it from the drawing room window, her fingers trailing along the keys of the old harpsichord she had once practiced so diligently upon. So much that had passed, so much never to be recaptured.

What gardens would she plant, she wondered, as Baroness Blomefield? What music would she play?

The idea pained her and brought tears to her eyes, but she would not allow them to fall, would not allow the stifled sobs to make noise, for she could hear her stepmother in the entryway, her voice echoing slightly as directions were given—directions that concerned her.

"Jane is not to be allowed access to the stables, do you hear, Mr. Ash? Anyone allowing her to set foot in a saddle, or obeying an order for the carriage that does not come from my lips, and my lips only, will be subject to the loss of their position. Is that understood?"

"Yes, my lady," came the old man's compliant answer, and Jane, no longer able to hold back the tears, stared through misted eyes at the steeple of the church where she was to be married in two days' time—on Christmas Eve, in the morning.

Chapter Twenty-six

The wedding day dawned bright and brisk, the ground gone white. Not snowfall—but ice upon the ground, a thin film of it—hard and frosty as Jane's heart. The frozen rain that had tapped at her window until the sun rose shone as flinty and bright as her resolve. She would make it through the day with thoughts of Miss Godwin to keep her strong, she decided, as she swung her legs out of bed.

If her old governess survived, full of vigor and good cheer without the use of her legs, surely Jane could survive without the use of her heart.

She would not think of the duke—could not—should not—ought not—she decided. For two days she had thought of nothing and no one else, hoping he would come, knowing he must, trusting in her love for him—in his for her—trusting without question. He would come. He must.

But he had not.

She had listened for a knock upon the door. She had sat by the window, watching, listening for hoofbeats. But the only carriage to arrive had been the baron's, who came with the special license, then her stepmother's solicitor, who came with the marriage settlements, written out in triplicate.

"You must sign them," her stepmother had insisted, carrying them up to her.

"I cannot," she had said. "Will not. You know I do not love him, that I will not marry him."

"You shall," her stepmother said coldly. "You must.

The wedding is arranged. There will be no backing out a second time, no running away."

"You marry him if you are so eager to please the man," Jane had challenged.

Her stepmother laughed. "Please him? That is not at all the point. It is his money I am after."

"And willing to sacrifice your own daughter to get it?"

"You forget yourself, Jane," her stepmother had scolded in velvet tones. "You are not my daughter."

"I speak of Rose," Jane responded, unruffled.

"Rose?" The baroness snorted and turned to the window. She stood quiet for a moment, lifting her finger to rub a clear spot on the fogged pane to look out at the cold countryside. "Rose behaved stupidly. And I blame you. She followed your example. Running away, into a life of poverty."

"Happy girl," Jane said wistfully. Far happier than I shall ever be, she thought. "She has found love."

"Love! Ha! Love will not feed her, nor put a roof over her head. Could she not love a wealthy man as easily as she loved this dancing master?" For the first time in this interview the baroness lost her composure. Abruptly, she turned her back on the view. "It is a favor I do you," she insisted, "in assuring you do not end in a poorhouse, Jane."

Jane had never understood the workings of the baroness's mind. "Was that all you wanted of my father?" she asked. "His money?"

"Money?" The baroness paced the room like a caged lioness. "Stupid girl! It is all entailed away from us. Do you not understand? All of it to go to your distant cousin's son, William. Do you know him?"

"No."

She waved her hands rather dramatically. "The house. The land. The investments—all of it sifts through our fingers like so much sand. All of it to go to a man neither of us have met. Just like the first time. Just like Lily's father." She stalked about the room, her face stormy.

Jane watched her, absorbing all that had been said. For the first time since her father had brought her home as his wife, she began to understand what drove the baroness.

"We cannot survive on what remains." The silken voice had gone ragged. "Certainly not in any sort of style. You should have been born a boy, you see. A dreadful shame you came out a girl. And so you must be the one to repair this mess we are in. You will marry the baron."

"No."

The baroness shrugged. "One way or another, you will see reason, Jane. Just as I did. A woman must be practical when it comes to turning away her very sustenance, which is what you propose to do in refusing the baron. That you may fully understand the consequences of such foolishness, I shall not allow dinner to be sent up to you, nor any food at all until you see reason."

"I can support myself sewing. You know I can."

"Ha. A pittance eked out by the sweat of your brow. I will not allow you to sell yourself so cheap. Nor Lily, either. The two of you, you see, must support me by way of your marriages, just as I supported two daughters by way of marriage. Just as your father supported himself—even bettered himself—in marrying your mother."

Jane could not combat such twisted and unyielding logic. She held her tongue and made no complaint of her growing hunger, but continued to refuse to sign the paperwork.

And yet, her wedding day dawned, bitterly cold, her stomach gnawing, her heart aching. The duke still had not come. She began to think herself a fool. She had better spend her time in trying to get away, or, at the very least, in writing a second letter—to the duke's cousin. Nigel was a clever man. He might have seen a way to set her free. He might figure a way yet.

Was it too late? She must set aside her naive trust in the childish dream of love everlasting, of a commitment to surpass Baron Blomefield's. She must abandon the idea of being rescued by the silver surprise of love. She must learn to live instead with heartbreak and despair. But the sort of despair might be of her own choosing. Could it not?

When the white ball gown she had sewn with her own hands was brought to her, the gown that was to have been part of Fanny's wedding trousseau, the gown in which she had first met the duke, Jane did not refuse to put it on. She did not fight the dressing of her hair, nor the rub of red flannel upon her pale cheeks. She drank from the pitcher of water that was brought and thanked Sue with a quick hug for the crust of bread she had slipped into the pocket of her apron. She reserved all of her energies for later.

She had decided. She would beg the vicar to put a halt to the wedding. If he refused, she must make a run for it.

Chapter Twenty-seven

The water had been laced with laudanum.

Too late Jane realized her knees had lost all their strength, that her view of the world was clouded, her hearing muted. She had no strength to struggle when her stepmother and Lily helped her to the carriage. The familiar countryside passed before her like a dream. Her head was too heavy to hold upright. She leaned it against the cold windowpane, trying without success to collect her thoughts. They kept wandering.

What was it she was supposed to remember? Something important. Something imperative, she recalled, and yet it would not come to her.

Christmas, she thought, as she was led into the chapel without protest, her stepmother's shoulder surprisingly warm, her stepsister's perfume sweet. It was almost Christmas, was it not? The chapel smelled of juniper and yew, and candles burning. Almost Christmas, and she wanted nothing more than to sleep, and might have laid herself down on the pew where they sat her, had not the chapel been cold enough to make her breath mist silver before the stained-glass window depicting Mary's visitation by an angel. The image arrested her attention, prodding her memory.

She rested her head against the poppyhead at the end of the pew to think. She opened her eyes to the sensation of a hand touching her shoulder, a voice whispering her name, to find no one there. Just the cluster of oak leaves and acorns biting into her cheek. It stirred her enough to raise her head.

"Who is there?" She squinted into the light, into the golden whirl of dust motes that hung upon the air. But the chapel was empty save for the alabaster effigies gracing the tombs of those wealthy, or important enough to rest inside the chancel, and the wooden wise men who stood beside the altar, gifts in hand.

Her stepmother and Lily huddled in the doorway, watching the road. Above the door a gilded star had been hung. A wooden angel, wings spread, seemed to hold it aloft.

"What keeps the man?" her stepmother was saying. *Did she mean Jesus?*

Jane could not help but echo the question in her mind. Not Jesus, the duke. What kept her savior from coming?

She rose. Supporting herself with the back of the pew in front of her, she staggered to the back of the chapel, where a wooden Joseph led a wooden Mary on a wooden donkey, past them to a raised alabaster casket. An alabaster figure reclined on top, hands folded. Such a peaceful expression Mama wore, her face familiar and sweet.

"Mother!" Jane whispered, and sank against the cold marble, shivering. "Help. I beg of you. I have not the strength to go on."

The memory of Juliet Nichol's last words resounded in Jane's mind, as though a voice called from the grave. *Promise me you will not wallow in despair, Jane.*

The wind whistled outside. Jane stiffened her spine. Mustering all remaining strength, she headed for the door, for the bar of sunshine that poured in from the graveyard.

As she reached it, a shadow blotted the sun, and the baron stepped between her and escape to say, "Running away again, are you, Jane? Not until the vicar says we are man and wife, my dear. Not until then do we leave. A Christmas eve wedding, my dear, a Christmas Day bedding. Come along now."

He took her elbow, his grasp strong, and led her back toward the altar.

Her voice no more than a hoarse whisper, her lips and limbs equally disabled, Jane threw herself upon her mother's tomb. "No!" she cried. "You cannot make me marry you."

"Come now," he coaxed impatiently. "Let us not make a scene."

"You would tear me from the arms of my mother?" she persisted. "You, who knew her?"

"Knew her, and wanted her, my dear." He pried her fingers loose, one by one. "It is justice that I should now have opportunity to capture her daughter instead. Have I ever told you, Jane, how much you look like her when she was young?"

"You cannot want a wife who despises you, my lord." She had not the strength to fight him. He pulled her away from her mother's arms.

"Too late for wedding jitters now, my dear. You have signed the settlements."

Jane shook the great weight of her head. "I have not."

He spoke slowly, as if to a child. "The paper bears a signature. Your stepmother's solicitor satisfied me it was indeed your hand."

"I did not sign." She shook her head even more vehemently, which only made the room dip and sway. "I will not say yes. I will not marry you. I mean to tell the vicar as much."

"Ah! Tsk-tsk. It is a great pity, but the vicar tends to forget from one moment to the next what has transpired these days with but a bumper or two of rum in him."

Jane looked at him as if from a great distance. Her tongue seemed too thick to form words. The baron was nodding, the carbuncle on the end of his nose catching the light.

"We breakfasted together, the vicar and I, and shared a bowl of Christmas punch, did I tell you?"

He sounded quite cheerful. His face loomed closer as he spoke, his breath smelling of rum. "Come along now, his gig is arrived, and the good vicar tumbled out. I will have you, Jane, willing or no," he warned.

The vicar appeared as if from nowhere, and with him her stepmother and Lily, and suddenly they were all talking, their voices like a Siren's song, and she was drowning, her lifeline the baron's arm. He would not allow her to slip away, to slip under, as she wanted to.

Her stomach growled, the gnawing feeling in the pit of her gut based on something far more compelling than hunger. The baron's grip was a vise. He patted her cheeks and said, "Come, come, Jane. No fainting away on your own wedding day. Be a good girl and I shall feed you figgy pudding and roast goose, and mincemeat pie. You are hungry, your stepmother tells me."

The vicar, fat, jolly old soul that he was, stared at the two of them blankly through rheumy blue eyes. He had seen Jane christened as an infant. He had watched her grow to womanhood. She had confided in him many a secret.

"Jane, is it?" he asked, smoothing his silky, white beard. He looked to her stepmother, and then to the baron, as if for confirmation, and in gazing deep into his eyes she ignited no spark of recognition there, no evidence of his memory of her.

"Shall we proceed?" he asked cheerfully, his cheeks ruddy as apples, his nose a bright red cherry.

Jane's head swam. Her knees gave out. The smell of beeswax and evergreens overwhelmed her. She would have fallen but for the baron's ruthless grip. He yanked her upward. Head lolling, she stared at the intricately carved medieval rood screen that had fascinated her as a child. Decorated with juniper and ivy, it rose above them in all its glory. To think that a man might carve a bit of wood into such exquisite lace. It awed her still, such artistry. It made her think of the

many pieces of lace and fabric she had molded into
dresses. She felt a kinship with the long-dead carver.
Oak leaves and acorns he had woven into the screen,
just like the ones on the end of the pew.

The vicar was saying, "If anyone should know just
cause why these two should not be joined in holy matrimony, let them speak now, or forever hold their
peace."

Jane opened her mouth to speak, "I . . ."

Her utterance was cut short by a sound behind her,
the doors being flung open. Heels came pounding
across the stone floor, accompanied by a high-pitched
squeal of protest.

She turned to look.

They all turned to look.

In walked a sizable white stoat. It grunted when it
spied them, and shook its head. Around its neck a
little silver bell tinkled.

"Is that a pig?" the vicar asked.

"It is," Jane found voice enough to whisper.

More footsteps echoed from the stone floor and a
jingling of bells. A second trotter joined the first, this
one not so large, and speckled with black, followed
by a third, a fourth, and then a veritable flood of pigs,
accompanied by suitably piggy noises and a growing
crescendo of bells ringing.

Christmas, Jane thought. It sounds like Christmas!
She stared in disbelief, head whirling. This must be a
dream. The pigs were followed by a man, something
familiar in the shape of him against the light. *A swineherd.* He carried a swineherd's crook. But no, it was
the duke, not a swineherd at all, and he was dressed
as if for a wedding, in a very fine suit of clothes.

He wore a coat of silver gray, a waistcoat worked
in glittering silver thread. Upon his feet, silver-
buckled and heeled shoes, and on his head a gray
feathered hat, banded in silver. Definitely a dream,
Jane thought.

"You bring pigs, Your Grace?" The baron's astonishment echoed above the noise of the trotters. His voice; the tightened grip upon her arm jerked her attention back to the nightmare of her reality.

"As you see, my lord."

The duke's calm voice proved so dear to Jane's memory it brought tears to her eyes.

"They are lucky pigs, you know," he said.

"Are they?" The baron's nose looked rather more snoutlike than usual as he turned it to the ceiling but he wore no silver bell about his neck. "All I know is that they are demned inappropriate at a wedding. In a chapel for God's sake, Your Grace."

"Inappropriate? I disagree, my lord. I am convinced they strike exactly the right chord," the duke said forcefully.

He turned to Jane. *Dear Edward.* He had come, if only in her imagination. At his most imperious he struck a pose. She remembered that mouth, that perpetually amused mouth, though it did not look at all amused at the moment.

"What do you think, my love?" He allowed his gaze to travel between her and the baron and back again before he said with a twitch of his lips, "It would seem you would be a swineherd after all."

She stared at him, confused. He had brought pigs, silver-belled pigs, and yet he would call her swineherd? It made no sense, as dreams often do not. She raised her puzzled gaze to the carved acorns above her and listened to bells ring. The light from the window struck her eyes so that all the world turned silver for a dizzying moment, and her mind rose from the fog, and she said with complete understanding, "Yes. I've leprosy, you see, and would not give it to those I love."

"Leprosy?" The baron recoiled at once, dropping his terrible grip on her arm.

Jane swayed, and might have fallen had the duke not leapt forward to take the baron's place.

"You said nothing of this!" The baron rounded on Lady Nichol, his face distorted with distaste. "Is leprosy the reason she ran away to Bath in the first place?"

"Leprosy?" The baroness sputtered in protest, trying to make her way through the noisy press of pigs. "I know nothing of leprosy. It is the first I have heard of this nonsense. You must believe me."

"As I was supposed to believe you when you said Jane had actually signed the settlements?" The baron's voice rose, disturbing the pigs, who milled about the baroness with increasing agitation, grunting, and jangling so loudly she pressed her hands to her ears, and shouted, "Believe what you will!"

The duke winked at Jane, who pressed a hand to her forehead and said faintly, "It is true. She knows nothing."

"Well, I will not marry a woman with leprosy," the baron announced to the baffled vicar. "It is too much to ask, though she may be in all other ways young and beautiful."

"I release you from any obligation," Jane murmured.

The duke nodded as she spoke, as she swayed again, against his chest, the room swimming.

"No acorns," he murmured wryly with a sad shake of his head.

"Have you any?" Jane asked, no longer convinced she was dreaming. His arm was too warm, the glow in his eyes too compelling.

Edward threw back his head and laughed. "Large ones," he said. "Care to cross the river to see, my love?"

"If I may wallow in the mud," she agreed.

He smiled and nodded, then said, "Wrap your arms about my neck, then. There's a cure in it."

She did as he asked, and he swept her up in his arms to carry her through the river of milling pigs.

"Have you no fear of falling?" she asked, gazing into his eyes, transfixed by the play of amusement across the lips she had been enamored of since first she met him.

"No," he said, pressing her tighter to him. "You see . . ." A smile tugged at the corners of those irresistible lips. "I've a very good seamstress to make sure my wings do not tear."

Wings, she thought, and smiled up at the angel over the door, and remembered, it is almost Christmas!

She kissed him. She had to kiss that smiling mouth, right there in the midst of the pigs, with the vicar, the widowed Baroness Orday, and the reluctant bridegroom, Baron Blomefield, looking on in shock.

And when she was warm from kissing him quite thoroughly, she laid her cheek upon his shoulder.

"Will you marry me, Jane Nichol?" he whispered in her ear.

She smiled. "Leprosy and all?" She cupped the apple of his cheek in her hand. "Will your kingdom welcome me, I wonder?"

His eyes closed as he savored the softness of her touch.

"But of course," he claimed. "We shall kill the fatted calf."

"Always feeding me," she said. "What of the queen?"

He smiled, then put her down in front of the vicar and removed the signet ring from his ring finger, slipping it onto hers. "She cannot refuse you," he said. "You wear the ring."

"Is it true?" She directed the question to the dowager duchess, who in that instant came walking toward them down the aisle, flanked by her daughters. "Would you welcome me?"

The duchess's features softened. She spread her arms and said, "Dear Jane, I would not stand in the way of my son's happiness."

The duke's sisters came running forward to embrace her, their enthusiastic voices coming from every direction.

"Oh, Miss Nichol!" Beth said. "We thought Edward mad to want to bring pigs to a Christmas eve wedding."

Celia nodded. "We were sure you would be angry with such a stunt."

"But you are not at all put out with him, are you?" Anne said.

"No," Jane said, her eyes for none but the duke.

"You have yet to give me answer, Jane," he reminded her gently, his gaze just as fixed. "But know this . . ." He dipped a hand in his pocket and taking something from it held his fisted fingers above hers. "I have your heart, my dear." He turned his palm upward, his fingers uncurling to reveal what he held. A silver trinket gleamed in the light, a little silver heart, a plum pudding heart. "I would but give you mine," he said.

Jane laughed, then took up the little silver treasure and said, "My dear Edward, I shall cherish it always."

The vicar married them right then and there, of course, with angels and pigs as witnesses, along with the duke's mother and sisters, three wooden wise men and a Miss Godwin, whom the duke had carried with him in his carriage. She later went to live with the new duchess and her husband.

And Madame Nicolette? She was never seen or heard from in Bath again, except by way of a legal document in which she made a Christmas gift of her shop to Marie and Mrs. Bell, who stitched beautiful dresses there for many years, designed, it was whispered, by an undisclosed patroness, a noblewoman of great taste who frequented the baths of Bath every Christmas Season thereafter.

There were rumors, of course. That Madame Nicolette had not been French at all. That she had been, in fact, Miss Nichol, daughter to the late Baron Orday, new wife to the duke of Chandrose. But, it was pointed out, quite logically by the duke's new stepmother-in-law the widowed Baroness Orday, that one must always consider the source of such rumors, for the very same gentleman who said as much, also claimed, in all sincerity, that there were pigs invited to the duke's Christmas eve wedding—a whole herd of them.

And who could believe such a curly tale?

Read on for excerpts from some other delightful
Christmas Regency romances from Signet.

Available at www.penguin.com
or wherever books are sold.

Father Christmas

Barbara Metzger

The Duke of Ware needed an heir. Like a schoolyard taunt, the gruesome refrain floated in his mind, bobbing to the surface on a current of brandy. Usually a temperate man, His Grace was just a shade on the go. It was going to take more than a shade to get him to go to Almack's.

"Hell and blast!" Leland Warrington, fifth and at this point possibly last Duke of Ware, consulted his watch again. Ten o'clock, and everyone knew Almack's patronesses barred its doors at eleven. Not even London's premier *parti*, wealth, title, and looks notwithstanding, could gain admittance after the witching hour. "Blasted witches," Ware cursed once more, slamming his glass down on the table that stood so conveniently near his so-comfortable leather armchair at White's. "Damnation."

His companion snapped up straighter in his facing seat. "What's that? The wine gone off." The Honorable Crosby Fanshaw sipped cautiously at his own drink. "Seems fine to me." He called for another bottle.

Fondly known as Crow for his anything-but-somber style of dress, the baronet was a studied contrast to his longtime friend. The duke was the one wearing the stark black and white of Weston's finest evening wear, spread over broad shoulders and well-muscled thighs, while Crow Fanshaw's spindly frame was draped in magenta pantaloons, saffron waistcoat, lime green wasp-waisted coat. The duke looked away. Fanshaw would never get into Almack's in that outfit. Then again, Fanshaw didn't need to get into Almack's.

"No, it's not the wine, Crow. It's a wife. I need one."

The baronet slipped one manicured finger under his

elaborate neckcloth to loosen the noose conjured up by the very thought of matrimony. He shuddered. "Devilish things, wives."

"I'll drink to that," Ware said, and did. "But I need one nevertheless if I'm to beget the next duke."

"Ah." Crow nodded sagely, careful not to disturb his pomaded curls. "Noblesse oblige and all that. The sacred duty of the peerage: to beget more little aristocratic blue bloods to carry on the name. I thank heaven m'brother holds the title. Let Virgil worry about the succession and estates."

"With you as heir, he'd need to." Crow Fanshaw wouldn't know a mangel-wurzel from manure, and they both knew it.

The baronet didn't take offense. "What, ruin m'boots in dirt? M'valet would give notice, then where would I be? 'Sides, Virgil's managing to fill his nursery nicely, two boys and a girl. Then there are m'sister's parcel of brats if he needs extras. I'm safe." He raised his glass in a toast. "Condolences, old friend."

Ware frowned, lowering thick dark brows over his hazel eyes. Easy for Crow to laugh, his very soul wasn't engraved with the Ware family motto: *Semper servimus.* We serve forever. Forever, dash it, the duke unnecessarily reminded himself. His heritage, everything he was born and bred to be and to believe, demanded an heir. Posterity demanded it, all those acres and people dependent upon him demanded it, Aunt Eudora demanded it! God, King, and Country, that's what the Wares served, she insisted. Well, Leland made his donations to the church, he took his tedious seat in Parliament, and he served as a diplomat when the Foreign Office needed him. That was not enough. The Bible said be fruitful and multiply, quoted his childless aunt. The King, bless his mad soul, needed more loyal peers to advise and direct his outrageous progeny. And the entire country, according to Eudora Warrington, would go to rack and ruin without a bunch of little Warringtons trained to manage Ware's vast estates and investments. At the very least, her annuity might be in danger.

Leland checked his watch again. Ten-ten. He felt as if he were going to the tooth-drawer, dreading the moment yet wishing it were over. "What time do you have, Crow?"

Crosby fumbled at the various chains crisscrossing his narrow chest. "I say, you must have an important appointment, the way you keep eyeing your timepiece. Which is it, that new red-haired dancer at the opera or the dashing widow you had up in your phaeton yesterday?" While the duke sat glaring, Fanshaw pulled out his quizzing glass, then a seal with his family crest before finally retrieving his watch fob. "Fifteen minutes past the hour."

Ware groaned. "Almack's" was all he could manage to say. It was enough.

Fanshaw dropped his watch and grabbed up the looking glass by its gem-studded handle, tangling ribbons and chains as he surveyed his friend for signs of dementia. "I thought you said Almack's."

"I did. I told you, I need an heir."

"But Almack's, Lee? Gads, you must be dicked in the nob. Castaway, that's it." He pushed the bottle out of the duke's reach.

"Not nearly enough," His Grace replied, pulling the decanter back and refilling his glass. "I promised Aunt Eudora I'd look over the latest crop of dewy-eyed debs."

Crosby downed a glass in commiseration. "I understand about the heir and all, but there must be an easier way, by Jupiter. I mean, m'brother's girl is making her come-out this year. She's got spots. And her friends giggle. Think on it, man, they are, what? Seventeen? Eighteen? And you're thirty-one!"

"Thirty-two," His Grace growled, "as my aunt keeps reminding me."

"Even worse. What in the world do you have in common with one of those empty-headed infants?"

"What do I have in common with that redhead from the opera? She's only eighteen, and the only problem you have with that is she's in my bed, not yours."

"But she's a ladybird! You don't have to talk to them, not like a wife!"

The duke stood as if to go. "Trust me, I don't intend to have anything more to do with this female I'll marry than it takes to get me a son."

"If a son is all you want, why don't you just adopt one? Be easier in the long run, more comfortable, too. M'sister's got a surplus. I'm sure she'd be glad to get rid of one or two, the way she's always trying to pawn them off on m'mother so she can go to some house party or other."

The duke ignored his friend's suggestion that the next Duke of Ware be anything less than a Warrington, but he did sit down. "That's another thing: No son of mine is going to be raised up by nannies and tutors and underpaid schoolmasters."

"Why not? That's the way we were brought up, and we didn't turn out half bad, did we?"

Leland picked a bit of imaginary fluff off his superfine sleeve. Not half bad? Not half good, either, he reflected. Crow was an amiable fribble, while he himself was a libertine, a pleasure-seeker, an ornament of society. Oh, he was a conscientious landowner, for a mostly absentee landlord, and he did manage to appear at the House for important votes. Otherwise his own entertainment—women, gaming, sporting—was his primary goal. There was nothing of value in his life. He intended to do better by his son. "I mean to be a good father to the boy, a guide, a teacher, a friend."

"A Bedlamite, that's what. Try being a friend to some runny-nosed brat with scraped knees and a pocketful of worms." Crosby shivered. "I know just the ticket to cure you of such bubble-brained notions: Why don't you come down to Fanshaw Hall with me for the holidays? Virgil'd be happy to have you for the cards and hunting, and m'sister-in-law would be in alt to have such a nonpareil as houseguest. That niece who's being fired off this season will be there, so you can see how hopeless young chits are, all airs and affectations one minute, tears and tantrums the next. Why, if you can get Rosalie to talk of anything but gewgaws and gossip, I'll eat my hat. Best of all, m'sister will be at the Hall with her nursery brood. No, best of all is if the entire horde gets the mumps and stays home. But, 'struth, you'd change your tune about this fatherhood gammon if you just spent a day with the little savages."

Ware smiled. "I don't mean to insult your family, but your sister's ill-behaved brats only prove my point that this whole child-rearing thing could be improved upon with a little careful study."

"Trust me, Lee, infants ain't like those new farming machines you can read up on. Come down and see. At least I can promise you a good wine cellar at the Hall."

The duke shook his head. "Thank you, Crow, but I have to refuse. You see, I really am tired of spending the holidays with other people's families."

"What I see is you've been bitten bad by this new bug of yours. Carrying on the line. Littering the countryside with butterstamps. Next thing you know, you'll be pushing a pram instead of racing a phaeton. I'll miss you, Lee." He flicked a lacy handkerchief from his sleeve and dabbed at his eyes while the duke grinned at the performance. Fanshaw's next words changed that grin into so fierce a scowl that a lesser man, or a less loyal friend, would have been tempted to bolt: "Don't mean to be indelicate, but you know getting leg-shackled isn't any guarantee of getting heirs."

"Of course I know that, blast it! I ought to, I've already been married." The duke finished his drink. "Twice." He tossed back another glassful to emphasize the point. "And all for nothing."

Fanshaw wasn't one to let a friend drink alone, even if his words were getting slurred and his thoughts muddled. He refilled his own glass. Twice. "Not for nothing. Got a handsome dowry both times."

"Which I didn't need," His Grace muttered into his drink.

"And got the matchmaking mamas off your back until you learned to depress their ambitions with one of your famous setdowns."

"Which if I'd learned earlier, I wouldn't be in this hobble today."

The duke's first marriage had been a love match: He was in love with the season's reigning Toast, Carissa was in love with his wealth and title. Her mother made sure he never saw past the Diamond's beauty to the cold, rock-hard shrew beneath who didn't want to be his wife, she wanted to be a duchess. There wasn't one extravagance she didn't indulge, not one risqué pleasure she didn't gratify, not one mad romp she didn't join. Until she broke her beautiful neck in a curricle race.

Ware's second marriage was one of convenience, except that it wasn't. He carefully selected a quiet, retiring sort of girl whose pale loveliness was as different from Carissa's flamboyance as night from day. *Her* noble parents had managed to conceal, while they were dickering over the settlements, that Lady Floris was a sickly child, that her waiflike appeal had more to do with a weak constitution than any gentle beauty. Floris was content to stay in the shadows after their wedding, until she became a shadow. Then she faded away altogether. Ware was twice a widower, never a father. To his knowledge, he'd never even sired a bastard on one of his mistresses, but he didn't want to think about the implications of that.

"What time do you have?"

Crosby peered owl-eyed at his watch, blinked, then turned it right side up. "Ten-thirty. Time for another drink." He raised his glass, spilling only a drop on the froth of lace at his shirtsleeve. "To your bride."

Leland couldn't do it. The wine would turn to vinegar on his tongue. Instead, he proposed a toast of his own. "To my cousin Tony, the bastard to blame for this whole deuced coil."

Crosby drank, but reflected, "If he was a bastard, then it wouldn't have mattered if the nodcock went and got himself killed. He couldn't have been your heir anyway."

His Grace waved that aside with one elegant if unsteady hand. "Tony was a true Warrington all right, my father's only brother's only son. My heir. So *he* got to go fight againt Boney when the War Office turned me down."

"Protective of their dukes, those chaps."

"And *he* got to be a hero, the lucky clunch."

"Uh, not to be overparticular, but live heroes are lucky, dead ones ain't."

Leland went on as though his friend hadn't spoken: "And he was a fertile hero to boot. Old Tony didn't have to worry about shuffling off this mortal coil without a trace. He left twins, twin boys, no less, the bounder, and he didn't even have a title to bequeath them or an acre of land!"

"Twin boys, you say? Tony's get? There's your answer, Lee, not some flibbertigibbet young miss. Go gather the sprigs and have the raising of 'em your way if that's what you want to do. With any luck they'll be out of nappies and you can send 'em off to school as soon as you get tired of 'em. Should take about a month, I'd guess."

Ware frowned. "I can't go snabble my cousin's sons, Crow. Tony's widow just brought them back to her parents' house from the Peninsula."

Fanshaw thought on it a minute, chewing his lower lip. "Then marry that chit, I say. You get your heirs with Warrington blood, your brats to try to make into proper English gentlemen, and a proven breeder into the bargain. 'Sides, she can't be an antidote; Tony Warrington had taste."

The duke merely looked down his slightly aquiline nose and stood up to leave. "She's a local vicar's daughter."

"Good enough to be Mrs. Major Warrington, eh, but not the Duchess of Ware?" The baronet nodded, not noticing that his starched shirtpoints disarranged his artful curls. "Then you'd best toddle off to King Street, where the *ton* displays its merchandise. Unless . . ."

Ware turned back like a drowning man hearing the splash of a tossed rope. "Unless . . . ?"

"Unless you ask the widow for just one of the bantlings. She might just go for it. I mean, how many men are going to take on a wife with *two* tokens of her dead husband's devotion to support? There's not much space in any vicarage I know of, and you said yourself Tony didn't leave much behind for them to live on. 'Sides, you can appeal to her sense of fairness. She has two sons and you have none."

Leland removed the bottle and glass from his friend's vicinity on his way out of the room. "You have definitely had too much to drink, my tulip. Your wits have gone begging for dry land."

And the Duke of Ware still needed an heir.

Heaving breasts, fluttering eyelashes, gushing simpers, blushing whimpers—and those were the hopeful mamas. The daughters were worse. Aunt Eudora could ice-skate in Hades before her nephew returned to Almack's.

Ware had thought he'd observe the crop of debutantes from a discreet, unobtrusive distance. Sally Jersey thought differently. With pointed fingernails fastened to his wrist like the talons of a raptor, she dragged her quarry from brazen belle to arrogant heiress to wilting wallflower. At the end of each painful, endless dance, when he had, perforce, to return his partner to her chaperone, there was *la* Jersey waiting in prey with the next willing sacrificial virgin.

The Duke of Ware needed some air.

He told the porter at the door he was going to blow a cloud, but he didn't care if the fellow let him back in or not. Leland didn't smoke. He never had, but he thought he might take it up now. Perhaps the foul odor, yellowed fingers, and stained teeth could discourage some of these harpies, but he doubted it.

Despite the damp chill in the air, the duke was not alone on the outer steps of the marriage mart. At first all he could see in the gloomy night was the glow from a sulphurous cigar. Then another, younger gentleman stepped out of the fog.

"Is that you, Ware? Here at Almack's? I cannot believe it," exclaimed Nigel, the scion of the house of Ellerby which, according to rumors, was more than a tad dilapidated. Hence the young baron's appearance at Almack's, Leland concluded. "Dash it, I wish I'd been in on the bet." Which propensity to gamble likely accounted for the Ellerbys' crumbling coffers.

"Bet? What bet?"

"The one that got you to Almack's, Duke. By Zeus, it must have been a famous wager! Who challenged you? How long must you stay before you can collect? How much—"

"There was no wager," Ware quietly inserted into the youth's enthusiastic litany.

The cigar dropped from Ellerby's fingers. His mouth fell open. "No wager? You mean . . . ?"

"I came on my own. As a favor to my aunt, if you must know."

Ellerby added two plus two and, to the duke's surprise, came up with the correct, dismaying answer. "B'gad, wait till the sharks smell fresh blood in the water." He jerked his head, weak chin and all, toward the stately portals behind them.

Leland grimaced. "Too late, they've already got the scent."

"Lud, there will be females swooning in your arms and chits falling off horses on your doorstep. I'd get out of town if I were you. Then again, word gets out you're in the market for a new bride, you won't be safe anywhere. With all those holiday house parties coming up, you'll be showered with invitations."

The duke could only agree. That was the way of the world.

"Please, Your Grace," Ellerby whined, "don't accept Lady Carstaire's invite. I'll be seated below the salt if you accept."

No slowtop either, Leland nodded toward the closed doors. "Tell me which one is Miss Carstaire, so I can sidestep the introduction."

"She's the one in puce tulle with mouse brown sausage curls and a squint." At Ware's look of disbelief, the lordling added, "And ten thousand pounds a year."

"I think I can manage not to succumb to the lady's charms," Ware commented dryly, then had to listen to the coxcomb's gratitude.

"And I'll give you fair warning, Duke: If you do accept for any of those house parties, lock your door and never go anywhere alone. The misses and their mamas will be quicker to yell 'compromise' than you can say 'Jack Rabbit.'"

Leland gravely thanked Lord Ellerby for the advice, hoping the baron wasn't such an expert on compromising situations from trying to nab a rich wife the cad's way. Fortune-hunting was bad enough. He wished him good luck with Miss Carstaire, but declined Ellerby's suggestion that they return inside together. His grace had had enough. And no, he assured the baron, he was not going to accept any of the holiday invitations. The Duke of Ware was going to spend Christmas right where he belonged, at Ware Hold in Warefield, Warwickshire, with his own family: one elderly aunt, two infant cousins.

Before going to bed that night, Leland had another brandy to ease the headache he already had. He sat down to write his agent in Warefield to notify the household of his plans, then he started to write to Tony's widow, inviting her to the castle. Before he got too far past the salutation, however, Crow Fanshaw's final, foxed suggestion kept echoing in his mind: The Duke of Ware should get a fair share.

Once Upon a Christmas

Diane Farr

The vicarage was small and shabby, and so was the girl. But when Her Grace placed an imperious finger beneath the girl's chin and tilted her face toward the light, the better to see her features, a certain something flashed in the child's expression—a look of astonished reproach—that slightly altered Her Grace's opinion. The girl met the duchess's eyes fearlessly, almost haughtily. *Just so,* thought the duchess, a faint, grim smile briefly disrupting the impassivity of her countenance. This milk-and-water miss may be a true Delacourt after all.

The duchess dropped her hand then, remarking idly, "You are offended by my examination. Do not be. A woman in my position must be careful. I am forever at risk of being imposed upon."

Ah there it was again. The flash of swiftly suppressed anger, the unconscious stiffening of the spine. She had spirit, this unknown grandchild of the duke's Uncle Richard.

She spoke then. Her voice was sweet and musical. At the moment, however, it was also crisp with annoyance.

"I am sorry, Your Grace, that I must contradict you, but there is little risk of your being imposed upon by me. I have not sought you out in any way. You have come to my home, ostensibly on a visit of condolence, and asked me the most extraordinary questions—scrutinized me as if I were some sort of insect—all but placed me under a microscope—"

Her Grace's brows lifted. "*Not* sought me out? What can you mean?"

Miss Delacourt's brows also lifted. "I mean what I say. I have not pursued your acquaintance. You came to me. How, then, can you suspect I wish to impose upon you? Forgive me, but the notion is absurd!"

The duchess gazed thoughtfully at the girl. Her confusion seemed sincere. An interesting development.

Her Grace sank, with rustling skirts, onto a nearby chair. "We have evidently been speaking at cross-purposes," she said calmly. "I received a letter, begging me to interest myself in your fate. Were you not its author?"

Miss Delacourt appeared amazed. "A letter! No. No, Your Grace, I have never written to you. I would never presume to— Good Heavens! A letter! And it begged you to—what was it? *Interest* yourself in—in—" She seemed wholly overcome; her voice faltered to a halt as she struggled to suppress her agitation.

The duchess lifted her hand, knowing that Hubbard would be anticipating her need. Sure enough, Hubbard immediately glided forward to place the letter in her mistress's palm, then noiselessly returned to her place near the door. "This is the letter I received," said Her Grace. "Someone has been busy on your behalf, it seems."

She handed the folded sheet to Miss Delacourt and observed the girl closely as she sat and spread the paper open with trembling fingers. Miss Delacourt then bent over the letter, cheating the duchess of a view of her face. Only the top of her head, crowned with a mass of dark brown curls, remained visible.

The duchess took the opportunity to look more closely at the girl's person. Although she lacked height, her figure was pleasing. Her fingers were smooth and finely tapered, the hands of a lady of quality. She kept her back straight and her ankles neatly crossed, even in an extremity of emotion. Despite the ill-fitting black dress, the cheap shawl, and the frayed ribbons on her slippers, there were marks of breeding in the girl. Given enough time, the right surroundings, the right company—and, naturally, the right wardrobe— she might yet prove adequate.

Given enough time. But how much time would be

given? These days, the duchess tired not to think about time in general, and the future in particular. *Would there be enough time?* The thought was disquieting, but Her Grace had a lifelong habit of steely self-control. This rigidity of mind enabled her to banish unpleasant thoughts—a skill that was proving useful of late.

She turned her thoughts away from the fearsome future, therefore, and studied the room about her. She required information about Miss Delacourt. Obtaining it firsthand was the whole purpose of her visit. What might the vicarage tell her about its occupant?

One assumed that a person of rank would be entertained in the best room in the house. If this was the best room in the house, it spoke volumes for what the other rooms must be like. The parlor, or whatever this was, was spotless, but oppressively small and low-ceilinged. Blackened plaster over the fireplace gave mute testimony that the chimney smoked. Those old-fashioned casement windows were completely inadequate; it was growing quite dark in here as the afternoon closed in. The single candle that was burning was tallow, not wax. And the furniture! Someone had polished all the wood until it gleamed, but the duchess's sharp eyes were not deceived. All of it was old, most of it fairly worn, and several pieces were visibly scarred.

Quite a comedown for a branch of the illustrious Delacourt family! Her Grace wished for a moment that her sole surviving son could see it. It might give him pause. This, *this* is what lies in store for those who defy the head of the house and indulge themselves in foolish rebellion! Poverty and ostracism, banishment from all the elegancies of life—not only for oneself but for one's descendants. It was a lesson in filial obedience just to see the place.

But the girl's face was lifting from her perusal of the letter. It seemed to the duchess that she had turned quite pale. "Do I understand you correctly, Your Grace? You have come here in answer to this?"

"Certainly I have. Quite an affecting letter, I thought. Do not be offended by my arrival so many weeks after its date. I am sure you will understand that the assertions it contained required investigation before I permitted myself to reply in any way. In my position, I receive appeals of this nature on a regular basis. One grows quite tired of them. But this one contained the ring of truth. I thought it my duty, as a Christian and a Delacourt, to investigate—and eventually, as you see, to respond. Our connection may be distant, but it is not so distant that I could, in good conscience, ignore it. The tale related in that missive is factual, is it not?"

Miss Delacourt pressed her fingertips against her forehead, as if trying to make sense of all this by main force. "Yes. But—why did you think I sent this letter? It is written entirely in the third person."

"I assumed, naturally, that that was merely a convention on your part."

Miss Delacourt gave a shaky laugh. "Oh! Naturally. As if I had my secretary write it! You will be astonished to learn, ma'am, that I have no secretary in my employ. I suppose that must seem strange to you."

"On the contrary, I did not expect that a girl enduring the circumstances described in that letter would keep a staff of any kind." The duchess glanced fleetingly at the nondescript female who was trying to make herself invisible in the darkest corner of the room. "It is not unheard of, however, for the author of such a letter—which is, if you will pardon my frankness, nothing more than a bald appeal for charity—to phrase the message in such a way that's gives the impression it has come from a third party when it has not. The signature is quite illegible."

The girl glanced briefly back at the letter in her hand. "Yes, I suppose it is. I recognize it, however. It is Mr. Hobbi's signature." She sighed, rubbing her forehead again. "I am sure he meant well. His conscience must have pricked him when he engaged the new vicar. I don't know why it should. What else could he do? He had a duty to the parish. It was kind of him to allow me to stay so long in a house that does not belong to me."

The girl's eyes traveled around the ugly room, her expression one of naked sorrow. She even seemed to be fighting back tears. Was it possible she was mourning the loss of this insignificant little house? Her Grace devoutly hoped that Miss Delacourt did not suffer from an excess of sensibility. There were few things more tiresome than to be subjected to continual displays of sentiment, particularly the sentiments of one's inferiors. True, the child had just suffered a series of tragic misfortunes, but it was high time she recovered the tone of her mind. Her Grace did not approve of persons who unduly indulged their emotions.

The duchess was not, by nature, playful, but in an attempt to lighten Miss Delacourt's mood she offered her a thin smile. "I am glad to hear that you are accustomed to dwelling in a house that is not your own. You will not find it objectionable, I trust, to remove to another house that is not your own."

The girl did not laugh, but Her Grace did not resent Miss Delacourt's lack of comprehension. She, herself, frequently misunderstood when those around her were joking. Miss Delacourt would understand the duchess's modest jest when she saw her new home. The absurdity lay in speaking of such a drastic change for the better as *objectionable*.

The duchess rose, shaking out her cloak. "I shall send members of my personal staff to assist you in packing. You will find them most efficient. I expect, therefore, to receive you at Delacourt this Thursday week. Henceforward, you may address me as Aunt Gladys, and I shall address you as Celia. I am neither your aunt nor your great-aunt, of course; I am the wife of your father's cousin, but that is neither here nor there. The disparity in our rank renders it disrespectful for you to address me as cousin."

Silence greeted this pronouncement. The duchess glanced at Celia, her brows lifting in frosty disapproval. "Well? Have you some objection?"

Celia had automatically risen when the duchess did, but she appeared to have lost the power of speech. Her mouth worked soundlessly for a moment before she managed to say, "I'm afraid I do not understand you, Your Grace. Are you really inviting me to Delacourt? What of the bad blood that existed between— between my grandfather and his family?"

The duchess waved a hand in languid dismissal. "You need not consider that. We shall be pleased to let bygones be bygones. The present duke has no interest in prolonging the estrangement. In fact, I am told that your grandfather was quite my husband's favorite uncle before the . . . unpleasantness. Do not fear that he will object to your presence. I can promise you that he will not."

Celia flushed prettily. "Why, then, I suppose I—I have to thank you. Pray do not think me ungrateful, ma'am! I am just so surprised that I—I suppose I was taken aback for a moment. My grandfather always spoke of Delacourt with great affection, but I never thought to see it with my own eyes. Thank you! I shall look forward to my visit with pleasure."

The duchess eyed Celia for a moment, considering whether she ought to correct the child. She decided against it. Let the girl think she was coming for a visit. Once she saw Delacourt, she would naturally be loath to leave. It would be an easy matter, once she was actually on the premises, to extend Celia an invitation to make her home there—and once she had seen Delacourt, Celia would understand the enormity of the gesture and be properly grateful.

It was extremely important that Celia be properly grateful. Nothing could be accomplished unless Celia was properly grateful. She seemed to have little understanding, at the moment, of the generosity being extended to her, nor any appreciation of Her Grace's

condescension. Her Grace found this vaguely irritating, and had to remind herself that Celia's ingratitude
arose from ignorance. That was easily mended. All in
good time, she promised herself.

Time. There was that word again. The ghastly spec-
ter she must face, and face soon, immediately clam-
ored for her attention. It was, again, swiftly banished.
Pish-tosh! She would cross the bridge when she came
to it, and not an instant before.

She bade Celia Delacourt a gracious farewell and
was pleased to see the degree of deference in the girl's
curtsey. She may have sprung from the black sheep
of the family, and she might be ignorant of the glories
in store for her, but at least she was not one of those
brass-faced young women one encountered so lamen-
tably often these days.

The nondescript female who had admitted them
emerged from the shadows, showed Hubbard and the
duchess to the door, and quickly effaced herself. Hubbard adjusted Her Grace's cloak and tightened the
wrap round her throat. The duchess avoided Hubbard's sharp, worried eyes and placidly smoothed the
creases on her gloves.

But the more devoted one's servants were, the more
impossible it was to hide anything from them. As
usual, Hubbard read her thoughts. "Will she do, Your
Grace?" she asked gruffly.

It was a fortunate circumstance that Hubbard was
so completely loyal. Her uncanny percipience would
be embarrassing otherwise. The duchess smiled se-
renely. "Oh, I think so. She seems a trifle strong-
minded, of course, but I daresay that's the Delacourt
in her." Her smile faded as she voiced the unpleasant
fact possessing both their minds. "She'll have to do.
There's no time to find another."

When Celia heard the door closing behind her visi-
tors, she let her breath go in a whooshing sigh of relief
and collapsed nervelessly onto the settee. "What a

terrifying woman!" she exclaimed. "Why do you suppose she asked me all those impertinent questions? My heart is hammering as if I have just run a race."

Elizabeth Floyd emerged from the shadows to flick the curtain aside. "Be careful, my dear!" she urged in an agitated whisper. "They have not yet gone."

Celia rolled her eyes. "Well, what of that? Even if she could hear me, which I sincerely doubt, I cannot picture the duchess unbending far enough to come back and ring a peal over me."

"I can," asserted Mrs. Floyd nervously. "There! The coach is moving off, and we may be easy. Well! I don't know what she meant by putting you through such a catechism, but it seems you passed the test. Oh, my dear little Celia! What an astonishing stroke of good fortune for you! At last!"

Celia did not move from her collapsed position on the settee, but turned her head far enough to peer at her former governess with a skeptical eye. "Are you serious, Liz?"

Mrs. Floyd's round eyes grew rounder. "Quite, quite serious! Why, how could I not be? I think it amazing, and really quite affecting, that you should come to such a delightful end after all your travails."

"I am not sure this is any sort of end, let alone a delightful one," Celia pointed out. "I own, it will be interesting to visit Delacourt—which I never expected to see—but do not forget that the duchess is in residence there! How am I to face her on a daily basis? I hope she does not mean to pepper me with personal questions every time we meet, for I am likely to say something rude to her if she does." Indignation kindled in Celia's brown eyes and she suddenly sat upright again. "How dared she question me on my religious beliefs? As if Papa might have neglected his duties! And why do you suppose she wanted to know my medical history? I almost offered to let her examine my head for lice. Do you think that would have satisfied her?"

"Oh, dear. Oh, dearie dear. I am so glad you did not. Think how affronted she would have been!"

"Yes, but what was her *purpose*? I don't believe she was worried about . . . what happened to my family. Nothing contagious was responsible for—"

Mrs. Floyd interrupted quickly when she heard the catch in Celia's voice. "No, certainly not. Not a contagion at all. No question of that. Very odd of her, very odd, indeed! But many people are nervous about illness, you know. I daresay she wished to feel quite, quite sure that you would not communicate some dread disease to her household. Smallpox, or typhus, or something of that nature."

"Well, I like that! Of all the—"

"Now, Celia, *pray*! You should be blessing your good fortune, and instead you are looking a gift horse in the mouth! She has invited you to Delacourt—*Delacourt*, my dear! Nothing could be more exciting. I declare, I am in transports! You shall have a family again, for they *are* your very own relatives, however grand and strange they may be. And you shall be surrounded by luxury—which I'm sure is no more than you deserve— and *I* shall be able to go home for Christmas, something I had not thought possible a quarter of an hour ago. Oh, I am so happy!" She whipped a handkerchief from her sleeve and dabbed briskly at her eyes.

Celia saw that her old friend was really beaming with joy. "Oh, Liz, what a wretched friend I have been to you!" she exclaimed remorsefully. "I have been so taken up with my own troubles, I never gave a thought to yours. Of course you would rather be home for Christmas than cooped up here, bearing me company for propriety's sake."

"For friendship's sake," said Mrs. Floyd firmly, perching her plump form on a nearby chair. "I have not begrudged a single moment of my time here, and well you know it. Why, Celia, you are like a daughter to me! I would no more think of abandoning you than—than anything."

The cap on the little governess's head fairly quivered with indignation. Celia smiled affectionately at her. "Even friendship has its boundaries, however.

Am I to keep you from your family forever? You ought to have told me you wanted to go home for Christmas.''

"I will be glad to go home, there is no denying it, but my brother's wife takes better care of him than ever I can, and I am only Aunt Liz there. Had you needed me for another month or so, they could easily have spared me. But, my dear, now that the crisis is past, I do not hesitate to tell you how worried I have been—for I was at my wit's end to imagine what would become of you when the new vicar arrives. I could not offer you a place with me, since I do not have a home of my own. There was no possibility of the new vicar being able to spare you a room, with such a large family as he has. And only think how difficult it would be to see another family move into the house where you have lived all your life—the house where you were born! After everything else you have been through, I feared for you, my dear, I really did. How unfortunate, that both your mother and your father had no siblings! With no aunts, no uncles, no cousins—where were you to go?''

Celia tried to smile but failed. "I suppose I would have found myself thrown on the parish. Although I do have four hundred pounds safely invested in the Funds, which will bring me the princely sum of—what is it?—about twelve pounds per annum, I think. And I might double that income if I hire myself out as a scullery maid.''

Mrs. Floyd shuddered. "Do not even jest about such a thing. I have been so anxious! And when we received that message from the duchess informing you that she intended to pay you a visit, I was thrown into such a fever of hope it was almost worse than the fear! And then she asked you so many questions, just as if you were being interviewed for a position of some sort, which struck me as so very—but now everything is settled, and quite comfortably. Celia, I congratulate you!''

Celia frowned. "Settled? Surely you do not think

that dragon of a female means to offer me permanent residence at Delacourt?"

Mrs. Floyd nodded vigorously. "Oh, yes! Yes, indeed! That is what I understood her to say. Did not you?"

"Certainly not! What an idea! After all—why should she? Her Grace did not strike me as the benevolent sort. In fact, I thought her the coldest fish ever I met."

"Well, she is, perhaps, a little high in the instep—"

"High in the instep! That woman has held her nose in the air for so many years, it's my belief she can no longer bend at the waist."

Mrs. Floyd fluttered agitatedly. "Celia, *really*! You mustn't be disrespectful. After all, she *is* a duchess. It would be wonderful if she did *not* acquire a great opinion of her own importance, the way everyone round her must bow and scrape. Such a handsome woman, too! I daresay she is accustomed to an extraordinary degree of deference."

Celia's eyes sparkled dangerously, and Mrs. Floyd hurried to forestall whatever remark her former charge was about to make. "Do not forget she is your aunt! Or something like it. And she will be showing you a great kindness."

"Aunt." Celia shivered dramatically. "I shall never be able to address her as 'Aunt Gladys,' try as I might."

"Oh, pooh. I daresay she is perfectly amiable when one comes to know her. And they do say blood is thicker than water."

Celia chuckled. "Yes, they do, but she's no more related to me than you are. She simply married my father's cousin—whom he never met, by the by! The old duke booted my grandfather out of the house without a farthing, cut him out of his will, and never spoke to him again after he married my grandmother. We never encountered anyone from that branch of the family, and never cared to. And now I know why! If that stiff-rumped Tartar is the present duke's choice for his life's companion, only think what *he* must be like! After a se'nnight in their house, I daresay it will be a relief to hire myself out as a scullery maid."

"I wish you would not talk in that flippant way, my dear, about matters that are quite, quite serious! And besides, Delacourt is not a house," said Mrs. Floyd severely. "I would own myself astonished if you encountered the duchess above once a month in that great sprawl of a place. Apart from dinner, that is."

"Gracious. Will it be so very splendid, do you think?"

"My dear Celia—! Delacourt is *famous*!"

"I suppose it is." Celia rubbed her cheek tiredly. "In that case, I've nothing suitable to wear. It is a bit much, I think, to have to take something so trivial into consideration just now."

Mrs. Floyd reached out and patted her young friend's knee consolingly. "Depend upon it, my dear, they will understand that you are in mourning."

"They will have to," said Celia defiantly, "for even if I had the inclination to purchase a new wardrobe right now, I haven't the funds." Her eyes widened in alarm as another thought struck. "What about Christmas? I hope I am not expected to arrive bearing gifts for a houseful of persons I have never met. And I cannot afford anything remotely fine enough!"

"Oh, they don't keep Christmas in the great houses the way we humbler folk do. A pity, I always thought—as if Christmas could go out of fashion! But that's what one hears."

"Yes, but we don't *know*. The way my luck has been running, I shall arrive to find every room decked with holly and mistletoe, and discover that I must give expensive presents to all my unknown relatives—and their servants! Well, that's that. The instant I step through the door I shall tell the duchess that I have other plans for the holidays."

Mrs. Floyd looked uneasy. "But you don't, my dear. They will think it odd when Christmas approaches and no one sends a carriage for you."

"Perhaps they will offer me the use of one. They doubtless have a dozen."

"How will that mend matters? You will have to direct the coachman to take you somewhere. Where will you go?"

Celia bit her lip. "I think I feel an attack of influenza coming on," she said mendaciously, pressing a hand to her forehead and falling back on the sofa cushions. "What a pity! I fear I shall not be able to visit Delacourt until the second week of January. At the earliest."

Mrs. Floyd's face fell. "Well, of course, you *could* plead illness," she admitted. "And Mr. Hobbi has promised us a goose," she added valiantly, "so I'm sure we will have a very merry Christmas here at the vicarage, just the two of us."

Celia's conscience immediately pricked her. She sat up. "No, no, I was only funning," she said hastily, and forced a smile. "The duchess is expecting me next Thursday week, and Thursday week it shall be. I would not dare to gainsay her."

Mrs. Floyd's relief was palpable. She immediately brightened and began chattering of her nieces and nephews, and how pleasant it would be to give them their little gifts in person rather than sending them through the post, and how there had never been a figgy pudding to equal the figgy pudding her sister-in-law made every year.

Listening to her, Celia felt ashamed. Her grief had made her selfish. It hurt to see how much her friend was looking forward to leaving her. But it was only natural, after all. Anyone who had a home would want to be home for Christmas.

Celia had not given Christmas a thought. Now she realized that she simply had not wanted to think about Christmas, any more than she had wanted to think about Mrs. Floyd leaving. Both thoughts gave her a painful, even panicky, sensation. But she would make an effort to hide that. She owed it to her friend, to let her leave for home with a happy heart, untroubled by the notion that Celia still needed her.

But she did. Oh, she did indeed.

Mrs. Floyd was the last person left alive whom Celia loved. The thought of Liz going back to Wiltshire and leaving her alone, completely and utterly alone, filled Celia with a blind and brainless terror.

It was useless to tell herself how silly she was being. She knew there was no logical reason to fear that Liz, too, would die if she let her out of her sight. But logic had no power over the formless dread, monstrous and paralyzing, that seized her every time Mrs. Floyd left the room. Since the first week of September she had been all but glued to Liz's side, following her about like a baby chick. How would she feel when Liz left the county? Could she smile and wave her handkerchief as the coach bore her only friend away? Or would she make a spectacle of herself, weeping and screaming like a child?

This surely was going to be the worst Christmas of her life.

REGENCY CHRISTMAS WISHES

Five Holiday Tales
by Barbara Metzger,
Sandra Heath, Edith Layton,
Emma Jensen, and Carla Kelly

Celebrate the joys of Christmas in Regency England,
with five stories by some of the most beloved
Regency authors. Ringing in the season with fireside
warmth, holiday wishes, and Yuletide romance,
these stories capture the spirit of Christmas. A
sparkling collection, it is sure to delight readers all
year round, with warmth, cheer—and love.

**Available wherever books are sold or at
penguin.com**

**From _New York Times_
bestselling author**

Jo Beverley

WINTER FIRE

Jo Beverley returns to the Georgian period and
the irresistible Malloren clan in this sumptuous
historical novel of sizzling tension, powerful
attraction, a false and forced engagement—and
the lavish use of mistletoe and rather
well-spiked eggnog.

From *New York Times*
bestselling author

Mary Balogh

UNDER THE MISTLETOE

Old loves rekindled, new loves found, and family bonds
strengthened...from the beloved, multiple-award winning
author Mary Balogh comes this compilation of four classic
Christmas stories: *The Star of Bethlehem*, *The Best Gift*,
Playing House, and *No Room at the Inn*, and a new story
exclusive to this collection—*A Family Christmas*.

**Available wherever books are sold or at
penguin.com**